THE

A NOVEL

JEANETTE
LYNES

Edited by Sandra Birdsell.
Book and cover design by Coteau Books.
Cover image: "Woman modeling high heels," CSA Printstock Illustration/ Veer.

Printed and bound in Canada at Marquis Imprimeur Inc.

Library and Archives Canada Cataloguing in Publication

Lynes, Jeanette
The Factory Voice / Jeanette Lynes.

ISBN 978-1-55050-401-9

I. Title.

PS8573.Y6 F42 2009   C813'.54   C2009-901029-1

10 9 8 7 6 5 4 3 2 1

COTEAU
BOOKS

2517 Victoria Ave.
Regina, Saskatchewan
Canada S4P 0T2

AVAILABLE IN CANADA & THE US FROM
Fitzhenry & Whiteside
195 Allstate Parkway
Markham, ON, Canada, L3R 4T8

The publisher gratefully acknowledges the financial assistance of the Saskatchewan Arts Board, the Canada Council for the Arts, the Government of Canada through the Book Publishing Industry Development Program (BPIDP), Association for the Export of Canadian Books, and the City of Regina Arts Commission, for its publishing program.

For David

"Oh, must we dream our dreams
and have them, too?"
— ELIZABETH BISHOP

Prologue

The Factory Voice
Fort William Aviation
December 11, 1941

Special Exclusive – ESCAPE OF THE YELLOW JACKETS! – By Ruby Frances Kozak

*Y*esterday, on December 10, eleven men sawed their way out of Angler Detainee Camp in northwestern Ontario's frozen bush country. The Mounted Police quickly captured four of the escapees. Search dogs then discovered two more men behind a clump of buckthorn. Tracks in snow indicate that of those still at large four are moving in a cluster which, according to the lead constable in charge of investigation, will likely speed their capture, and two are travelling alone. The two men are moving in the direction of the twin towns Fort William and Port Arthur at the head of Lake Superior.

One of these, thirty-nine year old Thaddeus Brink, is a noted political subversive who has, since the last war, distributed dangerous propaganda and socialist tracts. He has a youth prison record in Vancouver, and long involvement in antipatriot activities. Police are particularly keen to arrest Brink, and believe he may still be in the area of Fort William or Port Arthur. When asked how this prisoner might navigate miles of muskeg in brutal winter temperatures, the lead investigator described Brink as also being a man of extreme stealth and resourcefulness who stands six feet with an upright frame, a restless blue gaze and greying shaggy brown hair. He may or may not be beardless.

With these men on the loose, the aviation plant in Fort William has been placed on high alert against infiltration of subversives. Plant manager Frank Parks told reporters at The Fort William Daily Times Journal, "this factory is sealed so tight, a lady's hairpin couldn't slip through without authorization from Head Office." Let's hope Mr. Parks is right. It's widely known that the factory has been beleaguered by industrial problems and can ill afford further complexities. Meanwhile, a fifty-dollar reward is offered for any information leading to the arrest of Angler escapees – one hundred for Brink.

Last night Prime Minister King, in a radio speech, reminded the Dominion of Canada that vigilance must remain the order of the day, especially with respect to the northern problem. "In the underworld up there," King said, "any profiteer will be dealt with severely, for he is a menace to the Allied cause and all that is sacred in human relations."

As for the sawing, it had gone on for some weeks at the Angler Camp, according to chief of security there, Tom Bee. The prisoners had, over time, sheared away the bars of a small window and climbed out. During the aftermath of Pearl Harbor, guards at Angler kept their radio turned on, no doubt tuned in to news of that catastrophic event; the broadcast's high volume must have enhanced escape opportunities, and, said Bee, "out the vermin slipped."

To add insult to injury, a trumpet, a family heirloom of Bee's, was stolen from his quarters during the escape. How music would do anyone in the frigid wilderness any good is beyond Bee. Nor is it known how the prisoners procured the wire to saw their way free. Bee won't rest, he stated publicly, until he has gotten to the bottom of this ugly affair. He has already advised government officials that any future prison design not include windows.

The Mounted Police warned the citizens of Port Arthur and Fort William to be wary of strange men in the vicinity and, if any are seen, to notify authorities immediately. At the time of escape, the men wore the standard-issue yellow prison jacket with a large black circle on the back. No escapes were reported from Angler's sister camps at Red Rock and Magpie.

Dry Cold

I know where the moon lives now –
At the east end of the sky. Where the tip of Lake Superior meets the future.

You don't mind if I run hard while saying exactly where, do you? I'm in an awful hurry. I have a train to catch, the God's Country Express. The train will carry me east, away from this whistle stop, away from cave-era parents, away from the ranch hand. And I'm likely to leap over gopher holes along the way, so if my words wobble in the next few minutes, that's why. This ranch always was riddled with gophers. If I twist my ankle on one of their front porches, I won't be going anywhere. I'll miss my train. My life will be over when it's hardly begun.

I'm only sixteen, but I'm told I sound older. That's because I read. All Star Comics. The *Spruce Grove Examiner* (my parents don't take the paper; they already know the news and it's not good), Hollywood-star magazines, books about Ontario. Is *that* ever one dilly of a place – fast and loose, sounds like, and lots of work. Shiny pages filled with art. I have to sneak into town, to the library, to look at these. Sometimes I dip into novels there, but I can't bring them home so I catch

1

glimpses in town when I can. I *did* manage all of *Anne of Green Gables* in bits and pieces and it was swell. Still, I keep my reading a secret and breathe each new word I learn into the grass. The newest word is *heroine*.

This ranch goes on forever. You could dash in the direction of doomsday and still not reach the edge, but I'll make it. If I had the Green Lantern's power ring, I'd be there before this.

I'll tell you something else; the moon loves industry.

The moon is modern.

Gopher   hazard

There, I'm over it. Forgive me if I pant like a set-upon fawn. I'm built for speed, but my feet have been pattering over frozen acres faster than Gene Krupa's drumsticks. If my parents catch me leaving, they'll skin me. I could spout Bible verses about mercy until I'm blue, but they'd skin me anyway, my holy parents Horace and Daisy Foley. They've always called me a wild cork whistling in the wind – and *sly* – worst trait in a girl, according to my mother. They're right about me. You'd think they'd be happy, being right, but it frosts their brimstone socks, which doesn't make much sense when you consider. Stagger me I don't have time to consider. The train for Winnipeg then Fort William, Ontario, where the moon lives, stops here in twenty minutes, and only now do I scramble over the rail fence that marks our ranch boundary.

I've got to rest for a shake, though. I have small bones. This carpet bag drags me down. I've been hauling it across the pasture, along the ragged path through the darkening trees. Over frozen vetch. Knotweed.

Like I said, away from the ranch hand with the face like clabbered milk and huge, thunking hands that would wed me between yanking slick red calves out into the world (I can breathe better; on I go again). He talked to my father. My father talked to my mother. She talked to me. I talked to the moon.

I'll bet that sounds queer to you, but if you've ever been an only child like me it might sound less queerlike. A girl has to tell someone, and the red staggering calves aren't my idea of a good sounding board. My parents said "oh, dandy, you two can marry, carry on the ranch." That was more useful than finishing high school, they firmly believed. I told you they were cave-era parents.

All my life they've crowed "lo, the end is near." If that's true, I said, what does the ranch matter? They said we had to soldier on regardless. Speaking of soldiers, I guess they'd heard there was a war? There's always a war, my mother pattered on, patting the Bible.

And the ranch hand? All he did was smirk. He's been smirking since I was fifteen. Scheming with my parents behind my back. Making grabs for me in the barn. Calling me his dumpling, his colt. Then this whole wedding thing began to unroll like some crazy carpet I couldn't stop. They've got it all planned out, a simple service (*Audrey Leona Foley do you take*), perogy supper. *Carry on the ranch.* They used a fancy word for it, *vocation.* But let's –

Smallish   gaping   hole

call a spade a spade; I know what it's really about, begetting and begetting and begetting.

Here's little Audrey with her brood, roping her calves, cooking her flapjacks, living her Old Testament life when there's a swell modern world out there. Like I said, I read on the sly.

The Spruce Grove Library is the size of a fingernail. I'm supposed to be studying some special Bible for brides they keep locked in a glass case there. Comics beat Bible stories all hollow if you ask me. I just read my first Wonder Woman comic! At the library I always head for the shelf marked *New*, and there she was in her dandy outfit and her bullet-bracelet, holding her golden lasso, and wasn't she one glorious lady? I couldn't get enough of her. I'd give anything to be able to fly like Wonder Woman or, stagger me, even be *near* what, or who, flies.

Instead of reading at the library, I'm supposed to be peddling these little sheets of paper with Bible verses printed on them around town, a penny a verse. My mother says that will teach me the value of money, and the pennies will go towards my wedding ovenware from the Corning Glass Company. I'd rather stand with a cob of corn stuck in my ear than peddle those verses.

I told my mother no one was home, that's why I came home penniless. If I'd stuck around here, I'd have had to cook up a new story, for people have to be home *some*times, don't they? And where would they *go* in a speck like Spruce Grove? But the pickle I was in with the Bible verses faded that day when I saw the newspaper ad:

Girls Wanted to Build Airplanes in Ontario
Earn Good Wages. Apply in Person to Miss Ruby Kozak,
Head Office, Fort William Aviation

Stagger me if that paper wasn't lying open at the *Classifieds,* waiting for me to waltz in there like Matilda. Think about it. The next best thing to being able to fly like Wonder Woman would be spending time in the company of airplanes, wouldn't it? I'd so love to see how they fasten the wings. How they soar.

A cog cranked in my head that day. The ranch could ranch onward without me. The red calves could find their way out; Clabber-Face could save his big birthing hands for someone else. If I had wages I could find out about planes. I could do whatever I wanted. And I stayed so long in the tiny library, when I left it was dark and the moon had shifted. I haven't looked back since.

I'm nobody's dumpling.

Not that far ahead, the train station, lit by electric light. The lace of my canvas Jeeper comes unknotted, dangles, and could trip me. I won't let anything trip me. My shoes aren't fit footwear for winter, but I'll worry about that when I reach Fort William, the Dominion's industrial hub (said the newspaper). *Audrey, do you take* – Clabber-Face – *definitely, oh, for sure, take my* dumpling (me), his colt. His newly-minted missus (me) gets whisked upstairs to see what's under that white dress. I already know the story, and when you know it before it even happens, it's no kind of story and you should find a fresh new moon. *I want to be someone, so no, I* don't *take you*

Final   gopher

About the moon.

It hovers above the tip of can't miss this train, at the east end of the sky. Above Fort William Aviation. All I had to figure out was cash. Then, the day after the library, the solution hit home – since the thirties my parents had lost faith in banks, stocks or any modern to-do with money. They kept cash all over the house. Wads of rolled bills inside the cherry jar, the wedding fund my mother made a big *woo-hoo* over. I cleaned it out.

And while I was at it, I took her one sin, lipstick. The wages of sin. I used it to redden my cheeks on this, my journey to the moon, hoping lipstick will age me to eighteen and help keep away Nosey Parkers asking where I'm going, and why.

Just before I left the house I cut my brindled hair for speed, and now it falls like short rain poured from a bowl. They send Clabber-Face to find me, doesn't hurt if I look different. Too bad I can't stand taller. I'm a half-pint. They'll tell me that stealing the money was the worst sin a daughter could visit upon her parents. I can already hear what they'll say, that's what I mean about knowing the story beforehand – it's got to be better than that.

One last short stretch of road and I'll reach the station. My ears don't need lipstick; they're small, hot bundles of readiness. My ankles are untwisted. Gophers, good-bye – *ha!* – your little porches of pain didn't get Audrey Foley this time.

The moon is full, industrial. You could punch a hole through the sky, to the very spot where it hangs roundly, and touch it, but you'd need an airplane to reach that high. You'd need the longest ladder in the Dominion of Canada. Either that, or Wonder Woman's golden lasso. It would snag the moon and whoever's home in there would have to speak the truth, just like in the All Star comic. Maybe there's a chance, just a sliver of chance, I could be a tiny Wonder Woman, her third cousin. Sliver, but there for the taking.

Already I have wondrous ears. I can hear the train whistle miles away, west of me in alpine-framed Jasper, in Hinton's hilly saloons, the levelling-off lands. Best sound I've ever heard.

Here's the station. Shantylike, a sorry sign nailed over the door – S and P crumbled – *uce Grove Alberta* all that remains. My ticker's about to leap from my chest now that the moment is here. I lug my carpet bag to the ticket wicket. Elmer, the usual stationmaster, isn't working. The moon shot a ray of luck right down on me when I needed it. I flatten the roll of stolen bills. "Fort William, Ontario. One way. Please."

Mr. Not-Elmer spouts times, change in Winnipeg.

Do I want a berth? You bet I do.

The train comes now, a dark, moving deliverance. All steam and screech. Brakes. I grasp my ticket. A striped arm helps me step up with my bag. I find a seat away from other passengers, which isn't hard at all – the coach is empty except for a fancy lady poring over some papers. She looks pretty with her wire-rimmed spectacles and she's not *that* old and likely could smile if she wasn't scowling over whatever dire thing she reads (I doubt it's a novel). I sit a few rows from her (when she's not gone to the smoker) and I press myself into the coach's shadows. It strikes me full now. I'm a runaway bride, a prodigal. But only to my parents and to Clabber-Face. I know better. I'm swinging on a new moon.

The engine bucks out of Spruce Grove. I feel so few pangs. Alberta is too small for me. I take one last glance out the window; a place never looks shabbier than when you're leaving it, does it? A few boiled potato suppers through small, lit windows. The broken water tower. Poky little lives. I feel a dandelion-puff of pity for them, but then, *poof,* gone. The locomotive's *ka-choo* is the best song I ever heard. Sweeter than any tune by the Andrews Sisters. My parents are right; I *am* a wild, whistling cork. Let me be fully sly then. I'm the kind of girl Green Lantern would be proud of, a runaway success story, quite possibly a heroine. Yes. Wonder Woman's third cousin. Why not?

Town's behind me, moon's ahead. I notice, for the first time, a blanket folded on the seat beside me. I snatch it up, stuff my mouth full of wool to stifle – what? – my giddy, prodigal glee, or the higher joy-sob of a heroine on the loose?

You won't breathe a word of this to anyone, will you?

Muriel, B.S.E., M.A.E.
(Bachelor of Science in Engineering
University of Toronto, 1929;
Master's in Aeronautical Engineering,
University of Michigan, 1932)

*S*he is officially a spinster. Thirty-six years old. She has her work, though. Her Master's degree protracted by polio, but earned nonetheless. She thinks silver linings, thinks clouds, as she clip-clops with her cane along the sidewalk that leads to the main entrance of Fort William Aviation, while the wind bangs her satchel against her woolcoat-covered thigh. Thinks aerodynamics. She grasps the brim of her floppy hat against a sudden gust. Snow falls in hard pellets like pop rivets. Her plum new job begins today. After nine years in a fusty office at Fairchild, she, Muriel McGregor, is now Chief Engineer at this plant with a contract for three hundred northern model Mosquitoes and a sky-high security alert in the wake of recent escapes – *subversives* – from Angler Detainee Camp. She'd arrived yesterday and, hunkered beside her steamer trunk in her new flat, had inked, in bright red, this milestone in her diary – *he Lakehead at last! December 15, 1941. Threshold!* Below these words she'd sketched a horned cartoon devil and added, wickedly, *Watch out for subversives and monsters!*

The head office of Fort William Aviation stands apart from the plant, separated by a frozen courtyard about half the size of a Dominion-league hockey rink. Muriel notes, as she passes the courtyard's snow-covered benches, a Christmas tree listing crookedly as the bitter wind buffets tinsel and garlands of Union Jacks looped over its boughs. The pine's off-kilter stance gives it a forlorn look. She flips through her mental Kardex and remembers that she's to proceed to the reception area on the main floor of the two-storey office building. She stops for a moment to breathe the bracing air. Bears down on her cane. Before pushing the buzzer beside the office door, Muriel rolls her dream over in her mind – landing skis. Engineers have been trying to crack a foolproof design. This is how Muriel wants to be remembered, not as a spinster or a cripple, but as the brilliant engineer who perfected landing skis. Which is why the Fort William job is perfect; its long winters are ideal for testing skis.

She buzzes. Through the glass panel of the door, Muriel sees a girl with crimped hair skitter towards her. The girl introduces herself as Fraudena, the plant's switchboard operator, and urges Muriel to, "for pity's sake, come in out of that awful wind chill."

As Muriel stamps snow from her boots onto the mat inside the door, she recalls the long-distance telephone chat she had with this switchboard worker several weeks ago. The girl had warned Muriel that, since there'd never been a lady engineer at the factory, people were curious as cougars. Newspaper reporters from Fort William and Port Arthur had been ringing the factory, hounding Fraudena for information. The newshound from Port Arthur said he wanted to run a feature called "Queen of the Mosquitoes Lands at the Lakehead." Muriel had quipped back to the switchboard girl to tell reporters who call that she rises in the morning, makes hot oatmeal just like everyone else and does *not* bite.

The phone rings insistently on the switchboard, and Fraudena makes 'will it never stop' eyes and says whoever it is, they can just call back. She asks Muriel how her train ride was, all the way from British Columbia.

"Oh – grand, grand," Muriel breezes. "What a country this is." An odd thing to say, the engineer thinks, given it's her own country, but lately she's had the sensation of observing earth from outer space. As for the girl's query about her journey, Muriel leaves out a great deal.

She doesn't tell this crimp-haired creature with the funny name that she went to visit her mother on the west coast after receiving a telegram from a hospital there. She hadn't seen her mother, Annabelle McGregor, a prominent juvenile-court judge in Vancouver, recently retired and suddenly taken ill, for years. Nor had they been on speaking terms. Muriel had an account to settle with this mother of hers, but Annabelle was too weak to be taxed with any settling of accounts.

And then those interminable days on the train, nearly devoid of interesting characters, except for a fey girl with a carpet bag and a wild rodeo of hair who boarded at some speck of a place in Alberta. But the girl had huddled mute, or retarded, in her seat. The kid had also disembarked at Fort William, dashing rudely from the train in front of Muriel, not offering to help with her heavy satchel. Luckily, the plant had sent one of its young constables, a boy named Jimmy Petrik, to drive her to the Brodie Street flat the factory had rented, and to carry her luggage.

No, Muriel's trip to Vancouver had been futile, beyond the time it afforded to pore over the thick industrial folders the factory had sent her with their maps and protocols that wearied her, and the urgent *Possible Unauthorized Parts* memorandum that, while possibly grounded in rumour, distressed her and made her worry that her dream job might be slightly less dreamy than she'd anticipated.

"Miss McGregor?"

Fraudena offers to take Muriel's coat, hat and satchel. Muriel will keep the satchel; it contains files she'll leave in her new office. As Fraudena drapes Muriel's coat over her arm, she croons over its fine fox collar, then gives the felt hat a fondling sort of stroke. Muriel can only assume that textiles offer this frazzled soul, who handles telephone cables all day, some sort of comfort. Fraudena says Frank Parks will be down any minute to give Muriel a factory tour, and isn't that him now?

The plant manager's legs churn in their direction. He might have resembled Jimmy Stewart, in better days. These aren't better days. Frank Parks wears a shapeless grey suit with wide lapels. His face, with its prominent forehead, is 'light-bulb-like,' Muriel thinks. He joggles her hand and tells her she must be the new lady engineer. She beams at his brilliant deduction. Pointing to her cane, he confesses that her *affliction* had slipped his mind. He asks if she's heard about the escape from Angler.

"Yes. It's all over the news."

"Terrible business about Pearl Harbor," the manager remarks.

She agrees.

He says he wants her to experience the plant from *the worker's perspective.* Her coat is gone, but he supposes they can dash across the courtyard to the employees' entrance without getting frostbitten. She guesses he's already forgotten she can't dash.

They head outside and she picks her way over the courtyard's icy path as fast as she can while the pop-rivet snow continues to fall. She senses that Frank Parks finds it painful to watch her, and so, to spare his nerves, she sends words into the air.

"Is it always this cold?"

His laughter is like a decelerated flywheel, a sound so unsavoury she regrets her gesture. "*Cold?* This is nothing, Muriel – may I call you that?"

"Of course."

They've almost reached the plant entrance.

"Besides," he says, "it's *dry cold* we've got up here."

Frank Parks swings open the door for her. They enter a foyer he calls "the portal for each employee, the checkpoint." She quickly pegs him as one of those people who love playing tour guide. He tells her two thousand workers pass into the plant through the checkpoint every shift, and that, with the new Mosquito contract, the number is growing each day. This is the place where ladies' purses are screened. By screened he means checked for unlikely bulges (the inner compartments are left alone, in deference to feminine privacy, except in cases of extremely aroused suspicion). The morning shift is already under way, so the checkpoint security officer is on break. Once they've cleared the checkpoint, Parks explains, the workers click through the turnstile and stash their personal effects in the ladies', or men's, locker room, whichever the case. The manager assumes Miss McGregor's fine leather satchel sails above reproach. Muriel smiles and wonders if her Dr. Chase's Nerve Food would be confiscated if she were a regular line worker.

She shoves herself through the turnstile, slowly, careful not to catch her cane in the crossbar. Frank Parks navigates the barricade in one efficient thrust. He pushes open a saloon-style door. She steps through. He follows. They occupy a larger foyer now. Muriel muses, does this place consist only of thresholds? The first thing she sees in this foyer is a huge banner strung across the open area: ALL THIS COULD END TOMORROW. Below these words, in smaller letters: *Stay Alert. Report anything unusual, no matter how small.*

She'd been warned she'd have her work cut out for her. Her predecessor left a stack of industrial problems. Test flights had been crashing and almost crashing. Rumours that the test pilot, Orville Loftus, was on the verge of – *something* – had reached her ears. This frozen wasteland seemed built on rumour alone – anecdote, suspicion, gossip, radio news pumped with helium into the airwaves – stories of unauthorized parts, general skull-duggery, and now of unsavoury men, escaped subversives from Angler, lurking behind every spruce in Lake Superior country.

Muriel points to the words on the banner. "Surely it doesn't have to be this dire?" she asks.

Frank Parks stops the tour. She doesn't care for his look – it signifies how little she knows. He sighs. "We've had over a thousand girls start work here in the past few months, Muriel. Some local. Many not. They've blown in from everywhere. Hungry for work. Wild as colts. Away from home for the first time, often. Giddy. They spur the local girls on, too. They all need supervision. We don't know who they talk to after their shifts, what they blather to the rest of the world, who they *consort with* in the wee hours. For all we know, they could be *double agents.* Only thing we're certain of is that they're girls, and girls have *loose lips.*"

"What are you afraid of them letting loose with?" Muriel asks.

Frank Parks sends her a managerial scowl as he moves them past First Aid. Ladies' Locker Room. Men's Locker Room. He stops just before they're about to enter the first production bay. "Production secrets, for one thing. There's something you need to know, Muriel. Talk, in this neck of the woods, spreads like – " He moves closer, startling her. He cups his hand to whisper, which unsettles her further. Sends warm puffs of breath into her ear – "*venereal disease.*"

She gasps.

Frank Parks steps away. "I see I've got your full attention, Muriel. If the Angler menace isn't enough – after all, those men could be anywhere – this factory employs locals who, we worry, are either Red Finns, or are thick as bandits *with* Red Finns."

"Some kind of fish?" Muriel recalls hearing that this part of the country is heavily Finn. She supposes the mood of a brooding race could come to pervade the larger population. Perhaps these northerners are highly prone to doom. As for the general *heightened* air on these frozen streets, it could stem from an outpost suddenly finding itself part of a larger drama.

Frank Parks laughs. Then goes dark. His face hangs on a chain that he pulls to switch the light on, off. "You don't know much about our northern culture, do you, Muriel?"

She confesses she doesn't.

"Red Finns have underworld connections. In fact, they pretty much *live* under the world. Since the war started, that's a real threat and, when it comes to running this plant, a big fat thorn in my side."

Frank Parks flourishes open the double doors under the sign: 'A' Bay: Sub-Assembly. The immense noise jangles Muriel's nerves. She's used to working alone in an office with drafting instruments, blueprints, sometimes radio music playing softly. He shouts that the plant consists of three production sheds and sub-areas within them. His own secretary, Ruby Kozak, had sent Muriel an industrial floor plan; Frank Parks seems to have forgotten this fact.

Muriel lets the manager surprise her. "Three? Impressive," she calls back. She doesn't mention that the Fort William plant was based on a factory in Bouguenais, France, and is also similar to most industrial sites in England she's read about.

As they survey 'A' Bay, Muriel sees what Parks means about girls. This shed, the size of several stadiums, is a sea of yellow head scarves, shapely bodies in overalls, a blur of feminine hands, eyes that steal glances at her before turning back to their workbenches. There are a few men, older, in a recessed area under a large sign: *Caution: Sheet Metal Works.* So this is where they come every day. Muriel lifts her face to the shed's industrial-height ceilings, like those in airplane hangars, and its transom-style windows along the upper ten feet, or so, of the vast chamber. Windows that afford light but no view. No distraction.

Dust motes drift through the air as the manager escorts Muriel along one wall lined with bins as far as she can see. "Stores," he hollers, as they pass a dizzying number of containers, each numbered and labelled. Parks shouts over the din – "an airplane contains over twenty-thousand parts." She knows. Does he think he is giving a member of the Imperial Daughters of the Empire a tour?

They walk, observing contents of bins as if strolling through a gallery of art. Muriel recognizes these parts, could identify them in her sleep, but each brings new joy, nonetheless. To her, they're notes in a symphony. *Better,* for how many symphonies leave earth and fly? She gives her cane a chipper tap on the concrete floor as they make their way along.

The lovely things inside the bins – pulleys, sprocket wheels, trimming cables, cowlings, clevis bolts, Morse tapers, filler caps, trim cranks, manifolds, throttles, alloy castings, spools of red wires, blue wires, yellow wires, wood spars, snap jack gears. Rivets with countersunk heads, round heads, flat heads, brazier heads, raised tits. Grooved rivets. (She bends awkwardly to scoop a handful of grooved rivets and let them ripple, like silver rain, back into their bin.) Thimble-wired cable, bushing cable, shackles, cotter pins, grommets, cocks, castle nuts, plain nuts, wing nuts, slotted nuts, self-locking nuts (she marvels at the sheer variety of nuts in the world), thousands of small notes making the symphony complete.

Frank Parks wants to show her the larger parts now, such as spruce stringers, struts, fuselage sections and all that truck, housed in the second production shed, 'B' Bay.

She follows him, going past girls who are grinding undercar-riage sections and operating tube-bending machines. Other young women fit rubber stops on wing slat-tracks, coat hub bores with finish, sort rivets. It has always struck Muriel how solid rivets resemble tiny mushrooms. A sweet-faced worker picks through a tray of them, placing each bucktail end in the same direction. She looks up and sends Muriel a cautious grin. Muriel delivers a decidedly *un*cautious one back. The girl blushes. Nearby, a stout woman presides over a table of tubes – so many piles of snakes, coiled. She shoots pressurized air into them, checking for obstructions, Muriel knows. Good work. Down the line a tall, gaunt girl attaches skin-stressed stabilizers to a sub-section of fuselage. A severe-looking dame driving a crane whizzes by them as though she's on her way to a fire. A dark beauty checks for shearing on taper pins. Another, blonde (Muriel sees the wisps poking out from under her head scarf), assembles nose cones. The crane driver pulls a vicious U-turn before passing them again.

'B' Bay contains partly built cockpits, fuselages, wing and

tail pieces and the paint shop. Muriel would recognize the paint shop if she came through here blindfolded. She has a superb nose; it sorts, without difficulty, the various smells of flight. She fills her lungs with oxide primer, hot raw linseed oil, chromate primer, lacquer and enamel. She loves oxide primer best, and if she could dab it behind her ears she *would*. But the world, she suspects, isn't ready for industrial-smelling ladies. Frank Parks asks if her trek through the plant is tiring, given her *condition*.

"Not a whit," she says.

Hearing this, he hurries her along now, as fast as she can manage with her cane. They pass vast piles of plywood. Huge screaming saws operated by men whose eyes remain fixed steadfastly on their work. The sawdust makes Muriel cough. Smaller buzzing saws, more swirling sawdust, more coughing.

"Mosquitoes are built mostly of wood," Parks hollers.

She knows.

"And we've got nothing *but* wood in these parts. Trees," he adds.

She's noticed that, too. They leave 'B' Bay. More foyers, sign-plastered walls, such things as:

Buy Victory Bonds (spoken in word balloons by smiley squiggly cartoon-people)

Ask about our Employee Incentive Program

Regulation Parts Only

A rabbit warren of foyers. Frank Parks jerks his thumb towards a room to their right – "Forge in there." To their left – "Welding." Towards closed double doors – "Cafeteria." She glances at the notice beside the cafeteria entrance. *Please don't feed the mice.* All these signs could dizzy a person, Muriel thinks.

As Frank Parks swings open yet another set of double doors marked "'C' Bay, Final Assembly," he tells Muriel that some girls make dandy welders. They stop and survey the final production shed. This is where the music gets big, Muriel reflects; aircraft undercarriages rest on production jigs, while nimble workers in overalls rivet-gun inside, underneath, above them. Yellow head scarves bobbing, holding steady, gunning, bobbing again, with a fervour that delights Muriel.

"Mosquitoes," Parks shouts.

She supposes he's referring to the airplane sections, not the girls.

"I know," she returns.

"You'll hear 'em called 'Skeeters,' too."

She looks forward to that.

The far wall of 'C' Bay is one gigantic door, as in an aircraft hangar. Frank Parks tells Muriel that the finished Mosquitoes are rolled out of the shed onto dollies, test flown, then loaded into crates and shipped out on the Superior water route.

Then he steers her back through the factory, past the staring, curious eyes of workers, to 'A' Bay. He asks her how she feels about climbs. At first, Muriel thinks he's referring to flight; she has been climbing in and out of cockpits for almost a decade, test flights. She says she feels fine about them.

"Good," he replies. "Because your office is up there."

He points to an upper deck, a kind of glassed-in box poised above Sub-Assembly. Beside her office, also perched on high, is Plant Security, "Conrad Kozak and his boys," he brays, then quips that Muriel will hover over Sub-Assembly like a hawk. This being one of Frank Parks' first forays into humour, Muriel doesn't understand, initially. After a moment, she smiles to acknowledge his effort. Parks would now like to share a little plant folklore: Kozak has spent his life at the factory, the manager prattles. Even in the thirties, when the plant was shut down for several years and sections of roof and walls were torn open by storms, and mice ran rampant through the production sheds and grass grew through the jigs where the occasional wild buck grazed, Kozak would make his rounds with his flashlight to check on things. It wouldn't surprise the manager to learn that Conrad Kozak had been *born* inside that factory.

Muriel supposes the north is filled with cracked characters

like Kozak, but she saves this sharp thought for red ink in her diary.

As they ascend the long wooden staircase to her office, Frank Parks, bouncing upwards and ahead of Muriel, tells her that his son, Frank Junior, is overseas.

"Air, water or ground?" She puffs while working her cane expertly up the many steps. She has been carrying her satchel all this time.

"Ground."

She supposes they must chatter on ascent. He swings his light-bulb face back down at her, and says if his boy wasn't overseas, he'd be sorely tempted to do some matchmaking, given that his own personal secretary, Ruby Kozak, "Con's daughter," is the prettiest girl in the plant by a long shot. Muriel doesn't know what to say. She's here to build planes.

They reach the door with her name on it – *Muriel McGregor, Chief Engineer* – the brass plate so newly affixed, metal filings still sprinkle its rim.

So this is her domain. They step inside. Muriel's heart dive-bombs. The large room looks ransacked. The temperature has fallen far below rational thought. In one corner, a chesterfield coughs up its insides. Near it, a gaggle of empty whiskey bottles, left by her predecessor no doubt. Large sheets of paper – bend-allowance tables – stabbed to the wall with tacks hang askew. Last year's calendar – 1940 – torn at the edges is gallowed to a nail. Wooden filing-cabinet drawers gape. A tower of files on the drafting table is labelled in an oversized scrawl: *Problems never solved.* The office reeks of cigar smoke. Dust scrims both sets of large windows: the one overlooking the production shed below, and the one on the opposite wall, facing a sawed-off mountain hazed in snow. The dust clogs Muriel's throat. She coughs.

"I'm sorry," Frank Parks says. "I ordered this office scrubbed from stem to stern. I don't know what happened."

Muriel tells him oversights occur. She stifles her disappointment at not being able to get to work. She sets her satchel on the desk; the heavy bag detonates a cloud of dust.

"What happened to the last chief engineer?" she asks.

Frank Parks stands, shifting his weight in the messy room. "Karl Wilkins? Bad nerves. The more trouble with test flights, the deeper he dove into his bottle."

"What happened on those flights, Frank?"

"Your answer is probably buried in there." He points to the huge stack of files on the drafting table. "But it'd be faster to talk to Orville Loftus, the pilot. It'll have to be by phone, though, he's out of commission with a broken ankle from his last test flight."

Muriel had heard Loftus was difficult – or odd – or *something*. She sends this cautious word-balloon in the manager's dusty vicinity.

"Loftus is Loftus," he shrugs.

Muriel can see that, on the subject of the test pilot, she'll get nothing more from Frank Parks. He's drifted over to the dusty window overlooking production. She makes her way there too, and clears a patch of glass in the way someone would rub a viewing square in frost. They survey the hundreds of workers down there, moving with the rhythms of an enormous engine. Muriel sees, for the first time, several girls wearing red kerchiefs instead of the usual regulation yellow.

"What about the red tops?" she asks the manager.

"They're trainees," he says. "Or on probation. Or both."

One red-kerchiefed girl, riveting directly below them, catches Muriel's attention. The girl is a wonder with her rivet gun. She's light-years speedier than any other riveter down there, which Muriel finds all the more surprising given the girl's huge, pear-shaped body, and gigantic feet. The riveter moves in awkward, fumbling steps when she refills her tray from the stand behind her. But when she plants her platypus-like feet back into gunning position, she's a marvel.

Muriel, mesmerized by this clumsy grace, points to her. "Who's she?"

"Florence Voutilainen. Local girl."

"What's she doing on probation? She's astonishing with

that gun."

The manager agrees. "And she's only just started. But, frankly, there are some problems with her background check."

"Such as?"

He sighs. "Her mother."

A ratchet wheel turns in Muriel's stomach. She understands problem mothers. Her conviction that a daughter shouldn't have to atone for the sins of her mother surges through her anew. She feels for the big girl down there with the rivet gun. She asks the manager, "What's the hitch?"

"Her mother is a Red Finn. Henni Voutilainen. She's well known around here. She sews, takes in mending, but that's only a front for her underground activities. We're not sure who her cronies are, but we know they're enemies of the state. She's a bottom-feeder, an eccentric, a cramp in our collective side – in short, a threat to security. There's a file on her next door." He thrusts his thumb in the direction of the security office.

"But you can't be *that* worried," Muriel challenges. "You hired the girl, after all."

Frank Parks frowns. "We can't build planes fast enough. I hired her with reservations and, I admit, some pity. She's dirt poor. Wants to work badly. We're keeping a very close eye on her, though she doesn't know it."

"We, who?"

"Plant police. Young Jimmy Petrik's special detail is to watch her. After the escape from Angler, we can't afford to take any chances. The plant could be in jeopardy. All this could end tomorrow." He sweeps his hand through her shambles of an office.

The manager's dumb echo of the factory banner, for some reason, inclines Muriel towards laughter. She submerges the droll surge boiling up inside her. "Save it for your diary," she reflects – *hey speak in slogans here*. Instead, she says, "Jimmy Petrik is a plant constable? The boy who met me at the train?"

"I don't think you should hold the lad's youth against him."

"Of course not," Muriel says, chastened.

Frank Parks grouses that the government will soon send some intelligence big shot from England, some Scot, to the plant. Why can't the top brass just leave them alone to build planes instead of miring them in red tape? Muriel can only click her tongue in sympathy. The manager looks at his watch. He has a meeting with a reporter. Because Muriel's office isn't ready, he'll ask Jimmy to drive her back to her flat to settle in there, maybe show her a few local sights along the way.

"That's the beauty of Jimmy," Parks huffs. "He's a jack-of-all-trades."

They return in silence to the reception foyer of Head Office, where the telephone rings and Fraudena chirps "Fort William Aviation." In the brief space between calls, Frank Parks asks her to page Jimmy Petrik in the security cage. She does so. "Jimmy will be right down," Fraudena says. She then announces that two reporters – one from *The Fort William Daily Times Journal,* the other from the *Port Arthur Herald* – have been calling yet again, asking for an interview with Muriel, a feature story on the new lady engineer. Each reporter wants first crack.

"You'll have to get used to the newshounds," Frank Parks advises. "*I* had to."

"Tomorrow," Muriel promises.

She is about to reassure him that she's dealt with press when she notices a poster hanging near the switchboard. Emblazoned across its top: *Wanted and Dangerous.* Beneath this, the face of a handsome, unshaven man. That knocks the wind out of her. Along the bottom of the poster, *Reward leading to any Information Towards the Arrest of Thaddeus Brink, Escaped from Angler Detainee Camp December 10, 1941.*

Vertigo rushes in. Muriel makes for the chesterfield near the switchboard. Barely reaches it. Fraudena drops her telephone cable and scurries over to steady Muriel onto its cushions. Frank Parks watches, stunned, an odd expression in his eyes.

He glances at the poster, then back at Muriel.

"Was the plant tour too much?" he asks.

"Yes, that must be it." Her voice shakes. Fraudena dashes off into the small staff room behind the switchboard and returns with a glass of water. As Muriel drinks, she dismisses the whole thing as a dizzy spell, and remembers the Dr. Chase's Nerve Food in her satchel. At the first private moment, she'll take some of that calming white powder.

Jimmy Petrik breezes in, flicking snow from the epaulettes of his plant-constable uniform. He looks different to Muriel in his working gear, his peaked blue hat with its gold braid and F.W.A. crest. Yesterday, when he'd met her train, he'd been dressed in a flannel shirt and worn trousers. He's ready if she is. The switchboard operator casts concerned eyes on Muriel. The manager delivers more odd looks, a mixture, Muriel discerns, of concern and suspicion. She assures them both she's fine, now. She thanks Frank Parks for the factory tour. Just as well her office isn't ready. She'll go home, rest.

The manager calls it a nerve-wracking time for everyone. He trots away towards the stairs leading up to his to office. Jimmy Petrik says a dirty wind's blowing outside. Fraudena asks Muriel once more if her spell has passed. After Muriel repeats, "yes, yes, it was nothing" several times, the switchboard operator fetches her coat and hat. Muriel puts them on, along with her best chipper act.

Muriel and Jimmy leave Head Office and walk through frigid air that revives her. To take her mind off the poster, Muriel studies the Petrik boy as they make their way across the packed-snow path towards the plant parking lot where his fine jade green De Soto waits. Jimmy asks what was going on in the reception foyer? Why was everyone all twitchy? Her long train ride to Fort William had caught up with her. Simple as that, she tells him.

The De Soto's seats are ossified with cold. During Muriel's factory tour, snow has accumulated on the streets of Fort William. Jimmy Petrik propels the automobile expertly through white drifts, past a trolley that shudders along the

Neebing Avenue tracks. He tells Muriel all about the Lakehead – his mouth working like a pneumatic rivet hammer between puffs from his Lucky Strike. He points out Mount McKay (the big sawed-off sill of rock to the south). "Covered in poison ivy," he says, "Indians call it thunder leaf. You wanna stay away from *that*." He laughs, and Muriel, glancing at her cane, assures him she has no intention of scaling Mount McKay any time soon. Jimmy explains that the aviation factory is boxed in by Gore Street to the north, Neebing Avenue to the west, Mountain Avenue to the south, Algoma Road and the railway tracks to the east. Muriel's head swims. Jimmy says the Kam River – short for Kaministiquia in case she didn't know – runs near the factory and, past the plant, it splits into two smaller rivers, Mission and McKellar. These pour into Lake Superior. These rivers loop around two islands with the same names. Jimmy chirps on that if the factory didn't make this, it would make that. In fact, if Frank Parks said tomorrow they'd be gutting the plant and flooding it for hockey, it wouldn't surprise Jimmy. But he guesses the big Skeeter contract will keep everyone busy for a while. The plant used to manufacture boxcars – some people use the old, leftover ones for car garages. "There's one right there, for crikey sake," Jimmy exclaims, pointing to a wooden shed – basically, a large, rough box that looks like it rocketed through turbulent air and landed, more than a little worse for wear, beside a house of no great distinction. Jimmy assures Muriel that she'll see that a lot up here – using something for something else, what didja call it – imp – imp–

"Improvisation?" she offers weakly.

"Yeah, that."

They drive on. To Muriel's eyes, the place is drab – small houses, rail spurs, hostile rocks. The sole thing of beauty they pass, as far as she's concerned, is Vickers Park, snow heavy on dark firs – a stately square flanked by the grandest homes she's seen so far. But even this spot of beauty doesn't bring Muriel back to where she needs to be in order to steady her nerves. The man's face on the poster is all she can think about.

A much older face than the one she'd once loved, but the same features, nevertheless. The age he would be now. Muriel's vertigo threatens to return. She fights it back. As they motor along, she tries to focus on the snow. Snow troubles her, too. On the one hand, winter is what she needs to crack landing-ski design. On the other, snow tells stories. Wanted men like Thaddeus Brink leave tracks, are more easily captured. She hasn't seen him for so many years, yet she already prays for wind to wipe away his sought-after footprints. The factory tour fades from Muriel's thoughts. She loses sight, temporarily, of the great industrial symphony she's come to conduct. Forgets the big girl with the rivet gun, her Red Finn mother. Everything vanishes except *his* face on the poster. *Wanted and Dangerous.*

Jimmy Petrik shifts gears. Chatters. Smokes. But all Muriel hears is a gavel bashing down on a wooden magistrate's stand in Vancouver in 1918, the gavel in her mother's hand, the words "Thaddeus Brink, guilty as charged" thudding from her own mother's mouth.

Audrey
Under the New Moon
Temperature: ⁻ 26 F
Wind Chill: ⁻ 40 F

The wolves howl not far from town.
The wolves howl bluer than Billie Holiday, but they don't spoil my song.

*Y*ou're probably wondering what happened to me. Tickled to tell you I made it all the way to Fort William even without the Green Lantern's magic ring. That's pretty good for a half-pint, wouldn't you say? The whole time on the train I pretended I was a deaf-mute so nobody would bother me. Nobody did. It was kind of a sorry excuse for a Christmas, though, rumbling along alone on a train, and I felt low, thinking about my parents back in Spruce Grove, wondering where I'd gone. But then I thought of Clabber-Face and the sneaky way they'd planned my whole life out for me, and I wasn't blue anymore, and each grain elevator shone like a little peak of hope. When the train finally stopped at Port Arthur, I dashed out of the coach so I wouldn't get tangled up with anybody, snagged a taxicab, told the driver – young and thin like me but much taller and what a case of acne – to take me to decent digs that didn't cost the earth. Talk about going in style, or *coming,* in my case – weren't those plush seats swishy-swash!

25

The driver took me to the Royal Edward Hotel in down-town Fort William. What a *palace,* with its Christmas pine boughs wound around the banisters and its white linen table-cloths in the dining room!

I had to register, dream myself a new name right there at the high desk while swanky big-band music played in some room behind another room, all classy-like. The desk I could hardly see over. All those hours on the train, I could have worked out a name. But no. I had to stand there racking my noodle while snow melted on my canvas Jeepers onto the lobby's plush red carpet. First I thought, "Diana Themyscira – Wonder Woman's real name" – actually, *Princess* Diana Themyscira – but I didn't want to draw attention to myself. Rolling into town and announcing myself as royalty seemed foolish when I thought twice. The man behind the desk was already gawking at me hard enough. I figured people would always spell Themyscira wrong, besides the bother I'd have, for the rest of my life, being asked was I Greek or Russian or what *was* I when the whole time I was just Canadian. So I wrote Diana Prince in the hotel book, and liked the sound of it, and *fully* loved it when the man behind the desk said, "let me show you to your room, Miss Prince." He carried my carpet bag. I sashayed after him in my old canvas Jeepers and I was ready to bust, I was that happy. Clabber-Face would never find me.

My room is a princess room. That's where we are now. Look at this *bed!* – it has a cloth roof over it, and it's almost as big as the Spruce Grove Library –

leap – soft –

no gopher hole here, only a

fine Ontario bounce   *Whoo hoo!*

quite the cozy royal square, all right

and mine all mine.

I dump the rest of the money from the cherry jar onto the tufted bedspread and count how much I have left. With any luck, enough for two nights in the princess room, a pair of boots, some grub, trolley or taxi fare. I take the newspaper ad from the pocket of my slacks: *Girls Wanted to Build Airplanes.* I didn't come all this way to jump on beds, so let's get moving! I toss some warm water at my face and – turn your eyes away for a minute – I leap into my only other set of clothes. When I get back downstairs, I ask the man behind the desk if he'll call me a taxicab – you know you're in a *real* place when the person you ask to do something asks someone *else* to do it. The man behind the desk hails another chap in a red jacket, and says, "Call Miss Prince a taxi, will you?" – and he does.

Stagger me, the same taxicab that dropped me off from the train station picks me up. I tell the driver, "Take me to a boot place. After that, Fort William Aviation – Head Office." The cabbie's nosiness has nudged upwards a notch since my last ride with him. "Where're you from?" he wants to know.

"Prince Edward Island," I say, thinking of *Anne of Green Gables.* (I read it at the Fingernail, like I told you.)

"What're the winters like?"

(The taxi bottoms into a big frost-heaved hole, wallows back out.)

"They're cold." I figure I can't go wrong.

"But *wet* cold," he urges. "So, colder than our northern *dry* cold, I'll bet –"

"Cold is cold," I shrug. He tells me his name, Reggie. He's from Rainy River. I say that's nice. I gaze out the window at icicles long as spears hanging from the houses' glassed-in front-porch eaves. This Reggie-driver brakes in front of the biggest store I've ever seen – Chapples Department Store.

"Wait here," I say.

I beetle in there. Look at this store! It's so huge, I'll have to study the map to find where to go... *Ladies Footwear, Third Floor.* I race up there. Buy the sturdiest pair of boots I can – hobnailed with heel irons. I'll need them for building planes. I pay for them and that puts a dent in the cherry-jar money, all right. But the ad for Fort William Aviation said good wages. Good boots.

Everything's good in Ontario.

I stuff my old canvas Jeepers into a brown paper bag they give me. Shove my feet into my new boots and leave the store. Clomp clomping across the snow, I'm an ant in chains. I'll get used to my weighty feet quick enough, I'll bet.

Reggie spins me along. My new boots are all spit and shine, and I feel like a hundred dollars when the taxicab stops at Fort William Aviation – *look* at this place! It's bigger than Jonah's whale.

My driver's nosiness nudges up yet another notch. He asks me who I am.

"My name is Diana. Diana in hobnailed boots," I say.

He wants to know if I'm old enough to work. I ask him if he's old enough to drive. Saucy, aren't I? There must be a bit of Ontario in me already.

Cold air rushes into the cab when I open the door. I land my new boots on the packed snow at the edge of the driveway.

This is it – we're off to see the Wizard. I hightail it up the factory's driveway towards the large sign that says Head Office, my scarf flopping. The taxicab driver calls out his window, "You need anything, Diana in Hobnailed Boots, you let me know." I turn and wave. Isn't this a swell place? And before I know it, I'm lindy hopping up to some girl at a switchboard. The ad said to see Ruby Kozak about work, and so I ask the switchboard girl where Ruby is, and the girl, holding a telephone cable, points to a set of double doors a hop, skip and jump away, marked *Employment*. I'm through the doors lickety-split

and then I see her.

There's a big placard on her desk – *Ruby Kozak, Head Stenographer.* Some other girls type away at desks behind hers – dull, shapeless blobs – chittering dishrags I barely notice. I only see *her* –

Look at her, typing.

Tapping. Slapping the carriage like it's a bee trapped in an invisible bonnet. In two shakes I can tell she doesn't care one bit for the words dropping, like a dripping tap, off the ends of her fingers onto the page. She's typing, but it's almost like, except for her hands, she's not there. She doesn't even hear the clatter of my hobnailed boots as I approach her desk. I stop a few feet in front of it, beside the empty chair. I can tell by her bones and her hands and her hair and her shape that she's older than me, but then everyone is. I'd give her twenty – she must be smart as a whip to be twenty and *Head Stenographer.* Her typewriter is the big black fancy kind. They've got one just like that at the Spruce Grove Library. But that's not what I mean to say about Ruby Kozak.

I mean to spell out her beauteousness, but my tongue's too tangled.

My boots are frozen to the hardwood floor. Even though she's not yet lifted her face – her eyes bore into the keyboard – I can tell by how the air kind of shimmers around her shoulders, hers is the face of an angel. I take a peek over the desk at her trim waist.

I'm having about eight litters of kittens – why? – one reason – there are *no* lookers in Spruce Grove, Alberta. I repeat: *none.* Even Miss Spruce Grove 1941 is built like a heifer. Why does Ontario get all the lookers? Clearly, they do. I can only stare, and try to untangle my tongue. Once I saw *Hollywood* magazine. Its pages were stuffed with dreamy pictures. Stars. Heroines. Veronica Lake. Ruby Kozak's hair flows down in the same kind of shiny river, the same long, smooth bang curtaining one eye. Ruby's hair is dark blonde, and I like that (I worry about blonde people; they're so white, I'm afraid they might fade away).

I clear my throat. Ruby Kozak stops typing. She looks up. A mix of misery and pique makes her even prettier. She's got Gene Tierney's eyes – eyes that look like they could eat you, but won't. I'm so rattled, all I can think is, satin skin, deep green pools.

She sighs. "And who might *you* be?"

(Wonder Woman's Third Cousin, I think.)

"I want to build planes," I say.

She brushes her long bang aside. "Child labour went out last century. Haven't you heard? How old are you?"

"Eighteen." Doesn't seem right to fib to Ruby Kozak – it would be like standing before that Mona Lisa painting I saw in a book, and telling a lie. I don't have much choice, though.

The air still shimmers around Ruby's shoulders. Listen – her voice is birdsong. What kind of bird? I don't know, but I heard it, once – I couldn't see where it came from. The best bird-singers make themselves scarce and hide high in the branches.

Ruby. She extends a slender hand, motions for me to sit down in the chair. Her arm soars sideways like a picture I'd seen of a ballerina tipping out a slow dance. I'm glad to obey, since I'm pretty sure I look smaller standing than sitting. *Ruby* – a name the colour of Dorothy Gale's slippers. Ruby reaches into her desk drawer, retrieves a piece of paper and a Parker pen, and gives both to me. Her hand is so close to mine, time has slowed right down and gotten big.

She's saying something – "Eighteen? Then I suppose I shall have to interview you. Here's an application blank. Fill it out, please. You never did say your name."

She sounds so blue, like her voice comes from under water. I don't know why interviewing me would make her blue. I roll the Parker pen in my fingers, feeling so bad about bringing her down that I can't fib again, so I tell her I'm Audrey Leona Foley, because I am, although I'm sticking with the Prince Edward Island story. I want to be true to her beauty, but I can't take any chances. Last person I wish to see around here is Clabber-Face, his big ugly hands hauling me back to Alberta.

I scratch away. I can answer all the questions until I reach

HOME ADDRESS _____

Once more invisible bees swarm Ruby as she resumes her typing. I rumble my throat again. Her fingers freeze mid-air.

"Excuse me, Miss Kozak – I don't have a home address."

Her long bang falls across her eye again, and I feel bad about having worsened the swarm of bees.

"Are you saying you're in need of accommodation?" she asks.

I nod. She gropes in her drawer once more and draws out another sheet of paper. This form, I discover, is called "Application for Single Room – Churchill Ladies' Residence, Fort William Aviation." The plant will deduct my room and board from my pay, she says, and remembering the cherry jar, my dwindling roll of bills, I say the sooner the better.

She types.

I write.

I write neat as I can. I want to make a good impression. It takes me a long time, I think, though I can't really tell. Ruby has rolled a sheet of paper out of the big black typewriter, rolled in a new one – she looks like she might cry, and I'm confused. She clatters some words on the fresh paper and rolls it out. I don't know why someone so beautiful, with such a plum job, someone who lives right under the moon, smack in the Dominion's industrial hub, would have anything to be sad about.

I give her the application papers. She snaps them on a clipboard. She reads what I wrote, which gives me another chance to take a good gander at her. She's sad, yes, but there's some vinegar in there. Bee. Bonnet. Mad. Sad. This doesn't spoil her beauty – the opposite. She chews her pencil as she reads, her teeth pillars of pure ivory. How does she get her lipstick on so perfect like that?

"I'm sorry," she says, her Gene Tierney eyes looking more like the eating kind now.

Gopher   Hazard

Deep, dark

"Hey? – I mean, *pardon?*" I promise to kick myself later for the hayseed *hey*-sound my mouth just blurted. I've been trying to learn to speak Ontario. I want to blend in here. Do you think her "sorry" means she doesn't want me?

Ruby drums her pencil against the clipboard. "Under 'Preferred Type of Work,' you can't write, as you have, 'I want to see how they fasten the wings.'"

"Well I *do*," I say, forgetting my Ontario manners again.

She sighs. It sounds the way a falling apple blossom might; it worries me.

"Look," Ruby says, "wing assembly is too heavy for you. But we need" – (oh most divine pause) – "heavens *yes*, we could most certainly use – a *snack-wagon girl.*"

"Snack wagon? Is that like a chuckwagon?" I am honestly stumped.

She laughs (more birdsong), and assures me it's steady enough work, making the rounds through the production sheds at staggered break times. I'd also be taking a smaller tray, a sampler of muffins, candy bars, cigarettes, coffee and tea upstairs to the security cage, the chief engineer's office, and then to Mr. Parks' digs in Head Office. "You've certainly got the boots for climbing," she quips. And between rounds, there are pots to scour – the cafeteria's kitchen would be grateful for my help.

I can start work tomorrow.

I must look more disappointed than a figure skater on slushy ice, because all of a sudden Ruby tries to cheer me up. She calls the snack-wagon a foot in the door. She says lots of plant workers shift from one job to another, or waltz between jobs. She adds everyone's moving all the time – except *her* – and I wonder if this accounts for her buzzing bees. She adds I'm young – a *kid* – I'll have lots of chances to fry bigger fish.

If Ruby Kozak were a heifer like Miss Spruce Grove, 1941, I'd tell her I didn't travel three provinces just to serve muffins. But she isn't, so I don't. Ruby must know I'm still down in the dumps about the snack wagon because she says that pushing the wagon could actually have an air of *glamour* to it. "What the dickens is glamorous about *muffins?*" I ask, and then mumble "sorry," because I am.

For the first time, Ruby's face lights up fully. She leans forward, crosses her swell elbows on the top of the typewriter, rests her chin on her arms in such a sweet way, like she's going to tell me a secret. My breaths come in short gallops.

"Listen to me, Audrey. There are *skunky dealings* in this plant. There could well be bad people here and, who knows, escapees from Angler Camp lurking as *spies* right within these industrial walls –"

I feel my eyes grow wide as Packard hubcaps.

"As the snack-wagon girl, you'll have a bird's-eye view of the factory. You'll *look* like you're just pushing your cart, but all the while you'll be seeing what your eyes can see – you'll be helping *me*, do you understand?"

"No."

She smiles for the first time. "Do you *want* to help me, Audrey?"

"Yes."

She rises from her chair. I was right – Ruby is tall, and flows, like a mermaid in a blue wool dress, out from behind her desk. She's wearing platform sandals in winter. I'm not astonished, as she can likely sail over the frozen white earth. Unlike the rest of us, she doesn't need boots. She comes round to the front of her desk and perches on its edge, crosses her ankles, swings her feet. She's even closer now, this Ruby – shining down on me like sunglow. She says her days are numbered, speaks words that sound like Greek or Latin or Ontario-educated. Tempus something...

She *is* smart as a whip. I'm dumb as a post. "Uh *huh?*"

"I'm an illusion, Audrey."

She scares me.

Beauty   hazard (?)

Then she tosses me a golden smile. "I'm not *really* a stenographer" – she drops her voice – "I'm an investigative reporter, a mighty good one, and once the world finds out, I'll never take dictation or type another letter or – no offense to you, Audrey – interview employees again. I'm one big story away from – "

(and now I *really* can't breathe)

" – blowing right *out* of here, this factory, this *whole pokey town.*"

She sweeps her ballerina's arm around the office and, the

hint is, beyond. The blobs typing at the desks behind her don't even look up. There's only Ruby and me in this room, in

the WHOLE WORLD.

She says the plant manager lets her write a little in-house newsletter called *The Factory Voice* – it offers some light entertainment, but it's nothing compared to the *real* writing she'll be doing once she gets her *big journalistic break*. She pitches me another smile, and I'm trying to think what I did to deserve this kind of swell treatment. But then her words sink in further, and I'm close to tumbling into the dumps again.

"You'll be blowing *out* of here? Where will you go?"

"Port Arthur. I'll have my own flat there. Imagine. With a view of the Sleeping Giant. I've been setting money aside for a maroon chesterfield set at Chapples Department Store. The Port Arthur newspaper doesn't want me now – I've tried – but it *will*. Once I land my big story, it'll dawn on them at long last that I'm the pearl among the swine."

I brighten. "Port Arthur's not so *very* far."

"Oh, that's where you're wrong, Audrey. It's worlds away from *this* backwater, Fort William, where I've been stuck all my life. Do you know what they call Fort William?" She doesn't wait for my answer. "They call it the *Swamp*."

"I could visit you."

"Sure you could, Audrey."

Ruby reminds me that, until that day arrives, she needs me to be her eyes in the factory. She'll depend on me to ferry information on whatever goings-on go on in those production sheds. Something is bound to happen; one of the *skunks* will make a mistake. Then she'll write her big story.

"I'm hungry, Audrey. Famished for every scrap you can feed me. *Will* you feed me?"

"You'll never be hungry again, Ruby." Tiny, excited horses canter inside my small rib cage.

Suddenly, a female voice snipes through the open door behind us – "Ruby, can you please *finish* with that girl? The whole reception area's crammed with people waiting to be interviewed for work, and I can't think straight!"

Ruby rolls her eyes my way and I see we're friends. What's more, I've already learned to read her eye-code. It says, about the girl who just called in through the door, *She can't think straight anyway.* I stifle a laugh.

"All right, all right, Fraudena!" Ruby grouses back. "We're almost done."

Ruby turns her full attention back to me. She says I'm hired. Snack-wagon girl. I'm to report to her every Wednesday on the matter of my other detail. Oh, isn't she the wizziest wiz if ever a wiz there was? Will eight dollars a month do? I clap my hands, hearing this fortune. I can move into Churchill Ladies' Residence that very day. I should report to work at the cafeteria tomorrow morning to load my wagon at seven-thirty sharp, after clocking in at the plant security portal. They'll give me a long white apron in the cafeteria along with a factory orientation. And finally, Ruby wants to be sure I'm clear on the glamour detail of my work.

"I'll be your eyes," I vow (oh your hungry green Gene Tierney eyes). "And you'll never be famished again."

"Clever girl," Ruby replies. The shimmers of air around her shoulders grow brighter. "Watch everyone, Audrey. The probation-girls in their red head scarves – and I'm sorry to say my own childhood chum, Florence Voutilainen, falls into that group. Even the brass and the new lady engineer. The plant constables, especially one called Jimmy Petrik – *that* snake. Even my own *father,* for heaven's sake – I'm sure that sounds harsh, Audrey, but the world of investigative reporting is a ruthless one."

It *doesn't* sound harsh, the parent part. I mean, no one knows better than me that you can't predict the stunts they'll pull when you're not looking.

Parental   hazard!

Ruby trills on – "Oh, and let's keep the glamour detail of your job between the two of us, shall we? It will spoil everything if I can't trust you. To the rest of the world, you're just the snack-wagon girl. But *you* know and *I* know you're *so much more* than that. Got it?"

I've got it. I ask Ruby how I'll know if I see something skunky, since I've never set foot in a factory before. Ruby says I'll be able to tell by their eyes, the guilty way they skitter sideways like an insect. Sounds odd to me but she's twenty and head stenographer. She must know.

I promise Ruby she'll start feeling a lot fuller soon. I'll feed her well. This is the best day of my whole life.

Thank you, thank you, thank you – buckets of thanks!

Let's just waltz right out of her office. Why was I foolish enough to think the snack-wagon job was a bit *lowlier* than I would have liked? All this time, I was only one pair of boots away from so much *industrial glamour*.

*A*nother Christmas. Another dreary blur. Another day of typing done. At least Ruby has the house to herself. Her mother is out selling Victory Bonds. Her father is still at the factory, working overtime due to the brouhaha around the Angler escape. Neither of them knows that the word stenography comes from the Greek word, *stenos* – Narrow Writing System. Of *course* they wouldn't know something like that.

Ruby sighs for their worldly lack, and stretches, on her stomach, across her neatly made bed. She likes her room to resemble a hotel as much as possible, to remind her that she's destined to fly this coop, and the factory, and her tiresome boss Frank Parks with his strangle of cigar smoke, and the whole unenchanted machine that's supposed to be her *life* and falls so short – except for the singular highlight of being crowned Miss Fort William 1939. She couldn't give a fig about Mosquitoes or scary-monsters-on-the-loose security alerts unless there's a story. The only bright spot in all this is, with so many workers trucking into the factory every day to sign on, there's got to be a few rotten apples in such a huge barrel, and the reporter in Ruby knows bad apples make good stories.

She peruses her dismal, chipped nail polish. Factory work is all right for someone like Florence Voutilainen, her girlhood friend who didn't finish high school or seem to have a single aspiration beyond the Swamp. Ruby fans her hands out and sighs. Stenography has been ruining her nails for a year now, ever since she graduated from Fort William Business College (her mother's idea). Even joining the Canadian Women's Army Corps would probably have been more interesting, though they'd have preached about how she should wear her hair. Ruby shifts on the quilt; her long Veronica Lake bangs fall over her left eye. She remembers the advice her grade thirteen English teacher, Miss Izza Sawb, delivered on how to live their lives – keep the zest keen. This was harder than Ruby might have imagined. Yes, a whole year and still stuck in the Narrow Writing System. *Dear Sir, Our Sub-Assembly Department regrettably awaits an order for one hundred arrestor hooks placed in September 1941. Dear Sir, Concerning our order for DH propellers. Concerning our order for chocks. Concerning our order for catapult spools. Concerning our order for trim cranks.* Template. Guff. Cookie-cutter work. All it does is blacken Ruby's fingers with carbon. And to top it, Frank Parks piled on the interviewing and registering of new employees in addition to Ruby's regular dictation, typing and filing. She's busier than Medusa's hairdresser.

Once in a blue moon, something worth noting befalls Ruby. Like the strange girl who'd blown into her office, looking for work. Audrey Foley. She'd claimed to be eighteen. *Yes, and I am Mata Hari,* Ruby thought. She'd been inclined to send this Audrey packing, at first, for the kid was too young and small for most line work, though Ruby supposed the half-pint could have sorted rivets or something equally light. The factory had enough rivet sorters. Ruby had puzzled, for a moment, over what work might be offered to this odd-duck kid, and then her own brainstorm clobbered her with the force of a Lake Superior gale – the chap who'd been working the snack wagon had given his notice, and there were no muffins or smokes or drinks, and much crankiness over this, in all three production sheds. Ruby had astonished herself with her stroke of brilliance. She'd kill two whiskey jacks with one stone – the workers would get their snacks and, with any luck, she'd have a journalistic *source,* a running girl. Everyone gets fed. And the girl had been so eager and *compliant.* Who would have thought a waif in boots might help burst the stenographic shackles around Ruby's pretty wrists, could hold the future's very key?

The balance must shift. Ruby feels this more every minute, and the pleasant pulsing in her temples that arises when something important is about to happen comes over her. A moving picture of Ruby's happy future flickers above the two trunks situated beside each other against the opposite wall of her bedroom, her hope chest and her hopeless chest. She rises from her bed, crosses the room and lifts both lids.

HOPE CHEST:
Buffed birch. Filled with creamy old goods that must not, under any circumstances, be used before she marries. Primly folded pillowcases, sachets, dresser scarves, baby bonnet (if her mother only knew), all manner of tatting, embroidery, needlepoint, crocheting handed down and down, intricate as spiderwebs. Ruby's mother encourages her to peek into this chest once in a while, a reminder of what the future holds (the future being when Ruby meets a nice boy, when the war ends). Frieda Kozak: maternal tourist stirring through the mothballs and sachets, her hushed voice, *Heirlooms,* spoken like a prayer. 'Little of interest in the hope chest,' Ruby thinks. Even her Miss Fort William tiara saddens her, that crown of splendour past.

HOPELESS CHEST:
Stodgy, stained dark. Held blankets, once. Musted, now, with blasted dreams, this behemoth broods, a diamond pattern inlaid along its front like some poky picket fence. Ruby fills it with her life's disappointments. It's full enough for a girl who

is only twenty. Third-place ribbon from the Domestic Science Fair. Bell belonging to poor old Puss. Carbon copy of the note she'd sent to Joan Alexander, the voice of Lois Lane (never answered), carbon copy of letter to the editor of *The Fort William Daily Times Journal* asking for a place as a journalist, answered: "no openings anticipated in the foreseeable future." Box filled with lilacs from a boy, a terrible mistake, Jimmy Petrik (the slightest puff of breath would send the tiny, shriveled blooms into tragic brown confetti). A doll with a broken foot. Her lively essay, "Should Women Ride Bicycles?" that should have won first prize but didn't because the jury was stacked with Port Arthur judges. Baby booties her mother had given her for some misty married future. Pressed between the worn pages of *Emily Climbs,* three maple leaves collected on Ruby's only trip to Toronto. The saddest trip she ever took, a visit, in the guise of a stenographers' convention, to a special doctor, a secret. Even her friend Florence Voutilainen didn't know. Ruby's mother certainly didn't. The baby's father, Jimmy Petrik, *knew,* had wished her luck before she left. His name is mud to Ruby. He'd told her, that night of the high-school graduation prom, to trust him. Trust, dust. A baby would have ruined Ruby's dream of becoming an investigative reporter. Investigative reporters did not have babies. What else does that hopeless chest hold? Ruby's stenography diploma, conferred on her by Fort William Business College – Stenography a dreary, stopgap measure until her life as a journalist gets under way. An entry, torn from her diary, August 11, 1939, again, over two years ago, "The Sad Shortage of Civilized and Well-Proportioned Young Men in Northwestern Ontario." Nothing has changed. More torn entries, noteworthy laments in her brief fizzle of an existence, folded, yellowing.

Ruby lowers the lids of both chests. Yes, the balance *must* shift, the contents of her hope chest will swell, grow to greater proportions. In Ruby's new resolve to keep the zest keen – her reinvigorated personal exit procedure – a running girl couldn't hurt. No, she couldn't hurt at all.

Auld Acquaintance
Should Definitely be Forgot

*M*uriel's office gleams. It has been scrubbed and refitted just as Frank Parks promised. She admires her engineering diplomas inside their polished wooden frames, brightening the wall where the old bend-allowance tables sagged in tatters. Both sets of windows, those overlooking the production shed and those facing the sawed-off mountain, sparkle. Her hardwood floor has been varnished; her heels now hobble with hopeful authority over the buffed boards. Lemon oil delights her nostrils. The kettle boils cheerfully. She'd read the sorry excuses for test-flight reports Orville Loftus had sent to Karl Wilkins, things such as: "SHE DON'T FLY WORTH COW-PIE." She would set the test pilot straight. This was no kind of reporting at all, and the fact that her predecessor, Wilkins, was afraid of heights and hadn't accompanied Loftus on test flights was scandalously unprofessional. No, she'd fix this. She lives to fix things. Even the problem files Wilkins left look less menacing stacked neatly, as they now are, on Muriel's tidy desk. She's read his twitching calligraphy, his lists of frayed cables, stressed ball joints, filler-cap leakages, deformed washers, broken fairings, fatigue failures of spring drives, taper pins incorrectly secured to starter magnetos thus shearing them, wrong rivets (why countersunk he couldn't imagine), wrong this, wrong that. Tailwheels that didn't retract fully – yes, he'd hit on something with that, she has to confess – Mosquitoes are notorious for that. Flutter and vibration. He'd circled *deficient wire gauge, thirty-one cases.* Muriel had absorbed his gloom with grains of salt. She'd get to the bottom of these hitches, soar past her predecessor's pessimism and perfect her winter landing gear design in the bargain. She'd inked these New Year's resolutions in red in her diary. And: *We'll never win this war with defeated minds like Karl Wilkins.'*

No, *her* office sings undefeated mind. Her refitted digs have granted fresh distance from the man on the *Wanted* posters. She'd seen his face the day this office was a shambles. This office is reborn. And as for the man on the poster, it has been twenty-three years. He is nothing to her now. He is best forgotten (on first seeing the posters she'd gone home and, foolishly, had a good cry, then wrote in her diary – *what are tears – mere sodium chloride + lysozyme* – that inked, she'd moved past him). Since then, when Muriel delivers her memoranda to Head Office, she assumes a tunnel vision and stares straight ahead to avoid the *Wanted* posters there. This mostly works, though it strikes her that a messenger pigeon would be even better.

She makes tea. While it steeps, she opens her mail. Christmas card from C.D. Howe, Minister of Munitions and Supply, with a stamped signature. *Season's Greetings* swirled across a Vancouver skyline from her mother (so she had recovered). A report from Orville Loftus, convalescing from an accident, the details of which Muriel unfolds: *Report of Test Flight, Fort William Aviation, November 14, 1941. Result: Crash.*

Post-crash engine pretty scorched but gauge of wires looked fishy. Rogue wires possibly. Plane lost altitude at twelve thousand feet, took sharp dive into trees at north end of Bishop's Field Airstrip. Bruised. Ankle snapped. Out of commission until 1942. This matter requires follow-up. No spring chicken.

Fed up flying sick birds. Orville Loftus, Test Pilot. P.S. Am sending new lady engineer slender volume. She should read it. Sure enough, a package wrapped in brown butcher paper, return-addressed O. Loftus, nests in the bottom of Muriel's mail basket. She opens it. A small, worn book. *The Rime of the Ancient Mariner* by S. T. Coleridge. She thumbs through a few pages before setting it aside. How this is meant to help Muriel solve aeronautical problems she can't fathom. She keeps hearing, through the industrial grapevine, about Loftus' gruff eccentricities. She begins to grasp the vine.

Muriel ferries her tea to the window overlooking Sub-Assembly. In seconds, the bell will clang the end of the shift. If she had no clock, she'd still know. She can already read the workers' bodies. Even the big Voutilainen girl with the zealous rivet gun slows in the waning seconds before the bell tolls, and it does. The machines stop. The workers stream out of the shed, a mostly yellow flow except for some men and several girls' red probation scarves, including Florence Voutilainen's crimson top. Over in Head Office, the stenographers will have scrubbed the carbon from their fingers. Then it will begin again tomorrow; the labour-river will wash back in on cue, the fingers take on carbon, bells sound, and already the pattern wins Muriel's affection. Nevertheless –

She welcomes the peace the empty factory brings; she often works after hours. No distractions. Con Kozak, the night watchman, shuffles past her office without disturbing her. Shines his flashlight and is gone. The snack wagon has braked for the day – thank goodness. Muriel had to ask the queer girl to make fewer stops at her office. Audrey used to blow by every few minutes it seemed, bursting with curiosity about planes, peeking at blueprints, asking, "what's this for?" – "what are you doing now?" And each time the girl would finally leave, she'd shout "keep 'em flying, Miss McGregor!" which simultaneously rattled and charmed Muriel. She'd felt badly about admonishing the girl, especially since the two of them shared a bit of history, and it was this – they'd both taken the same train to Fort William. Muriel had to put her lame foot down by saying she needed only one muffin each day – morning break – and she made her own tea in her office. She'd tried to be as gentle as she could, for studies show that industrial workers thrive on kindness, and clearly the kid, hardly dry behind the ears, regards Muriel as some kind of conjurer, or exotic species of bird, or *heroine,* even, and Muriel doesn't necessarily wish the spell broken.

Petrik's Autobody, Fort William
James Petrik, Proprietor
Hours Spotty for Dour-ashun of War
Light On Means Open

*L*ight On.

Jimmy Petrik slides out, on his back, from under Daisy and thinks, 'one thing's for sure, there's no sweeter sight in the whole Lakehead than a well-oiled chassis, seen from below.' Daisy is a Packard. Jimmy has been working on her in spare hours and holidays like today, New Year's Day. Free hours, he realizes, levering himself upright and wiping the axle grease from his hands onto his coveralls, that shrink with each passing week. He'd hoped to have Daisy fit to sell, reconditioned, by spring; she's only part of the fund Jimmy has been accumulating by taking on extra work. He has big plans for his garage – one day to have the largest autobody shop in Fort William. Now he's not sure Daisy will be ready. For one thing, she needs new tires. Tires are getting scarce as rocking-horse manure. He'll have to troll for those. The dump piles on the edge of Fort William. Wrecking yard out that way. Tomorrow. Good thing he's got a bit of steady money coming in from the special-gauge wire he's been selling to that crazy old coot, Mack, out in the bush.

A fire chatters in the small wood stove a few yards away. The shop has warmed up nicely. Jimmy settles himself on his smoking stump, a slab of tree trunk he'd carted into his garage one day. He'd also lugged a second, lesser stump, in case anyone visits (any minute) or he brings a girl here (in due course, surely – for what girl wouldn't go goo-goo over a chap's autobody shop?). He lights a Lucky Strike and stares across the garage at his pet crow caged on top of an old crate.

"Whatcha think, Einstein – will Daisy be ready by spring?"

The crow hops sideways once, and squawks a sour note Jimmy takes for no. He's not that surprised. He won't have the time to spend on the Packard. They need him too much down at the plant. So many Fort William boys have signed on with the Lake Superior Regiment, the plant is left top-heavy with giddy girls. Dim Doras. Pinch hitters, but who knew for how long? As far as Jimmy's concerned, the regiment can wait until every last pile of moose scat in the bush turns to bricks of gold before the army gets *him;* the last war took his father. That's enough for one family. Besides, Jimmy's leg suffered a pellet-gun injury ten years ago when he was sixteen. It doesn't slow him down and he's used to the little hitch in his step. Since Canada went to war, the handicap has proven a bonus; when the girls down at the plant nag Jimmy about whether he'll sign up, he points to his leg. Sadly. The cross he must bear.

Jimmy inhales, holds, releases smoke in the smart way he's honed on the streets of Fort William. His mother had done her best, raising him alone, but most of what he learned, he learned on those streets. They were no place for pansies. He exhales – not some prissy smoke-wreath – more a shape like a foxtail. No question, they need his sound head at the factory. He's *in-disposable* there. He'd started out as a wire cutter, but his talents shone through quickly. He'd moved up to plant constable, but had been decent enough to cover in the wire area until they hired someone to replace him. He really should ask for more money. Not everyone can juggle as many balls as he does: security, chauffeuring, pinch-hitting, training. Balls that just keep getting bigger, and this doesn't even count his helping out with parts when they run into shortages while waiting for some ship from Boscombe Down that's never going to come. He keeps those birds moving down the line for the good of everyone.

Bigger balls. A couple of weeks ago, Frank Parks asked Jimmy to train the Voutilainen girl to weld because she's so fast with her rivet gun; she gets way ahead and just stands around. So, after her riveting shift, Jimmy shows her the ropes in Welding (all the while keeping his eye on her Red Finn reputation as he'd been ordered). He used to weld, summer jobs during the couple of years he wasted in high school. Jimmy could have told Parks he didn't have time to train Florence Voutilainen, but he's learned that a favour, once done, can be cashed in some day, and though Florence is a tub of lard and has bad teeth and clown feet, her hazel eyes shine his way with endless gratitude for training her, so he puts up with it.

Still, she's a drain on his time, with her slow mind. Not to mention her physical eyesores. She caught onto rivet work quickly enough, but welding is a different story. Jimmy told Frank Parks that maybe Florence could turn out to be a one-gun wonder. Parks said give her time, so Jimmy must. And his plant-constable work demands more of him every day with new workers signing on, along with the dust his boss, Con Kozak, keeps kicking up about the Angler escape. And Jimmy has to wonder what his boss's daughter and his own one-time girlfriend, Ruby Kozak, is *doing* up there in Head Office lately, considering the simpletons and maniacs she's been hiring, like the kid who pushes the snack wagon, an ugly little human mosquito with porcupine hair, who stares at him so hard he wonders if she (he assumes she's a she though there's little evidence to point either way) shouldn't be in the Lakehead Lunatic Asylum instead of the factory, for crikey sake. When he'd asked the mosquito for a muffin the other day, she'd narrowed those beady eyes of hers and come back at him, "*Why* do you want a muffin? What is it about a *muffin* in *particular?*" No, she's most definitely one bulb short of a chandelier, that kid. If Ruby Kozak weren't so high-strung, and stuck-up, and his boss's daughter, and if she didn't despise Jimmy for a little slip back when she was in high school, he'd ask her what she was thinking, hiring human mosquitoes and retarded kids too green to show proper respect for a plant constable. Hiring mosquitoes to help build Mosquitoes, what a joke. But bouncing *that* rubber ball into Ruby Kozak's court isn't worth Jimmy's trouble; he'll have to teach the snack-wagon girl some manners himself.

This is only one example of what Jimmy must contend with day in and day out. They really *could* appreciate him more, down there. At least when Frank Parks had asked him to be the new lady engineer's driver before Christmas, Jimmy had had the sense to say, "All right, but if I'm driving *her* around like she's the queen, I'll need extra gasoline ration coupons," and Parks at least had had the gumption to agree. And at least Ruby Kozak had hired a new wire cutter named Reggie Hatch from Rainy River who, while green as the snack-wagon girl, knew enough to pay Jimmy some respect. And Jimmy had done the decent thing and taken Rainy Reg, a scarecrow of a small-town boy, under his wing. And Jimmy continues to train him, even today, any minute – on New Year's Day when Jimmy's not even clocked in at the factory.

Three timid knocks. Rainy. Jimmy butts his Lucky Strike inside a sardine can on the floor. This is Reggie's first visit to Jimmy's garage and, just as Jimmy predicted, the boy brims with awe the minute he steps out of the bitter wind, teeth chittering, and into Petrik's Autobody. Shivering, he wishes Jimmy a happy new year. Jimmy wishes him one back.

"Is this all *yours*?" Reggie unwinds his scarf one turn. His eyes, roving from the small wood stove in the corner to the 1942 calendar's pin-up girl with her head thrown back, to the crow in its cage, to the Packard with one end jacked up, to the heaps of radiators, mufflers, hoses and wires along one wall in piles, are suitably amazed. He pulls off his blue grey toque. His black hair is pomaded in a bumpkin way that looks foolish on someone so young. Reggie can't be more than nineteen.

Jimmy nods. He points to the visitor stump. "Sit, Reggie."

Reggie removes his thin cloth coat as he lowers himself gingerly onto the small circle of wood. He drapes the coat over his bony knees. He calls Jim's garage *darned impressive* and his Adam's apple bounces so much, as he continues to stare around the garage and mutter *swell*, and *nifty* and *jeepers*, Jimmy wonders if it will fly right out of his throat and land on the tire iron propped against the opposite wall.

Reg can't stop gawking. He asks if the crow has a name. "Einstein," Jimmy says. "Named so because that bird is smarter than most people. All it has to do is sit there, in its cage, and get fed." Reggie's eyes fix on a big pile of wires against the far wall. Hundreds of strands, chopped into lengths of about ten inches or so. They remind him of the wires he cuts at the plant.

"What's all the wire for, Jim?"

Jimmy resumes his smoking stump. "Special assignment, Rainy." He asks Reg how his wire-cutting job at the plant is going. Reggie says it sure beats driving a taxi over those frozen, rutted streets: a taxi filled with cranks who smell, or don't tip, or old vets who ask to be driven out to this shanty on the edge of Fort William to see some "sewing lady" and half the time don't have enough fare once they get there, or crazy girls blown in from who-knows-where who don't know where they're going, only the occasional looker, and in the end mostly riff-raff who treat him like he's some kind of *taxi driver* –

"Well, you *are*," Jim interjects "– or, *were*."

"Those days are done. I'm liking it at the plant. I'm liking it a lot. It pays decent. I'm helping bring down Hitler's boys. And for once I'm getting a little respect."

"Good, good," Jimmy says. "That's what a man wants, respect."

Reggie scans the contours of the 1942 pin-up girl on the wall. "That's not all, Jim."

Jimmy twigs, fast as lightning, to the object of Reg's gaze. "You got a girl?"

Reggie shakes his head. The ladies don't like bags of bones like him, and he has no car. Reg faces some obstacles, no question, Jimmy admits, but *he* could lend a hand in the date department, and it could start tomorrow, if Reggie wants to know more.

Reggie wants to know more. Like *where* will it start?

"Use your head, Rainy. At the plant. You're swarmed with girls there. Regular Jane Mansfields in overalls." Jimmy tips his stump seat back to observe the wire cutter from a fresh angle – "that factory is one big house of *love-potential.*"

Reggie asks him what he means by house of love-potential. Clearly, Jimmy's latest apprentice is as thick as the Voutilainen girl.

"Think about it," Jimmy urges. "You've seen the names of some of those parts. Couplings. Screws."

"Rivets with tits."

The two young men laugh. Jimmy slaps his knee. "That's right, Reggie, my boy. Sex *oozes* from the walls of that place."

Reggie Hatch wants to know how a bit might ooze in *his* direction. Jimmy says it's just a matter of Reg doing him a small favour; the rest will fall into place. And when Jimmy finishes fixing the Packard, he might even let Reggie borrow it to drive his date around. "Would you like that, Reggie?" Reggie nods, and his shining eyes tell Jimmy he can't believe his good fortune in finding a friend like Jimmy.

Jimmy says all Reg has to do is bring a bundle of wires from his work station bin to Jimmy's De Soto in the plant parking lot every Friday after work – he'll meet Reg there – as many wires as Reg can stash in his jacket pocket without a bulge. Then Jimmy will give Reggie wires to carry back into the factory the next day, again, in his jacket pocket. When Reg reaches his work station, he'll simply blend the new wires in with the rest, and before he knows it, he'll have dates coming out his ears. Wire out, wire in, piece of cake. Reggie asks what happens if they find the wires in his jacket pocket at the employee check point when he's on his way into the plant. Reggie is so unswift, Jimmy can't help lobbing him a look that says so.

"Who do you see when you go through the check point every morning, Reggie?"

"Uh, *you*, Jim."

"Right on the money, Rainy. You think I'm going to haul you aside and make you empty your pockets when I already know what's *in* them?"

Reggie's eyes are contrite and confused. "No?"

"Keep up, Reggie. And mum's the word, all right?"

Reggie says all right. "But what do you *do* with the wires?"

Jimmy glowers. "I help people. All right?"

"All right. There's something else."

Jimmy ogles his wristwatch. "*What?*"

"I *already* know which girl I want to take on a date."

"Moving fast, Rainy. Which one?"

"The girl who hired me. She's a slice of heaven, Jim."

Jimmy groans. "*Her?*"

Reggie's cheeks pinken. His Adam's apple pulses. He nods. "I think her name is Ruby. Yes. How many wires will get me a date with *her?*"

"That's not a good idea, Reggie. You wouldn't like Ruby Kozak. Besides, she thinks she hung the moon. Double-besides, she doesn't like me, so it'd be tough to convince her."

Reggie asks how could Ruby Kozak not like a swell chap like Jimmy?

"Ancient history," Jimmy says. "She holds grudges. You don't want a grudge-holding dame, Rainy, trust me."

Oh yes, he *would*, Reggie insists.

Jimmy can see that in the dating department his apprentice needs even more guidance than in the realm of wires. The plant should pay Jimmy a bonus for all the advice he dishes out to employees, but he'll give Reggie some for free today: "Don't grab the first fish that swims past." Instead, Reg should take a long, hard gander at the *whole ocean*, a few months, say. And new girls are tramping in every day. Jimmy probes: how much experience has Reggie had with women?

(Rainy: silence)

"That's what I thought," Jimmy says. "So remember what I just told you. Gander hard. All right?"

"All right."

They shake hands. Jimmy says there's a tin canister of dried corn and sunflower seeds on the shelf above the crow's cage. He tells Reggie to feed Einstein.

"Will he bite?" Reggie asks.

"Only if you provoke him. But believe me, he can rip your skin off."

Reggie takes some seeds and corn. He opens the cage door. He tosses the food in as quickly as he can before shutting the door.

"Now give him some water." Jimmy points to a tin cup hooked over a bucket of water by the wood stove. "Ice in the bucket should be thawed some by now."

Reggie fills the cup and approaches the cage again. His fingers, grasped around the cup, quiver. The crow is too busy devouring the seeds to notice the hand watering him. Reg closes the cage door in relief. What sissies, those Rainy River boys. Then Jimmy says, "Crikey sake, fifteen minutes ago I was supposed to fetch the lady engineer from the dumb winter-carnival parade. She was riding on a float – Queen of the Mosquitoes. I'm late." He won't be able to drive Reggie back to his rooming house on Syndicate Avenue. Reggie remarks how powerful busy Jim is, even on New Year's Day, and Jimmy says, "What can you do?" He snuffs the fire, and grabs his coat on the hook by the garage door. He yanks the light chain and the shop drops to darkness. Reggie pulls on his flimsy coat and rewinds his scarf, forgets his toque. He tells Jimmy walking is no bother; he's got lots to chew over along the way. He heads into the wind.

Motoring past him Jimmy geisers up snow to reinforce his late state, glances into his rearview mirror and sees the long, hard gander Reggie Hatch sends his way, sees it despite the winter day's dimming light.

Florence
where the Road
Fizzles, the Sow
Roots and the Rooster Crows

*W*ith each step along the cold road home, Florence Voutilainen hates the red scarf more, the vile rag they've made her wear since she started working at the factory five weeks ago. The money's more than swell, it's salvation itself, but the probation scarf makes it hard for Florence to keep her young chins up – yes, *chins* – for she's had, sadly, a double chin since she was twelve years old. When she wears the scarf, people stare at her strange and some line workers call her the big red fish, and this one geezer she has to pass to go to the bathroom likes asking, "Are you a red hun, honey?" And maybe even worse are the factory girls who pretend they don't see the probation scarf but whose pity rings through loud and clear. At the first clang of the bell ending her shift, Florence sticks the cursed red triangle in her overalls pocket. *Probation.* Florence knows what that spells. Hell's bells, that spells bottom-feeder.

She trudges, now, along a road carved through trees thickening with night. Pushes herself into wind that won't stop biffing her face, even after she's turned onto Rosslyn Road and hoped it might hit her backside. The wind has turned with her. To make matters worse, today her wool cap got lost in the women's locker room. Someone must have grabbed it accidentally, and now she can't feel her ears in the sub-zero air. Her forehead has frozen into a big, numb headache. And her head was *already* throbbing, crammed with welding words she's been having the worst time trying to jam in there and make stick. *Alloy. Arc blow. Blowhole. Inoculants. Parent metal. Slip lines. Wormholing. Yield strength.* Jimmy, the boy who is teaching her to weld, is a dream; this makes the words even harder to remember. He watches her when she rivets, too. Florence can't tell if her imagination is tricking her, or if Jimmy makes his security rounds past *her* more often than the other girls, but she's pretty sure he does. Jimmy looks so dandy in his blue plant constable's uniform he quivers the rivets in her fingers. Good thing she's got strong fingers. His passes make Florence blush, and only part of the flame in her cheeks comes from the shame brought on by the red scarf. *Ugh,* that scarf – it's made of some brand new material – *Dacron* says the tag – that itches, and suffocates her scalp, and while wearing the nasty scarf might save her ears out here on this day when she's without her wool cap, it will wreak too much damage on her pride even though no one's out here in the middle of nowhere to see her. Besides, Florence reflects glumly as she clinches her coat collar around her neck to stave off cold, she's already so homely with her rolls of fat, her cavity-ridden front teeth and clodhopper feet that frostbitten ears wouldn't worsen her looks that much more.

Florence's feet are snowplows. The wind clobbers her wavy brown hair – her best feature. Now that's frozen, too. Despite radio advisories telling everyone to watch their backs, to be wary of dangerous men on the roads, and young ladies in particular to check from side to side as they walk, Florence looks straight ahead in the manner of a traveller in a tunnel; if some criminal type comes upon her there, she reckons her looks will scare him away fast enough, so she doesn't invite more blasts of bitter wind by checking from side to side for hazardous men. Florence has lived out here, at the edge of Fort William, for the whole twenty-one years of her life, and there's nothing to see except the wrecking yard, about half a mile ahead and near her house, and dumping grounds. People bring things they don't want and leave them at the edges of places. If anything, Florence should think of the stingy light of winter days as a mercy, for it blocks out the great deal of nothing there is to look at, as well as the things no one wants to see, in Florence's neck, no, *armpit* of the woods.

Soon she'll reach her shambles of a house, sad digs where her nightmare mother might or might not be home, where the sow roots in the back shed near the old, rusted Model-T Ford (it has moldered there forever) and the rooster crows in the chicken hut even though there's nothing to crow over, where some gloomy Gus from the last war sometimes sits slumped at the kitchen table, waiting for "Henni Voutilainen, Veteran Seamstress of the Lakehead," just like the sign nailed to their mailbox says, to finish sewing his tragic mutant trousers. A cramped kitchen, its only decoration a crokinole board hanging on the wall. Or sometimes the veteran in need of mending waits behind the beaded doorway of Henni's bedroom, which he fills with tobacco smoke and sometimes low wailings that make Florence, in her own bedroom on the other side of the thin wall, stop her ears. No, Flo never knows what she'll find when she gets home, or whom. Thanks to her mother, Florence must endure the red scarf that marks her as a bottom-feeder, as trouble, while the other girls work away in their happy daffodil tops, their "I'm-no-problem-at-all" yellow scarves. As soon as Florence earns enough money to get her teeth filled, if it's not too late to save them, and then saves some more after that, she'll tell her mother no more sewing; they won't need the income and Henni can try, for once, to be a normal mother.

Florence repeats the welding words as she tramps along. She's talked to herself or to rocks or vegetables as long as she can remember. She's an only child. Lonely child. Repeating the welding words will help them sink in once and for all. She knows she's made her mark riveting. If she can prove herself in the Welding Department and convince Frank Parks and the rest of the brass that they *really, truly* can't do without her and she's *really, truly* not like her mother, surely they'll issue her a regular yellow head scarf. Florence is so tired of sticking out like a sore thumb. Her oldest and best friend, Ruby Kozak, who hired her for rivet work before Christmas, said, "just give it everything you've got, Flo, and they'll forget the red-scarf silliness." *Ruby* knew Florence was a good person, but the war had frothed up suspicion in people, and the government kept everyone stirred up, too, so *sadly,* Ruby concluded, Florence must go the extra mile on the line. Ruby also said she'd had to do plenty of "spadework" to convince her boss, Frank Parks, to hire Florence, given what he called her mother's Red Finn tendencies and antipatriot leanings. Ruby had spaded. Florence had spouted tears of gratitude for having the world's finest, not to mention most breathtakingly beautiful, friend.

Florence had swallowed her shame and worn the red scarf. Trouble is, each week the red reddens.

It's almost dark. Florence approaches the outcropping of rock that flanks the entrance to the wrecking yard. That rock's shape always reminds her of the gnarled, crouching troll in the "Three Billy Goats Gruff" story in the only child-hood book she'd owned. Ruby had given it to her for Christmas in 1928, when they were still little girls – well, Florence a biggish little girl. The same year they vowed to be each other's maids of honour when they married – *if,* in her own sorry case.

Just as Florence reaches the Gruff rock, a car suddenly rolls alongside her and scares her almost into conniption fits. She hasn't heard its approach or even seen its headlights, and hasn't been checking from side to side, as the radio advised, for dangerous men.

She keeps walking. The automobile inches along. Even the near dark can't conceal the vehicle's swank. The driver cranks down his window and if Florence's face hadn't been frozen, she'd have laughed with relief to see Jimmy Petrik, her hand-some welding teacher and plant constable. Strains of some snappy radio tune reach her. She's pretty sure it's Glenn Miller, though cold bends the music. The song, whatever it is, suits a car like that. Jimmy Petrik calls to her over the saxophones –

"Hey – you look like you could use this" – he tosses her a toque through the open window (the very toque Reggie Hatch left in his garage yesterday, and that Jimmy had found when he'd zipped by there to feed the crow this morning).

She catches the toque. So few acts of kindness have been bestowed on Florence Voutilainen, Jimmy's gesture ripples a deep place in her. She pulls this moment close, certain it means something. The toque. The darkening road. The fact that *his* car – and such a dandy jade green De Soto – is the only automobile she's encountered since turning off Neebing Avenue on her lonely walk home. Her earlobes are so cold she can't feel them as she puts on the toque. She thanks Jimmy. She watches his hands move to his mouth to light a cigarette. The car crunches along slowly, at her walking speed. So he's the considerate type, matching his pace with hers.

Jimmy calls out through the window again – "What in crikey sake is my welding apprentice doing way out here where Christ lost his sandals?"

"I live near here." Florence flicks her mittened hand down the narrow road, a zipper in dark trees. "Just past the wrecking yard. I'm going home – and I've never seen Christ around here."

She slogs onward on her tired clown feet. Jimmy tells her she shouldn't be out here, with those Angler men on the loose. She should take a taxicab home. Florence says that'd eat too much of her pay. She confides she's been saving hard. Jimmy understands that, all right. He's been saving like sixty himself. He's going to build onto his garage. "Golly, it must be something to have your own garage," Florence shivers. "It *is*," Jimmy returns.

He drives. She walks.

Suddenly it dawns fully on Florence – a *boy* is talking to her. A welding teacher. Plant constable. *Man.* Luckily, it's too dark for him to see her terrible teeth. She should talk back.

"What are *you* doing out here?" She calls in through his window.

He turns down the radio. "Tires. Salvaging. I was just going to turn into the wrecking yard when I saw you – or saw *somebody* crazy enough to be out in this wind without a hat. I was pretty sure it was you, though, even in the dark –"

"Uh-*huh*." Florence's tongue clogs with the shame of knowing *why* he was pretty sure; she can say no more. She's certain Jimmy recognized her because of her size, her billowing thighs, clomping clown-feet.

Jimmy has overshot the wrecking yard now, and will have to turn around and retrace his tracks. "Hey," he hollers. "Why don't you hop in and I'll drive you the rest of the way home?"

She shakes her head. Panic grips her. She can't let him see her shabby house on its crooked blocks, digs not much bigger than a hockey penalty box – her so-called home with its peeled paint and junk-heaped yard, or worse, her mother who might, just at the wrong moment, run steamy and pink, without a stitch of clothing, from the sauna hut in the backyard, around the front corner of the house, into the kitchen (her mother often takes a sauna before supper). Not to mention the ragged strands of yarn fallen onto the snow from the scarves of the last war's veterans who came to Henni for mending. No, he mustn't see where she lives. The place is full of shadows. It's grim. It smacks of death. Then there's the smell of pig, even in winter. Even outdoors. He *can't* see it, as much as sitting beside him in his beautiful car would have meant Florence could die without complete desolation.

"Oh no," she says. "I'm almost home. I'm so close. It'd waste your gasoline. But thanks, and thanks for the hat." She waves and turns away from his car and hurries as fast as she can down the final stretch of road. Jimmy Petrik hollers something. It sounds like "whatever blows your dress up," but his words stall in a sudden, bitter gust, and they might be "do you never dress up?" She can't be sure, and can't find out because that might open the can of worms about driving her home again, so she keeps walking and makes a mental note to do more with herself. To quell her nerves after the close call of a man of his calibre seeing where she lives, she makes a picture in her head of the perfect arc the blue grey toque made as it spun, in the air, towards her.

Human Interest Feature – By Ruby Frances Kozak

SNACKS ARE BACK; GOOD THINGS REALLY DO COME IN SMALL PACKAGES

y now you've all seen the new snack girl wend her wagon through our production sheds. Her name is Audrey Foley; she comes to us from a small, dreamy island on the Dominion's eastern shores. And what a loaded wagon she wields! It's a veritable movable feast. Hungry? Need a candy bar for extra fuel? Ask Audrey for a Milky Way, Snickers, Fat Emma or Butterfingers. I'll wager she's got a Baby Ruth bar or two tucked in that magic wagon of hers. Watching your waist, girls? Snag a warm bran muffin from Audrey's cheerful cart. Wash it down with a Root Beer, Fresh-up, White Rock Soda or Coca-Cola, or, for warm-blooded workers, coffee or tea. And no snack wagon is properly stocked without tobacco. Our girl's got that covered, too – Camels, Old Golds and Lucky Strikes. By now you're wondering how such a wee lassie can maneuver this pantry on wheels. Your trusty Voice inquired after her surprising strength. "It's from roping calves, I mean, hauling fish from the sea." She's clearly still dazzled by all the glamour around her (it's glamour to her eyes). Whatever the source of her strength, don't let our Audrey's size fool you; she's pure pluck, an inspiration to us all. And by the way, remember her tin cup – all tips go to Victory Bonds.

Muriel
In the depths of night
even engineers dream
(Actual Temp. – 22 F)
(Dream Temp. – 60 F
with a distinct pitch and yaw)

he blizzard's force is mythic, Antarctic. She is on her hands and knees, searching through wreckage and snow. She must find the bolt that bolted from the landing ski she'd hewn with her own hands, the bolt that flew that caused the crash. Only after she studies it for stress can she understand what went wrong. She is crawling through snow, her cold fingers panning for the lost bolt, her throat coughing away smoke that billows from the engine of the Mosquito, the beautiful bird in pieces now, because her landing skis failed to retract, plummeting the plane's nose into a bank of timber. The test pilot is still inside. His wails come to her: "You are a terrible engineer." The wolves howl; her fingers, sifting through snow, return empty to her. Crows already circle the plane. Its undercarriage burns. A Mahler symphony plays. "Don't leave me here," the pilot screams. "I won't leave you" she cries. Red ink rivulets across the snow, leaked ink from her diary. She can't do anything about that just now. She rises, lurches through the storm towards the shattered airplane. She is wearing a long Victorian frock coat; its iron weight pulls her down as she struggles through the wintry gale to where the test pilot pleads for help. She does not have polio. Still, she

moves so slowly, the wind. The pilot curses her landing skis. He
cries out once more, in the voice of her mother. She is repulsed,
yet has no choice but to extend her hand –

Muriel coughs. She gasps, frantically trying to unclog the
cinders from her throat. Her face is beaded with sweat –
strange, given the harrowing wind chill. Her Victorian robes
have turned into blankets. She hears a thud. A scorched
aileron falling? Her mother shouting more recriminations?
Muriel must reach the cockpit despite these. Must save whoever's trapped in there, mother or not. Another bang. Muriel
sits up in bed. She's shaking. A nightmare. More sounds with
edges. Knocks on the back-porch door of her flat. She remembers now. She resides here. Brodie Street, Fort William,
Ontario. She has lived in this snow and wind for more than a
month. This isn't her first nightmare in this northern wilderness, but it's the worst. She glances at the alarm clock on her
night table. A hair past two a.m. The door of the small
glassed-in porch off her kitchen, that's where the knocker
knocks.

She propels herself out of bed. Groggy. Stiff. She has polio
again. She puts on her bathrobe, grabs her cane, and a flashlight she sensibly keeps on her kitchen table. Sure enough,
someone stands huddled outside her door. Only a madman or
vagrant would be out on a night like this. Muriel shines her
flashlight into a man's face, what she can see of his features,
stippled with ice crystals. His beard stubble is barnacled with
frost. She slides the bolt to open the door. The wind eddies
snow around him. He averts his eyes from her harsh light.

"I'm freezing," he says. A voice drawn by frost. Rigidified.
She can see that. She tells him he can step into the porch if
he promises to keep quiet and not lay a hand on her. He
promises. Something in his voice Muriel trusts. She widens
the door's opening. He steps inside. The cold in the glassed-
in porch is dire, much like outdoors, only without the wind.
She can't stay here long, dressed only in her nightgown and
bathrobe. They will both freeze. The man sways on his feet –
from fatigue, hunger, illness, hypothermia, she can't tell. He'll

soon perish if she doesn't do something. He is weak. Muriel realizes he has little strength to use against her, even with her polio. She tells the man he can come into her kitchen to warm himself, but she'll sit right beside her telephone, and if he makes one wrong move she'll call the Mounties. She *can* call them, she warns, in a flash.

"You can but you won't," the ice-man says, following her into her kitchen. He leaves his snowy boots by the door and peels off his ragged parka. He sits down at the table. Muriel pours a glass of sherry to thaw him, and as she hands it to him his eyes catch hers, bitter, bright and, she suddenly realizes – *known.* The posters plastered throughout the factory. The security alerts. Muriel is fully alarmed now. A picture of a wanted man is one thing. A wanted man in *one's kitchen* is another. A wanted man one *loved,* once, in one's kitchen is something else entirely.

"Thaddeus," she whispers.

The sherry sloshes in his unsteady hands. He nods.

Muriel lowers herself into the chair across the table from his. "How did you find me?"

"You're easy to track down, Muriel. You're all over the newspapers. *"Queen of the Mosquitoes."* You might not think we saw newspapers in the Angler Camp, but we found ways. I read that you'd come to work for the imperial war machine right here in Fort William. Then I had my people follow you home from the factory, to find out where you live."

She chokes back her anger at being spied on. "Your *people?*"

He shrugs. "How do you think I made it out of Angler without freezing to death, Muriel? There are lots of our people around here. Friends of Rosvall and Voutilainen, the two men the Mounties shot in the bush back in '29. They helped me. Voutilainen's sister sewed me some clothes; I wouldn't have lasted a day in that yellow coat with its big black circle on my back. They're still helping me."

"You look terrible," she says, reaching into her bathrobe pocket for her Camels, matches. She holds back her deeper thought, which is that even in his gaunt, beleaguered state, he is as handsome as she, even as a thirteen-year-old girl, had once imagined he'd become. He sits now, a wanted man in a country at war, and stares at her. She hasn't even combed her hair. She had been thrust from a nightmare. A test-flight crash. The pilot, stranded in the cockpit, had called out in her mother's voice. The same mother who had sentenced Thaddeus Brink to two years of prison when he was only seventeen and, in doing so, had snatched the only friend, no, the only love, Muriel had ever known. And now Thaddeus sits before her, twenty-three years later, and she has not even combed her hair. She lights her Camel.

"You *don't* look terrible," he returns. "The duckling has grown into a swan. I'm sorry about *that*, though –" He points to her cane. "Accident?"

"Polio." How she hates that word. "You can't stay here," she says. "And you can't ever come back. There are pictures of you all over town, and especially in the factory. If they find out I know you, I'll be fired, Thad."

The sherry has softened the cold edges of his face. "Do you remember the first time we met?"

Muriel takes smoke into her lungs. She wants to assure Thaddeus Brink this is no Nostalgia Night, and *certainly* not the moment for a love story. Instead, she says, "Yes. Vancouver Library. Those high windows. That lemon light. The Canadians falling like leaves at Amiens."

"Another useless war."

"That's your opinion," she says. "I was going for my first library card. You were right behind me in the queue. You were so ragged and tall. But I remember thinking that your face was made of little lights. I asked you why you wore that black arm band."

"Brother Ginger Goodwin, gunned down by the Mounties."

Muriel can't help smiling. "I thought you meant your real brother. I was only thirteen, and didn't know the police went about shooting people's brothers. I heard the librarian tell you they didn't carry the *Western Clarion* "for security reasons.""

You said, "Why bother calling this place a *public* library?" I wanted to know more. You were already out the door.

"You chased me," Thaddeus says. "You tugged at my shirt sleeve." His face still holds some light.

"Yes, and we talked for hours in Stanley Park. I liked helping you deliver your special Socialist papers – until my mother found out and ruined everything." She butts her Camel down hard in her ashtray. She wonders why they must retell a history they both know, but it seems they must.

"Ruined everything for *you*?" Brink's echo is acrid. "Muriel, I spent two years in prison, thanks to your mother's sentence. My old man was locked up because of her, too. He died there, as a matter of fact. We were branded subversives, threats to national security."

"*Weren't* you?" She has no idea why she defends her mother in this small way.

Thaddeus glares at her. "All we ever did was write and distribute newspapers and broadsheets. Yes, underground, to keep the movement alive – and, as you just reminded us, you, the precious little daughter of the judge, *helped* me. I was good enough not to mention that in court, as you know."

She sees, for the first time, notched remnants of stitches, a scar, on his cheekbone.

"What did they do to you in Angler camp?"

"Muriel, they made us cut lumber for war shipping crates. They almost killed us with work. The boss there is a sadist. Man named Tom Bee. He blasted his wretched trumpet in our ears at five every morning to send us out into the cold. We hated that horn so much. We took it with us to spite him."

"Why are you still around here, Thad? You must know the risks."

"I'm needed here, Muriel. Men are dying in the other two camps, Magpie and Redrock. We won't stop until we help them bust out. Besides, I wanted to see you."

"Thaddeus, please."

"You used to call me your wild socialist boy. Did you just waltz off to engineering school and forget me all those years?"

The Mahler symphony from Muriel's nightmare has turned into violin melodrama in her head. She has never respected melodrama, its notes so unscientific, so useless to human progress. The violins must stop. She checks the clock over the kitchen sink. He can't remain much longer. The wretched violins persist. "*Forget* you? You got inside my hysteresis loop, Thad."

"Speak English, Muriel."

She lays it out for him. Her university notes are fused to the lining of her skull just as irrevocably as her mother's prison sentence pronounced on the boy, Thaddeus Brink. "In a hysteresis loop, the exciting current is increased continuously in one direction from zero to maximum value and then decreased to zero. The current is then reversed in the exciting coil in the opposite direction."

Thaddeus drains his sherry. "*English.*"

She tries again. "What excites, returns. I never forgot you –" (away, violins, stick to the facts) "– you surfaced in my thoughts at odd moments. While I typed my paper on flutter and vibration. Once during a test-flight spin" (enough). "After my mother financed my education, I sent her a polite thank-you note and told her I could make my own way from then on. I broke off all contact with her because I never forgave her for what she did to you. I didn't see her for ten years, until last fall. I thought she was dying. She wasn't."

"This loop business, does it work?"

"Every time."

His eyes are gentle, but spoiled by the tincture of pity. "That's why you love science, isn't it? You can be so sure of things."

"I'm *not* always sure," Muriel says, thinking of the aeronautical problems stacked on her desk; the test-flight crashes at Fort William Aviation; the fragile magic of each bolt secured in its rightful place; the chance of faulty assembly by human hands; the myriad of rogue air currents and climatic variables that can't be known in advance.

Thaddeus rises to leave. Right on the brink of a conversation she's hungered after for so long. At the factory she has to be all briskness and surety. Here, in the depths of night with an old friend, it's a relief to reveal a fissure in her armour. Suddenly it comes to her who she's talking to, and who *he* might talk to, and who that person might talk to, and so on down the line. No. The violins stop here and now. Muriel pushes herself out of her chair.

"You still have lovely hair," he murmurs.

"I could report you," she warns.

"But you won't. Just like you didn't telephone the police awhile ago."

She follows him into the chilly back porch. "Will you come back?"

"You're the one who believes in loops, Muriel – besides, earlier, you told me *not* to return."

Just as he is about to re-enter the darkness, she beckons, "wait." He stops. She goes into the kitchen and returns with a heel of bread, presses it into his hand. He regards her with sorrowing eyes. Bitter air buffets her throat. She grasps the collar of her bathrobe. No violin could survive that cold. Poised on the edge of leaving, he thanks her for the bread.

"Thad, how did you break out of Angler?"

"Industrial secret," he says, slipping into the night.

Plant Exclusive – by Ruby Frances Kozak

TOP BRITISH INTELLIGENCE OFFICER
TO BE STATIONED IN FORT WILLIAM IN WAKE OF MAGPIE

*N*ew Year's Salutations, workers! Your own industrial Voice last entertained you with a light-fare feature, the little snack wagon that could. Sadly, your Voice must now tune her chords to graver notes. The Japanese occupied Manila, as you have doubtless heard. Here at home, no stenographer now seizes a manila envelope without trembling fingers. So many new words have struck our ears in this past couple of years. Luftwaffe. An airy feeling, at first. We must keep those same ears to the ground more than ever in 1942! Closer to home, last week three men attempted to escape from the Magpie Detainee Camp not so many miles from here as the crow flies. The men were captured and locked back in their cells. YOU ARE READING ABOUT IT HERE FOR THE FIRST TIME; the foiled escape was classified information until now. Your Voice has just minutes ago received clearance to release it and she now duly releases it. Plant security alert has gone back to high. Ladies' handbags will now be fully searched on point of entry. ALL WOMEN EMPLOYED IN SUB-ASSEMBLY SHOULD REPORT TO WORK TWENTY MINUTES EARLY TO FACILITATE NEW SECURITY PROCEDURES. In the wake of the attempted escape at Magpie, the

British Intelligence Division has sent one of their experts, Lieutenant Colonel Roper McLaughlin, to monitor the northern problem. McLaughlin, a Scotsman, holds advanced credentials in intelligence with specialization in prison escapes. He is also a decorated flier from the last war. The lieutenant colonel will reach our snowy climes before this month ends. Your Voice, though taxed with her hectic schedule as a reporter, among other hats she wears, has accepted the assignment as his personal aide. McLaughlin will work closely with officials at Fort William Aviation to ensure plant safety. Everyone at Head Office hopes you will extend a warm welcome to this distinguished man from the land of bagpipes and brogues. We trust you will help acquaint him with our national customs and local delights... [Ruby can't think of any, hence the dots].

'Til next time and, as our snack-wagon girl is so fond of saying, "keep'em flying!'"

"Do ye ken 'dry cold?'"
"Where in the name of Robbie Burns
have ye brought us, Rope?"

*A*rtie Shaw's "Stardust" wafts through the lush grille work of the Philco radio in Roper McLaughlin's upstairs library in Fort William, Ontario, Dominion of Canada. Roper watches, through the window's leaded-glass panes, two skaters clinging to each other's coat sleeves as they shunt and reel, on unsteady blades, around the small pond in Vickers Park across the street. He can't fathom how anyone would willingly spend time out-doors in this wilderness; he has never experienced cold of this magnitude. The skaters must be lovers. He shivers even *thinking* about the climate's extremity, and moves the swivel chair closer to the vigorous fire lit by their maid. The chair was already there in the fine house secured for the McLaughlins by Fort William Aviation. Roper settles into it. He lights a cigar and admires the floor-model radio's gleaming burl finish. Roper is pleased the radio made it all the way across the ocean without so much as a scratch. The same can't be said for his bride, Glynis. She has cried herself to sleep every night since leaving Dumfries. She's found the Canadians they've met crude and boastful. In this opinion, Roper has to admit that his wife occupies firm ground; not even a week in their new country, and *he's* noted, *too,* their tendency towards blowhardism, their way of wearing the ruggedness, indeed, the general awfulness, of their country on their parka sleeves. Roper keeps this consensus with his wife's views to himself. Glynis had found the conditions on the colonial train that carried them from Halifax to Fort William far below satisfactory. That train ride had proven interminable. She'd turned her young, globoid face away from him during much of it, gazing outside the locomotive window despite there being, as Glynis put it when she deigned to speak to him, every five hundred miles or so, *nary a blessed thing to see, out there.* In the dining coach, she'd wagged her head in sorrow, and said, "Where in the name of Robbie Burns have ye brought us, Rope?" The miles had stretched Roper's patience. He'd explained it to her so often. He'd been sent to sort out the northern problem. The exact nature of his work was top secret, and Glynis must not ask him about it. They'd made their Canadian bed. They must lie in it, he'd advised her.

Now she is downstairs unpacking their wedding china, and her despairing wails, reaching Roper at regular intervals, tell him casualties run high. She unpacks slowly, to draw out the misery, he feels certain. Glynis has enlisted the maid to witness the dinnerware carnage and, between his radio's symphonic swells, Roper hears the maid's clucks of sympathy in the wake of his wife's virtuoso performance. He has deemed it wisest to stay out of his wife's way. His steady fingers had found the Canadian Broadcasting Corporation quickly enough, a civilized alternative to the local station, Sleeping Giant Radio. The CBC drowns out Glynis' laments, but not fully enough. Roper has had quite enough feminine bone-china histrionics – "Oh, Lord, no, *no* – not the gravy boat!" "God an it please ye, *not* the soup tureen!"

Roper puts the swivel chair through its paces, this way, then that. He turns and reclines. He tips the chair at a certain angle, hoping its high back will buffer the women's voices downstairs. It hardly helps. He realizes, quite simply, the chair will have to go. It doesn't tilt back sufficiently far to permit the broad scope of thought the upcoming months are going to demand. Roper will need to tilt back, *far* back, to think. Whether his physical and mental predilection for backwards leaning originated in his flying days in the last war, in the sweet, addictive sensation of ascent, or in some pressure applied to a particular point in his spinal cord that sent an encrypted message to the chamber or lobe of his mind that never failed, at the precise duration and angle of tilting, to hatch his most brilliant hypotheses, he can't say. He only knows he needs a better chair. He'll add this request to the list of tasks for his new secretary, Ruby Kozak, when he meets her at Fort William Aviation tomorrow.

Unable to bear the substandard chair any longer, Roper rises and moves across the library to the large map of northwestern Ontario tacked to the wall. What desolation. He sees the detainee camps, circled in red: Angler, Red Rock, Magpie. No wonder they stuck prisoners of war and other undesirables up here. Next best place to the moon, or so they'd thought, until the Angler escape late last year, and the more recent near-escape at Magpie. The Canadians might be blowhards, but he has to give them points for resourcefulness. He'd heard the men had cut their way out of Angler with wires. How had they procured them? This was improvisation of a raw sort, a shocking resourcefulness in the face of staggering odds. A kind of brute animal survival in the vast northern bush, a prison in its own right. Roper almost admired those men, their inventiveness. Still, in the grand scheme of things, what had the Canadians invented, other than distance? Aside from Fred Banting and some tinkering with foghorns, bowling balls and radios, they boasted few other accomplishments, whereas his Scottish compatriots had tapped into the exigencies of everyday life, into time itself. They'd dreamed standard time and the Mackintosh raincoat, not to mention the breech-loading rifle and the world's greatest lighthouses. Not small things.

Roper's finger scans Lake Superior's clotted mane of a north shore. Country so remote and inhospitable it makes his

Scottish birthplace seem positively tropical. This northern landscape differs drastically from the verdant west coast Roper had visited years before – a lifetime ago – on his only other trip to Canada, a country so vast it seemed, more than anything, a holding tank of many countries *within* it.

British Columbia. 1905. He'd been a young man then. Nineteen. A footloose adventurer. He'd met a breathtaking girl inside a tree, a great Douglas fir in Stanley Park. She'd just suddenly *been* there, daisies wrapped around her hat. Annabelle McGregor. A Canadian. The three months they'd spent together had changed his life forever. Now he'd returned, almost fifty-six years old, to change it again. He had to see his daughter, Muriel. He had not even known she existed until she was twelve when, out of the blue, Annabelle sent him a letter. The girl was winning science prizes across the country, she wrote, and it was possible that news of her accomplishments might make it across the ocean and Roper, being an intelligence man, might piece the thing together. Annabelle hadn't wanted him to find out that way. She hadn't written before because she was managing perfectly well in raising Muriel, and didn't want any interference. Muriel had been told she was adopted. Roper was in the service when that letter came, and he'd kept it folded in his uniform. After the war, he'd collected every news article about Muriel McGregor he could find. They were few and far between, at first. But he had a yellowed copy of "First Girl to Enter Engineering School in Toronto." "First Woman to Graduate as Aeronautical Engineer." After Canada joined the allies in 1939, he found more features on Muriel. "She Can Make Apple Pie and Build Planes." He read about her appointment at Fort William Aviation. Studied her papers on flutter theory and stress analysis. Read that she was working on a design for winter landing gear. Roper's file on Muriel grew thicker. He couldn't remember the exact moment he knew he must see her; perhaps he'd been walking briskly along Oxford Street on his way to work at the British Intelligence Office, and a young woman with chestnut hair and a folder under her arm had rushed past him. More likely, it was the Canadian newspapers that came into his office in London. They contained stories about Muriel McGregor, the first woman in Canada to earn a degree in aeronautical engineering and, recently, to head up the production of Mosquitoes in Fort William, Ontario. She'd be accompanying the plant's test pilot, Orville Loftus, on all flights, Roper had read. He could only hope the Canadian pilot had his wits about him.

There were photographs, too – Muriel standing beside a Mosquito in snow, waving. Muriel seated, smiling, at her drafting table. Roper clipped these out and studied them endlessly. She was pretty. She had Annabelle's rich, wavy hair. His chin. He marveled at how Muriel, stricken with polio, had graduated from engineering school. She must be very determined.

Roper studied the map again. Curious how a man could lose his daughter and then find her again in this wild place. After Roper read about Muriel's appointment as chief engineer, he'd asked Bill Stephenson to assign him the northern problem. Roper had expertise in aeronautics; he'd run the subcommittee on investigating the Japanese design for winter landing gear. It hadn't taken much to convince his boss to send him on Dominion work. No one else wanted to go there, Bill had chortled – "so it's all yours, Rope." Before they knew it, Roper and Glynis McLaughlin were on a steamer to Canada. Roper had told his wife that he was being sent to monitor security in Fort William and stabilize the situation around the detainee camps in that region. It was not in Roper's interests to tell anyone that the likelihood of the Angler escapees lingering in the Fort William area was remote, that when a man is being hunted like an animal he's going to run as far as he can. It *was* in his interests to tell everyone that in times of war national security could not be taken lightly – especially in places where airplanes were being built for the Allied effort. It *was* in his interests to find a way to Fort William and the daughter he'd never seen. The war had provided a fortuitous turn of fate, an opportunity he couldn't miss. He knew he couldn't simply charge into Muriel's office and introduce himself. He had to work slowly. Get to know his daughter gradually, earn her trust, before he revealed himself. She had important work. A sudden father could overwhelm her. He longed to watch her in action. For her to know him. Perhaps even grow fond of him. It would take strategic strokes of brilliance on his part. He'd been taking notes. Calling them Project Muriel. And if he let his plan unfold over time, he might one day hear that sweet word he'd longed to hear for so many years –

"Rope!"

He snaps his body to attention. New wailing from downstairs. Glynis – "no, *not* the serving platter" – then sobs. The maid's "there, there, Mrs. McLaughlin."

If only his wife would pull herself together, Roper could concentrate on Project Muriel. Tomorrow, when he asks his secretary, Ruby Kozak, for a new chair, he'll also request earplugs.

*M*y boots are wearing in nicely. No wonder! It's miles around this factory – witness with your own eyes. Hop aboard my snack wagon – you won't take much space. You might want to stuff a few rolled tissues in your ears; the noise is terrific, isn't it? I might be a deaf old woman someday because of it, but I've got to listen for anything unusual so I can report to Ruby Kozak. Besides, someday is such a long way away, isn't it? And, like the signs in the factory say, ALL THIS COULD END TOMORROW. The drills and compression hisses and hydraulic hallubaloos sound like home to me, now. After all, I've been making my rounds with this wagon for a month. But *your* ears probably aren't used to production, so if you cover them it won't offend me. I'll tell you if there's anything new to hear, something that sounds like a story.

"SNACKS – soft drinks   hard drinks   fried gopher hearts"

(I don't *really* have hard drinks or gopher hearts, but it gets their attention – besides, why can't *my* larder hold a couple of little stories, too?)

Roll on. Roll on. Ontario! The Dominion's industrial hub – what a place – fast and loose and I'm right in the middle of it.

It gets a person's blood pumping for better and worse. Picture the plant cafeteria on full tilt – hundreds of workers gobbling food and puffing on fags, girl-laughs pealing through the smoky air, chaps hooting over to girls' tables between thumping down their euchre cards and once in a while some fellow will step out onto an open part of the floor, between tables, and do a dandy little goose-step dance to please the ladies. All the clowning, in the cracks of work, gives me a kick. One disappointment, though, is that it has been a whole month and I still haven't seen how they fasten the wings. I've only seen *pieces* of wings. Ribs. Spars. Stringers. Struts. I guess you have to be there at the exact right minute. More chaps work in wing assembly than girls, and when I ask these fellows about the wings, they say they'll tell me later, they're busy (sure, busy buying snacks). Or when I'm in the wing area, trying to *imagine* how the wings click into place, these men flap their lips – "watch where you're goin,' kid!" They just want their Snickers and smokes. One day I held back an assembler's Lucky Strikes until he told me what some wing parts are called, and that's how I found out anything at all. I told him it's swell that wings have ribs. He looked at me like I was cracked when I only want to know what he knows.

Let's see if anyone hungers in the paint shop. Sure they do. Painters have sweet teeth. Hold your nose if you don't like the smell of turpentine. I'd rather smell paint thinner than cow-pies any day! All they ever buy in the paint shop is Milky Way candy bars. I told Ruby Kozak this in my last Wednesday report. "There could be something in all those Milky Ways," I whispered across her desk "– maybe signals they're sending into outer space, some spy code" (I love whispering to her, the whole world disappears). Ruby hoped I'd be bringing her more by now. She said give her something *real*. She can't build a story on candy bars, spun fancy. "This is a factory, not the funnies," were her words. Ruby's beautiful face shadowed over when I told her about the Milky Ways, and she looked so let down I felt like a louse. I've been trying to do better.

Today I *will* do better. Let's boogie-woogie this buggy.

The girl at the rubber press doesn't want a thing. She waves me on. The riveters are hungry. I can tell by the way they eye my approach. Have you ever seen muffins fly from hands as fast as they fly from mine? The stout girl in the red scarf is waving me over. Stagger me if *she* needs a muffin. Well, she may do something unusual I can report. She's wearing a red probation scarf, after all.

Wait, what's this? The crone driving the crane is zooming full-steam ahead, right towards my snack wagon. I've been giving her a wide berth ever since I started this job. Day after day she sits perched in her cabin-on-high and roars around the factory and thinks she's Goliath to my David-wagon. Doesn't she see my wagon? She's going to crash into me. She *doesn't* see me.

I bellow, "FRIED GOPHER HEARTS!"

She doesn't hear. She's bearing down on me. Closer. Louder. Larger. She'll squash me like a bug right here on the shop floor. It's happening fast *and* slow, the way accidents go – slow enough for me to think, "This is the miserable way you're going to die, Audrey Foley. You might as well have married Clabber-Face." And *then* to think, "*No* – *this* is not industrial glamour! *This* is not the end!"

Good thing I can think on my feet, as you know. If I had Wonder Woman's lasso, I could send its golden coil over to the crane's lever, pull on the lasso's rope, and shut down the crone's ugly engine. Instead, I reach over and pull the red scarf off the big riveter's head. I have to yank it so hard she hollers something fierce. "*Ow!* Hell's bells that *hurts!*" The knot part must have been tangled in with some of her hair. I don't want to hurt her, but no real choice. I wave the red scarf high over my head and scream, and the giant metal bull brakes inches from the snack wagon. The candy bars shake in their wrappers and me in my boots. The riveters' jaws have dropped open as they gawk at the close call, the near collision. Rivet gun still in hand, the stout girl rubs the back of her head – sore from my ripping, I guess. The wicked witch from the *Wizard of Oz* sticks her long sharp nose out the crane hut and shrieks, "Next time, if you don't get out of the way, I'll get you – and your little *kitchen,* too!" Then she jerks the crane into reverse and dissolves as she moves backwards into space.

I holler, "Oh, go eat a rubber chicken!" – but the crone is long gone.

The big rivet-girl eyeballs me and I think I'm in for it from *her,* too. Instead, she grins, her lips closed tight, and then informs me she's Florence and, for a change, she'd like a Butterfingers candy bar instead of a muffin. Not good for the cavities, she says, but she can't stop thinking about Butterfingers, lately. I sell Florence the candy bar and tell her I'm sorry about pulling her scarf like a roughneck, but waving something red in front of that bull-witch was the only way to stop her. Otherwise, Florence would be fishing through the rubble for her Butterfingers right now. Florence says it only hurt for a minute and, after that, she was glad to get rid of that *vile rag.* In fact, she tells me I did her a *favour.* She pays me for the candy bar and drops a small tip in the Victory Bonds tin. And that is another thing I wish – that they'd let me keep some of my tips. After all, as you just saw, I risk my neck in these production sheds.

The factory is surprise after surprise. My first week on the job I wheeled the wagon over to the west corner of Sub-Assembly where some chap sat hunkered, cutting wires, on a workbench. His head was bent over his task. I couldn't catch his eye. Instead, I hollered,

"SNACKS – soft drinks   hard drinks   fried gopher hearts" to get his attention. He almost sprang out of his skin. I've noticed this about industrial workers. Their hands and arms move but they're locked inside a dream. When the wire cutter returned to the world and looked at me, he turned out to be the very taxi driver who'd driven me to buy boots, then to this plant the day Ruby hired me. What do you know about that? How a person can keep bumping into the same people in such a huge country is beyond me (like the lady engineer who rode here on my train). The wire-cutter stared at me hard. Then at my boots. "Diana?" I told him I *was* Diana, now I'm Audrey – just like he used to be a taxi driver, now he's a wire cutter. His name is Reggie and he's from Rainy River (I'd forgotten that). Now, every day I ask him if he's dried off yet, coming from such a rainy place, and he tells me to dry up. Every day he buys a sardine sandwich and smiles and asks how my boots are working out.

They're scuffing in good places, I tell Reggie. Reggie's all right. I've never had a brother but if I did, I'd want him to be Reggie and not one of those stuck-up wing assemblers who think the sun rises and sets on their precious noggins.

There are no gopher holes here, but other kinds of holes. Sticky wickets. Mean plant constables. Jimmy Petrik is the worst. He told me when he buys something from the wagon to keep my skeeter-hole shut and stop asking why he buys what he buys. His snacks are his business. He gives me these biffs on the head, too, when he passes me, and pounces on my wagon from behind, and makes ugly mosquito whining noises. Jimmy has the same muskrat look as Clabber-Face back home – what I mean is, he'd just as soon chew on you as say hello. I hear girls in the factory say how suave, what a *dream,* Jimmy is. Stagger me on *that* score – they've inhaled too much red oxide primer! After Jimmy shushed me about his snack order that first time, he rapped my head with his knuckles like it was some kind of door. How I wished for Wonder Woman's bullet bracelets – *they'd* show that knuck-lehead's knuckles. Jimmy Petrik can rap me because he wears a uniform. If he does it again I'll lob a catapult spool at him. He'll soon find out that I'm more than the snack-wagon girl, just like Ruby said. That sounds suspicious to me anyway, to be so sensitive over food as Jimmy is, and I'm going to tell Ruby. He doesn't tip, either. To make SIXTEEN BUCKS A MONTH like he does, and not support Victory Bonds? It makes you wonder, and here I am, my tips going to the Allied cause. Ruby already warned me about Jimmy, so she'll want to know these things. Every Wednesday, she grills me on what I've seen (Wednesday would allow her time to Gestetner and distribute a story before the end of the week *if,* she said, I ever served up more than crumbs – *I will, I will,* I said – her skin is pure cream even when she grills).

I saw something sharp sticking out of Reggie's overalls pocket once, then again, about a week later. But I didn't tell Ruby. Like I said, if I had a brother I'd want him to be Reggie, and what decent human would squeal on her brother, even a pretend brother? No, instead I'll report that the crane crone is a witch who tried to use her machine as a battering ram to sabotage the snack wagon, weaken the workers and slow the war effort. While I'm at it, I'll inform Ruby that Jimmy Petrik's nerves seem frayed under the cover of his blue uniform. She'll have something real to work with, and she'll let me watch when she puts on her lipstick.

You don't know about this. Last week Ruby promised that if I started bringing her decent material, I could have a favour. I knew right away what I wanted – to see her paint her lips. I can't wait to witness how she gets the pink around that little dip in her top lip. In fact, why *should* I wait? I've got not one, but *two,* information morsels to report – Jimmy, and the crane crone. To blazes with Wednesday. I'm going to burn my boots up to Head Office *right now.* What I've got could be part of something urgent, and she wouldn't want to wait for urgent news if she's an investigative reporter, would she?

A Personal Request
Of a feminine nature
And it's only Monday

*A*re all Scotsmen this plodding? The stocky Scot seated across the table from Ruby Kozak dictates security memoranda so tedious they straighten her waved hair while her pencil scratches out shorthand strokes – heavy dots, heavy dashes, heavy subjects. *"Heightened Security Measures at Fort William Aviation."* *"R. McLaughlin to Attend Test Flight."* *"Further Security Procedures."* Measures like increased wattage in light bulbs in certain "critical" areas of the plant, the installation of matrons in women's washrooms, the posting of ALL THIS COULD END TOMORROW! banners above the cafeteria doors and steam table. Ruby bears down on her lead pencil and steals a glance at the mug shot of the escaped man, Thaddeus Brink, on the Wanted poster plastered on the wall of the meeting room. For a second she discerns an amused look in his criminal eyes, not present a moment ago, but she knows it's simply another flight of her gifted imagination.

Ruby stifles a yawn as she makes her leaden strokes. The only noteworthy features of this Roper McLaughlin are his accent and tartan tie. 'Intelligence Man strangled in plaid,' she thinks. Ruby's boss, Frank Parks, told her she must treat this

McLaughlin fellow well; he's a lieutenant colonel, a mucky-muck who's come all the way from Scotland (to change light bulbs?). He could sink their whole operation if he set his mind to it, Parks told Ruby.

She penetrates the Scot's ruddy face. She can see through people. That's why she's a writer. Beneath McLaughlin's Scottish bluster lurk notes of sorrow. He's telling her to copy all memoranda to Muriel McGregor, Chief Engineer. Ruby nods and leaves her dreary marks, his dreary remarks, on her notepad. She has already ordered a new reclining chair for his home on Selkirk Street. A pair of earplugs. What will he want next? New china? She fervently wishes for a surprise that fits *her* notion of surprise – journalistic *material*. A new chair does not a feature story make. Ruby has prayed so hard for the big story to catapult her beyond these factory walls. At this point, she'd settle for even a modest novelty, a bauble, to brighten the bleak winter day, January 31, 1942. *Surprise me, Man of Tartan.*

He does. They've finished with dictation for now, he tells Ruby. He has a request of a – *personal* nature. A florid branch flickers across his cheekbones; his swerve into more intimate terrain makes him appear, for an instant, interesting.

Ruby tosses her notepad on the table (a gentle toss, but still, that extra zest, keened). She pulls her pencil skirt over her knees. She's pleased to be wearing her lapis angora sweater: lapis, the colour of mystery.

"Request, sir?"

"It pertains to the feminine sex."

The tips of Ruby's ears tingle. Some spice at last.

Just as Roper McLaughlin is about to make his request, the door bursts open and Ruby's running girl, Audrey Foley, careens into the room, gasping for breath.

"I've got *two dilly items* for you, Miss Kozak!" she blurts. "The switchboard lady told me you were here – she warned 'don't go in there,' but I –"

"Can't you read, Audrey?" Ruby snaps. "The sign on the door says 'Do Not Disturb.' Besides, today isn't Wednesday, in case you haven't noticed." Ruby glances at the intelligence man; he sits stunned, most likely peeved. Ruby hopes the girl's intrusion doesn't cost her a dressing-down from Frank Parks. She still needs her stenography job, sadly. Her escape nest egg must gain greater girth. This lieutenant colonel from Scotland was about to spill some personal beans of a feminine nature and in bursts Miss Will-o'-the-wisp with, undoubtedly, another irrelevant crumb, which is all the kid has served Ruby these past weeks.

"Who's the Little Orphan Annie?" Roper McLaughlin asks.

"She's no one," Ruby says. "Only the snack-wagon girl."

Audrey Foley cowers, puppy whipped, in the doorway. Her rodeo of hair is particularly unkempt today. Grime is streaked across her quivering chin (how she gets dirty selling snacks Ruby can't fathom). Her apron is soiled and drags downwards on one side. And *"dilly items?"* – what must Roper McLaughlin think of their backwater operation? And now the snack-wagon girl seems incapable of speaking at *all*, or apologizing for her intrusion, so Ruby must lower herself and do it for her.

"I'm sorry about this, Mr. McLaughlin," Ruby says. "It won't happen again."

Audrey finds her voice at last. "Should I go now, Miss Kozak?"

"Yes. Go," Ruby answers. "Come back on Wednesday."

The sheepish snack-wagon girl looks at them. "Do you want a candy bar?"

They shake their heads.

"Muffin?"

"*No,* Audrey," Ruby carps. "Just *leave,* and let us get back to work."

Ruby doesn't miss the tear-globe on the kid's cheek. The quiver of her lip. She'll have to sort this out in a couple of days, at Audrey's Wednesday report. The girl shuffles her boots contritely, then breaks into a run. She forgets to shut the door. Ruby rises and closes it. She resumes her seat and apologizes to Roper McLaughlin once more.

"I think you've hurt the girl's feelings," he remarks.

Ruby assures him she'll have the snack-wagon kid back to rights in no time. "She worships me, you see, which makes it hard to discipline her," Ruby explains.

"Ah yes, *worship*," Roper McLaughlin echoes in an oddly melancholy and faraway tone, and just when Ruby frets that he'll continue in this vein, he tells her he'll dictate an "Interruption of Meetings" memorandum later.

Oh, joy. Another memorandum. Ruby corrals the lieutenant colonel back to his personal request of a feminine nature, and is relieved that the girl's intrusion hasn't stolen his thunder. Roper McLaughlin tells her his request requires discretion, and asks if she's up to the challenge.

"Absolutely," Ruby says. She wonders why he can't task his wife with this personal feminine request, but she's glad he, for whatever reason, can't. To his credit, he obviously sees her – Ruby – as more than a stenographer.

"I need to give a woman a gift."

So this is why he can't task his wife. Heavens, he's only been in Fort William for a couple of weeks, Ruby muses – these Scotsmen move fast. She furrows her brow empathetically. "Can you tell me anything about her?"

"She is Canadian. Young – much younger than me, but not as young as yourself."

"Lingerie? Chapples Department Store right here in Fort William carries decent quality."

Roper McLaughlin laughs for the first time. A decade drops from his face. "Nothing that personal. I haven't met her, but I've seen pictures of her; she has a fine figure, no need for a corset."

"I didn't *mean* corset," Ruby remarks. "More like satin bed jacket, or some such thing. But let me say that she *must* have a good figure if she's older than me and doesn't need a corset."

The lieutenant colonel chuckles; a couple more years gallop away. Perhaps romance *is* possible, even in the Swamp, even for someone as old as him. Ruby wonders if there may be a news story here. Her reporter's instincts soar as high as her curiosity –

"What do you know of this woman?" she asks.

"She's educated. Brilliant. Pretty. What kind of gift would she like?"

"Flowers?"

"Rather predictable, Miss Kozak. And rather too much like a – suitor."

"Novel?"

"I suspect her reading tastes don't run towards the fictional," Roper says. "She's the pragmatic type."

"Then I've got it," Ruby replies. "Food. We all need food."

He asks for elaboration.

"Sugar will be rationed soon; I heard that on the radio. Give her something sweet while you can. Something – *Canadian* – butter tarts. Golly, *yes* – have some tarts sent to her on Valentine's Day, unless you're worried that's too suitor-like, too much like love." Ruby sits back, beaming, in her chair. Her mind's deep well has never once run dry.

Roper McLaughlin looks pleased, relieved. "Tarts. You are brilliant, Miss Kozak. And on the Valentine's question, there are many kinds of love."

"Oh, and don't have your wife bake the tarts," Ruby advises. "Have your cook make a double batch, so as not to stir your wife's suspicion. Then divide them in half."

"Can you tell me how I might deliver the – *secret half*? I can't take them myself for reasons of discretion and – mystery."

Ruby furrows her brow again. She's never had this much fun at work. Wonder never ceases when it comes to herself. She can't imagine why it doesn't occur to such an intelligent man to have the baking sent in a taxi, but she's not going to spoil things by suggesting the obvious.

"How far are we talking about, Lieutenant Colonel? Where does this pretty, educated woman live?"

"I don't know. But I know where she works. That's where I'll send the tarts."

Ruby leans across the table conspiratorially. "And she works – "

"Right here in the plant."

A whiskey-jack feather could topple Ruby Kozak, given that Roper McLaughlin has only visited the plant once since his arrival in Fort William. He really does work fast, but not as swiftly as her gazelle mind –

"The plant? Then we'll simply have the snack-wagon girl deliver the tarts on her rounds. The kid who just blew in here – Audrey – the special detail will make her feel important, bring her back on track after her unfortunate intrusion today."

Roper looks skeptical. "Can she be discrete?"

Ruby assures him that the girl will do anything she asks. A herd of rampaging elk won't drag the secret from Audrey Foley if that is Ruby's wish.

"But the kid burst through a *Do Not Disturb* sign without a second thought," Roper points out, referring to the recent infraction. "Perhaps she's not as obedient as you think."

Ruby sighs. She should have known this Roper McLaughlin would not be fully attuned to her powers; after all, he is under the sway of two other, most likely, lesser women – his wife, and *the pragmatic lady* right there within the factory walls. Even the mind of an intelligence man can only contain so much. Case in point; he doesn't remember that she has employee interviews in five minutes, even though Frank Parks briefed him in advance. And the lieutenant colonel has clearly forgotten that Ruby was assigned to him on top of all her *other* work. She gathers her notepad and pencil. She will put it to him straight.

"Audrey Foley lives to see me apply my lipstick – she will never trespass forbidden doors again. She'll deliver the tarts to your pragmatic-type lady on Valentine's Day and no one will be the wiser."

Roper McLaughlin thanks her for the reassurance. He rises. He assumes any talk of tarts will stay right in that room. Does he assume correctly? Ruby stands and shakes his hand. "Of course," she says.

The moment these words leave Ruby's mouth, a literary surge swells within her. This could be her big story – this secret love affair between an official from British Intelligence and – who? Some lowly riveter in Sub-Assembly? Some pot scrubber in the plant cafeteria? Ruby doesn't believe Roper McLaughlin's "not a suitor" nonsense for a minute. This story is a hot pepper, and it's landed in the palm of her hand. She is about to dash away to her desk when the lieutenant colonel calls her –

"One more thing, Miss Kozak – what are '*dilly items*'? The girl spoke of them when she barged in."

Ruby winks. "Oh *those*. Heavens, Mr. McLaughlin, I can't tell you *that*. Those are items of a personal, feminine nature, don't you see?"

She has already begun to click away on her high black heels before she can discover whether he sees, or not.

Saint Valentine Carries an Axe

*F*lorence Voutilainen no longer walks home in darkness. It's the middle of February. She waves at the Gruff rock – these days of longer light have altered its crevices. The face etched in stone belongs more to a kind old woman than a troll now. Today, Florence had welded better. Jimmy Petrik had told her so himself. She'd kept her slag caps small, same with her weld pools. She'd come close to solving crater cracks. She'd welded seams, then spots, with little clumsiness. At the end of the session, Jimmy had slapped her shoulder and said, "Well welded, Voutie," and she'd blushed with pride. During her riveting shifts, Jimmy continues to pass her work station more often than those of other riveters, she feels sure. 'That's not the *only* plum,' Florence thinks, as she covers Rosslyn Road on lighter feet. The moment the snack-wagon girl yanked the red scarf from her head, the few seconds of pain quickly gave way to a feeling of – dignity? Yes. *Bliss.* She'd felt, for the first time since starting her job at Fort William Aviation, like an ordinary girl instead of a circus freak. She wants to be rid of that probation scarf for good, and to feel that way every day. "I'll *do* it, Old Rock-Woman," she calls over to the outcropping – "I'll prove I'm no probation case!"

Light lowers a notch when she reaches her mailbox, her mother's painted wooden sign – "Henni Voutilainen, Veteran Seamstress of the Lakehead." Florence tramps down the snowy laneway. Someone has gone before her – tracks larger than her mother's feet, their edges softened by wind. Must be a couple of hours old. Florence groans. She'd forgotten, until seeing those big prints, that the dead-eyed veterans liked to visit her mother on Valentine's Day. Every year Henni cooked a large pot of what she called her *special love soup*, but it was really only broth with cabbage. Why can't her mother just go to the Valentine's supper at the Finnish Hall in Port Arthur? No, her mother has to get more cracked every year, while Florence worries and rages, and all that maternal queerness lands, as the colour red, on Flo's head at the factory.

A whiskey jack skreels from the murky bank of firs behind her small house. Florence follows the boot prints up the rickety, snowy front porch steps. A healthy set of tracks. Two feet. No sign of a walking stick or the dragging of a prosthetic device, like so many other days. Whoever this visitor of her mother's is, he's whole from the waist down.

Just as Florence is about to unlatch the front door, a man holding a hatchet bounds around the corner of the house. She gasps. Her sturdy legs turn into gelatin. The man steps backwards quickly. Florence grasps the door's latch, thinking she'll dash inside the house. This stranger could be one of the escapees from Angler Camp the radio's been warning about. Dash inside, slam the door and heave the kitchen furniture against it, even though his hatchet gives him an edge. Everything about her house is so flimsy and hack-through-able. Something about the man makes Florence hesitate, grant him the benefit of the doubt. Probably it's the blue paisley handkerchief around his neck, like an artist would wear it, she imagines, or it's the benign way he boards the bottom porch step (even though he holds the hatchet) towards her.

"Heavens, you scared me," she says. "Did you come for mending?"

He's sorry he frightened her, he says, and there's no chord of danger in his tone. He's not there for mending. He's only helping out her mother. "Come and see for yourself," he urges. He retraces his steps around the house to the back yard. She follows. The lengths of timber that were scattered near the Voutilainens' wavering fence for weeks have been axed into stove-sized pieces and neatly stacked. The woodpile towers above Florence. Likely enough wood to get her and her mother through the rest of the winter.

"You did all this today?" she asks.

He nods. He's no amputee, that's for sure. He tells Florence that if she would make him a cup of tea, he wouldn't toss it into the snowbank. She says tea it is, yes, what was she thinking in light of all his chopping?

Florence places two steaming cups on the kitchen table, sits down across from the woodcutter and, as he begins to sip gratefully, she gets a better view of him. She guesses he must be forty, but in a pleasant way. He's removed his parka, revealing prominent muscles under his worn plaid shirt. His hands have their own intelligence. His teeth are solid, unlike hers. He has a small scar on his cheekbone. He looks at her, too.

"You must be the daughter," he says.

"I guess you mean daughter of Henni, Veteran Seamstress of the Lakehead. I'm afraid so," she sighs. "Where *is* my mother, anyway? She's usually here today of all days, feeding her Valentine's Day soup to the cripples." He can't say where her mother is – only that, as the daughter must know, Henni hops around like a jackrabbit. Florence knows, all right. She studies her visitor more. "Are you a drifter?" she asks. His negative reply doesn't surprise her. The way he drinks his tea, without slurping, like gentlemen from down east, Toronto, likely drink tea, tells her as much. "Do you work at the plant?"

"That would be supporting the war," he replies.

Florence guesses this means no.

"*I* work there," she says, "and it's the best thing that ever happened to me, if *only* –" And before Flo knows it, she's telling this stranger about the red probation scarf, and the ugly words sometimes hurled at her when she wears it, but she's recounting the goodness of the place, too, like the plant constable Jimmy Petrik who watches over her work station and teaches her arc, seam and spot-welding and how she'd give anything for him to take her for a spin in his green De Soto. And how hard everything was in the thirties and that she's earning her own money for the first time and soon she'll get her teeth fixed if it isn't too late. She loves how the shining rivets hiss and make a song as she sinks and countersinks them. Last summer, the Mosquitoes they'd built with their own hands spun and flashed through the sky at the Victory Bond Air Show at Bishop's Field and now *she* is part of that too, and more than she'd ever thought she'd be, after failing grade thirteen, but less than she *will* be, the moment she can convince them to lift her probation.

The man drinks his tea and lends his ears. His face fills with little lights as he listens. It's so much nicer talking to this woodcutter who doesn't slurp than chattering away to rocks, vegetables or, for that matter, her*self*. Suddenly, though, a dark notion flits across Florence's mind. "What are you to my mother – besides her lumberjack?"

"I owe your mother, so I suppose that makes me her debtor – she did some sewing for me," the man says. "Sewing that saved my life. I'm repaying her by helping out around here."

Florence can't figure how sewing could save a life, so she leaves it. "Does that mean you're coming back?"

"One woodpile does not equal a saved life. I've got more debt left to repay your mother."

Florence guesses this means yes. She is suddenly sleepy. The exhaustion of a day's riveting and welding always descends on her swiftly. But her earlier dark, nagging notion returns to stab her into a momentary alertness. She has told this man her dreams. Made an open book of her life. Wondrous as this stranger is (and what a grand listener), he has dealings with her mother that most likely go beyond sewing. "I can't get into trouble for talking to you, can I? – at the factory, I mean?" (Darn her spineless, pleading tones – pitiful mewls more like a scared child than a crack riveter.)

"No," the man says, rising from the table and pulling his parka back on. "Because you never saw me. You don't even know my name."

"True enough," Florence murmurs as the stranger strides for the door. "You could be Saint Valentine himself for all I know."

He says he's flattered that the daughter places him in such high esteem. He thanks her for telling him her story. The world would improve if there were more people like her, the stranger remarks.

Florence is so worn out she places her head on her arms, right there at the table, just long enough to think of something good enough to say to *that,* since no one has ever paid her such a compliment, and when she raises her head, he's gone. The clock behind the wood stove has leapt ahead a whole hour, and the fire has fizzled into a few critical, enduring embers.

Flutter & Vibration

The wolves howl blue among the saucepans.
The wolves howl bluer than Billie Holiday –
But not as blue as Audrey Foley.

*D*id you ever want to crawl into a louse hole and die? It's a rotten feeling, isn't it? It makes you quiet and small. In a sorry case like mine, smaller than I already am. And here I am, scouring pots. That's what I do between snack-wagon rounds – scrape away at the miserable porridge crusted to the morning's dippers, or worse, yesterday's wretched rice cemented to the stockpots. The steel wool rubs my hands raw and pink. I scrape away in the back corner of the utility kitchen behind the cafeteria, and nobody sees me, and there's such a mountain of greasy metal, I only start to catch up when Lucy Fell, the head dishwasher everyone only ever calls Dish, rolls in more dirties piled willy-nilly on one of those metal carts on wheels. To tell you the truth, she's been grating on my nerves. Have you ever met someone who seems to know only one song, and they sing it over and over until you want to fling a skillet at their one-trick-pony mouth? That was Clabber-Face and begetting
and begetting
and begetting
and begetting –

Now it's Dish. I'd never do a low thing like that to Dish, of course. Instead I stick toilet-paper plugs in my ears to drown out her singing – "Row, Row, Row Your Boat" (and stagger me, not even on key!) The toilet paper helps just a bit. It's hard not to hear what you hear. I could shove my ears full of steel wool, and I'd *still* be bombarded by those terrible words, Ruby Kozak saying – "oh, she's *no one,* only the snack-wagon girl."

Oh I know what you're thinking – you're thinking, stop feeling sorry for yourself, Audrey Foley! – so you made a little mistake – that was weeks ago – and you were only trying to help Ruby Kozak – besides, you learned a lesson, didn't you? I learned a lesson, all right – *two* lessons, as a matter of fact –

1. In the industrial hub of the Dominion, never be early! But also don't be late. Appear exactly when you're supposed to appear, predictable as sunset.

2. Life is like a smorgasbord during times of rations. If there's lots of meat, expect scrimping on pies. If it's a feast of sweets, you're not going to have lobsters piled to the sky. Works the same way in the Looks Department – if extra effort goes into making someone very beautiful, that person will fall short somewhere else. A looker might be mean, for instance.

Sure, I'm talking about Ruby Kozak. She doesn't know that when she sent me away I ran to the utility kitchen, to the farthest, darkest corner, and sank onto a sack of flour, *bawled* because I knew then that I'd never be Wonder Woman's third cousin. All I heard inside my head was "*oh, she's no one, she's no one*" until finally Dish trucked in, row-rowing that darned boat gently down that blasted stream, until she found me on my sack and said, "Well, and what are you doing sitting there *blubbering,* Miss Audrey? There are pots to scour!" Just my luck that day's menu was blood sausage and the smell nearly made me sick.

No, Ruby doesn't know that. On Wednesday Report Day, I slunk back to her office. Her desk was decked out with red crêpe-paper streamers and foil hearts scalloped across its front. Maybe there was a Cupid, too. I was so rattled it was hard to take it all in. Ruby wore that pinched expression she always wears when she types, slamming the carriage like it's a skunk that has just sprayed the Stenography Department. She scowled at me over her typewriter, lifted her long, graceful fingers from the keys. For an instant, I thought her Gene Tierney eyes really *would* eat me. Her voice was a carving knife sawing into an Audrey-sized roast.

"What do you want?" The blade sliced down and down with each word.

"It's Wednesday," I said.

Slowly she lowered her beautiful hands. "Ah yes, Wednesday. Sit, Audrey."

I sat in the same wooden chair as I had when Ruby first lifted her glowing face to meet mine. Only a couple of months and how different things are now. And yet, she was still so pretty, like an angel. I figured it was over for me. She was going to fire me – fry me in the fire. I thought about having to pack up my sweet little room in Churchill Ladies' Residence, and this nearly made me cry, so I planted my boots firmly on the hardwood floor so I wouldn't bawl.

I waited for the horrible words – YOU'RE FIRED – but they didn't come. Instead, her eyes (those green pools matched her emerald dress) took on light and (stagger me) a look of *pity* entered them.

"I'm hungry, Audrey."

"I know," I said.

"*Ravenous.*"

"Yes."

Then Ruby rolled her chair out from behind her desk. She propelled herself towards me until we were face to face, and both in front of the red crêpe-paper streamers and, yes, it *was* a Cupid, poised to shoot an arrow.

"I guess you know what you did wrong, Audrey."

"I think so. When the sign says *Do Not Enter*, I don't. And I only report to you on Wednesday."

"Correct, Audrey. Not Monday. Not Thursday, Tuesday or Friday. *Wednesday.*"

I started to think I could come out of this *employed,* but I felt lower than a vole in a mine shaft in spite of it. I wished a trap door would open under my chair and swallow me up. I couldn't help sniffling a bit. "Do you *really* think I'm no one?" I asked.

Ruby laughed and the birdsong returned to her voice. "Don't be silly. Of *course* I don't think you're no one. You are a very important person in this factory, Audrey" – and then she –

took my hand in hers (hers

smelled faintly of lilacs, not carbon!)

and Cupid's arrow

got me I think you know where –

And then I *did* start to bawl. Did I *ever* bawl – so hard, my tears could have floated Noah's very ark. Ruby's eyes, flooded with pity, shone down on me. She withdrew her hand, rolled her chair back behind her desk and passed me a tissue. This, too, smelled of lilacs.

"What do you *want for yourself?* What's your *wish?*" Ruby asked.

"I just want everything to be the way it was," I sniffled. "How *can* it be?"

She swished her hand, wandlike. "It's a cinch, Audrey. We can make everything the way it was before. Just tell me about those *dilly items* – now that it's the right time and place."

I told Ruby about Jimmy Petrik's high-strung, nasty ways on the shop floor. She said *that* was nothing new, he'd been a louse since high school. Then I whispered that I was pretty sure the old crone driving the crane had meant to take out my snack wagon, and *would have,* if I hadn't scared her off with a red flag. The crone clearly had evil designs on snacks, but lost her nerve at the last minute. I changed a few things to make the story better – I made the crone's nose way bigger, her eyes burning coals. 'If *any*one should be made to wear a red probation scarf, it should be *her*,' I added.

Ruby said that there *might* be something in the crane business – that for once I'd brought her something worthwhile. She told me to keep a close eye on the crane crone and, as usual, everyone else, and to report to her next Wednesday. So I *wasn't* fired. Ruby Kozak's directions were catnip to my kitten ears, and to prove I'd learned my lesson, I tossed her earlier words into the air like a song –

"Wednesday. Not Monday. Not Thursday, Tuesday or Friday."

Ruby went serious. "There *is* another task I must ask of you, Audrey, and you can't tell anyone. She smiled, and her teeth were divine pillars of pure ivory. She leaned towards me and whisper-spoke that on Valentine's Day, the very man I'd seen in the boardroom that day would give me a box to deliver to someone in the factory. The man would tell me not to reveal the name of the person receiving the box – but despite this, after I delivered it, she wanted me to tell her immediately who'd received the box. I was to disclose this to no one else, though – did I think I could manage this?

"I won't let you down this time, Miss Kozak."

"Good, Audrey. Now, is there anything else?"

I reminded Ruby of what she'd promised if I brought her something good. She'd liked the crone's crane story. Yes, she recalled her promise. She crooked her finger, signalled for me to come around behind her desk. I did, then lowered myself on my haunches so I was level with her on her fancy office chair. She pluffed a tissue from her purse and scrubbed off the lipstick she already wore. She wanted to give me *the full demonstration* from scratch. Then she reached back into her purse and took out a tube of lipstick and a small brush – the kind with only a few fine bristles, used for hard-to-paint places. So *that* was the secret of her perfect lips! She loaded the brush with poppy red lipstick and slowly drew a line around her mouth. So *this* was how she outlined the dip in her upper lip so perfectly, with the *brush*. Then she coloured in her lips from the tube until the brush line blended with the rest. It's the most artistic thing I've ever seen, this painted mouth of hers, it's –

Art   Art

Art   art   art

Art!

Ruby pressed her new poppy lips together quickly. Once. She blew me a kiss, then said, "There, you've had your favour, and isn't it time for your snack-wagon round?" She was sending me away. But while her words were tang, her tone was chocolate, and according to the clock on the office wall, it *was* time. I thanked her for the show. Then I beetled off to get my wagon and turned, just before leaving Head Office, to see her again.

"SNACKS – soft drinks   hard drinks   fried gopher hearts!"

I made my rounds. Noted nothing of note – after Ruby's lips, what can be news? The usual workers yelled the same old things at me – "Hey squirt, are you deaf? Over here!" Jimmy Petrik bought Lucky Strikes, and sized me up like I was a cockroach, and the crone flew down from her crane and cackled and lit into me all over again when she paid for her egg sandwich. The wing assemblers were their typical high-hat selves. One crusty riveter snapped that I hadn't given her back enough change from her candy bar when I knew full well I *had*, and that *she* was lying – and where was Wonder Woman's golden lasso when I needed it? The Chief Engineer had her "Do not disturb – No snacks wanted" sign on her door after I'd climbed all those stairs with a small, but heavy, sampling of my wares. By the time I'd finished my rounds, Ruby's spell had worn off, even though I repeated silently, in my head, "you are a very important person in this factory, Audrey." (The only kindness on my snack-wagon round came from Rainy Reggie, the wire cutter – he said I looked so glum he'd have to buy me an ice cream sundae after work. I argued that ice cream is wrong for winter, but he told me we're getting some anyway. Rainy's sundae promise, though nice, doesn't lift me high enough.)

Now I'm back where I started. Scouring pots. In fact, I never really left. My boots have been planted in front of this sink the whole time I've been bending your ear. Even so, the dirty pans keep pouring in. I'm low as ever. I'll bet you're wondering why I feel like this after I've seen the wonder of Ruby's lips – not to mention smelled her lilac hand. I imagine you're thinking, "why are you still blue, Audrey Foley?"

Because I can't help feeling like Ruby pulled some kind of string, and I danced. And she *did* tell that man I was "no one" – all the lipstick in Ontario can't make those words go away. Stagger me, the rice is stuck something *awful* today. And the harder I scrape, the more I wonder if that fine paintbrush Ruby Kozak uses on her lips isn't a *bit* like cheating.

Well, now you know.

*M*uriel McGregor flicks tart crumbs from the test-flight report form. It's the last tart. She wouldn't normally eat stale baking, but butter tarts preserve well. And these were especially tasty. She hadn't taken her mother's ancient advice into account, to refuse sweets from strangers. Any maternal counsel had long run its course – not that she'd ever listened to her mother anyway. No, Muriel had polished off every last tart. The neatly penned note fastened to the bow around the box they arrived in had beguiled her – *Valentine's Day Greetings. I greatly admire your work, Miss McGregor. Respectfully yours, R.* Muriel dreamed, with each bite, "R., R." She'd been working late these last few nights, and the tarts had been her sustenance and supper. Man can't live on bread alone, but woman can, apparently, live on butter tarts. Muriel's scientific mind revels in these occasional flights of fancy, the twisting of maxims. She was so fond of her man/ woman-bread/tart formulation she'd penned it in her diary, and then, *"Tarts from R.! Who is R.?"*

Muriel scrubs at a butter spot on her ski-pedestal drawing, beside it, her new test-flight report form. The test pilot,

Orville Loftus, might have gotten away with writing, "SHE DON'T FLY WORTH COW-PIE" in postflight memoranda to her predecessor, Karl Wilkins, but Loftus won't get by with shoddy, unprofessional slang as long as he's flying with *her*.

And Loftus *will* fly with her – that very afternoon. He'd sent a decidedly un-eloquent message through Fraudena at the plant switchboard – *Bust ankle mended, Loftus ready to fly, test flight Feb. 22/42, tell lady engineer be there if she insists.* Sadly, the man can barely muster a sentence. His blunt missive reminds Muriel of how, since arriving in northern Ontario, she's grown to appreciate the value of eloquence. The note accompanying the tarts had brought this realization home to her. R. is eloquent. As to discovering his identity (*his*? Not *her*? Ruby Kozak? – no – that girl is too vain for such a gesture), Muriel is torn. Part of her is happy to keep R. frozen inside a dream. She has sensed his presence, heralded by the tarts, and that has been enough. It has helped her push distressing thoughts of Thaddeus Brink into the recesses of her mind, has almost made her wonder if Brink's appearance hadn't simply been an extension of the nightmare she'd had on that bitter night. She's so glad *R.* is not *T.* It means there's no chance that Thaddeus sent the tarts – that would have been unlikely, given that he lives like a fugitive (where would he get tarts?). In fact, since the tarts, Brink has occupied Muriel's thoughts less, and she owes this mercy to R. who, without even *appearing*, restored her focus on the aeronautical tasks at hand. Her landing-ski design, to take one instance. How impressed R. would surely be with the ski pedestal she'd been devising (he *greatly admired* her work, he'd said so in his note).

Yes, the very fact of R.'s existence is enough for now, but Muriel may yet quiz the snack-wagon girl who, with doleful eyes, delivered the tarts last week – on Valentine's Day. The girl had knocked timidly, on hearing Muriel call "enter" had shuffled in contritely, no doubt chastened by Muriel's earlier admonishments on the subject of excessively frequent snack stops, her warnings not to intrude after morning break – especially if *No Snacks* hangs on her office door. When the girl, Audrey, brought Muriel's morning muffins, she no longer blurted out questions about airplanes, and the truth was, Muriel missed these childish queries so acutely she'd noted in her diary just the other day: *re-cultivate kid's curiosity – make her feel wanted again.*" No, the girl, on Valentine's Day, had dragged her boots into Muriel's office, carrying a box tied with a red bow, a card tagged to its ribbon, and had muttered – verging on tears, Muriel thought – "I'm so sorry, Miss McGregor, I saw the *No Snacks* sign, but I was told to deliver this *no matter what* so here I am – I guess the card will say what you need to know –"

Eager as Muriel had been to open the box and its card, sealed in an envelope, she was as keen to correct the snack-wagon kid, for there was no place for a hangdog attitude like the girl's in the Allied endeavour. "Look, Audrey," she'd said, "would you like to see what I'm working on?" The girl had raised her eyes with that half-distrustful, half-hopeful look of scolded dogs, sent her thin human shoulders upwards into a slight shrug.

"Leave that on my desk," Muriel had instructed, pointing to the ribbon-bound box, "and come over to my drafting table." Audrey had moved her boots gingerly across the floor, and left the box on the desk, then raised herself onto her toes to see the papers spread over the drafting table's sloped surface. She still seemed hesitant, and Muriel had to reassure her that it was all right.

"These are skis, Audrey. I'm figuring out how to fasten them to planes."

"They already *got* skis on planes – I saw it in a magazine."

"Quite right, Audrey. But most skis haven't worked. The check cables have snapped. Same with shock cords, especially at extreme temperatures. Trimming gear, when exposed, has fallen loose. Then there's the problem of freeze-down. The Japanese have had the best luck with winter landing equipment."

"The Japanese? What did *they* do?" the girl probed.

Muriel was pleased that Audrey seemed to have left her frazzled nerves behind. "Ah, if only we knew – if only *I* knew," she'd answered. "But somehow, they've cracked freeze-down."

Audrey's eyes had been immersed deep in the drawings, and Muriel caught her childish mutterings, her "tagger bee"s or "stigger me"s, or whatever they were. Then the girl had gazed hard at Muriel – "How are you going to *fix* all this, Miss McGregor?"

The girl looked so worried, Muriel hadn't been able to hold herself back from laughing. "I have a few ideas. Keep this to yourself, will you?"

Audrey nodded fervently.

"All right. I'm going to make a pedestal container for all the loose cables and trimming gear – it'll be like a little house to help keep out snow and slush. I'll keep the pedestal towards the front of the plane. That should prevent drag. I'll add more curvature to the back of the ski, more than other designs – that will improve drag and movement –" She stopped herself. She'd clearly overwhelmed the kid, whose mouth gaped open and whose eyes shone wide as two full moons.

"Can you make this – little house, and everything?"

Muriel had told Audrey she sincerely hoped so, and soon. And if Audrey wanted to come and see more drawings and check the progress of the little house, she could, whenever the *No Snacks* sign wasn't hanging on the door. Then she gently told the kid that she'd better get working on the design. Audrey's eyes danced. She'd sung, "Yes, you'd *better!*"

"But one other thing before you go, Audrey –"

"Anything!"

"You won't tell anyone you delivered a parcel to me, will you?" Muriel pointed to the box, with its bow, on her desk. "I have so little privacy, you see."

"They could run over me with a crane, Miss McGregor, and I *still* wouldn't tell," Audrey crowed.

"Good girl," Muriel said. Beaming, Audrey waltzed out of Muriel's office, calling, "Keep 'em flying, Miss McGregor!" And after she'd penned her thoughts on men, women, R., bread and tarts, Muriel had written in her journal that night, "*the girl is back.*"

Muriel glances now at the empty baking box on the drafting table, at the battered book the test pilot, Orville Loftus, had given her. *The Rime of the Ancient Mariner.* She hasn't read it. Hasn't had time for poetry. She's spent the morning brushing up on flutter theory. Rereading Green's 1936 study, "Status of Wing Flutter." Hollinger's 1937 treatise, "Conditions for the Occurrences of Flutter." Rackwell's seminal work, "The Two-Dimensional Problem of Aerodynamic Vibration" (1937). She'd read her own report, penned while still a graduate student at Michigan, on flutter and vibration. She'd wanted to be ready for today's test flight. Though she'd have liked more prior notice, she *is* ready – armed with Green, Hollinger, Rackwell and herself. Ready to meet the un-eloquent Orville Loftus. She'd reread his report on the test flight that had crashed three months earlier, and feels sure he's off the mark with his notion of substandard wire gauge. Based on the last engineer's designs, Muriel has grown convinced that the centre of gravity needs adjustment on these Mosquitoes. Moving the centre forward is bound to mitigate vibration. Her own study showed that for fixed surfaces such as wings, stabilizers and fins, it's desirable to keep the centre of gravity location of the surface as far forward as possible, and she'll tell Orville Loftus this. And the tailwheels need work, no question. He'd sounded wary of her during their short phone conversations. Muriel hadn't needed to conduct extensive calibrations to understand his wariness; it came from her being a woman. She *does* need Orville Loftus to trust her.

She swallows some Dr. Chase's Nerve Food, smokes a Camel and gathers her cane, coat, hat and new test-flight report forms. She picks her way through Sub-Assembly's clank and roar, to Head Office where Jimmy Petrik, her driver, meets her. They walk through the plant parking lot towards his De Soto. Snow is falling like pop rivets again, and a gust of wind sends Muriel's floppy hat spinning through the frigid air. Jimmy chases the hat, cursing, across the icy lot and retrieves it. As they motor along Arthur Street, Muriel tells him some snow won't matter on the test flight, but she'd rather not have felt that wind.

Jimmy smokes a Lucky Strike and asks Muriel if she thinks there's "anything wrong with the wires in them planes, like some said." When Muriel answers more likely a problem with centre of gravity, Jimmy calls her hat the dandiest one he ever clapped eyes on, and he's glad the wind didn't shoot it over the top of Mount McKay, never to be seen again. Muriel had pegged him as a queer chap right from the start; he keeps reaffirming her view.

They turn into Bishop's Field. Scrub timber snaggles along its perimeter. Closer, a windsock whips itself into a frenzy. A shining Mosquito is parked on the runway. Silver, with black spinners. 'Oh she's a beauty,' Muriel thinks, admiring the sweep of the plane's fifty-four-foot wingspan, its fin-flash catching the light. The mechanics at the airstrip have built a wooden step-way for Muriel, its top step flush with the cockpit door. Hearing the De Soto's arrival, they pile out of the maintenance shed. Jimmy Petrik cuts the automobile's engine, hops out and starts jawing with them. Muriel despairs at the callow boy's chauffeuring skills as she propels herself out of the car, clipboard wedged under one arm, cane under the other. It's much colder at Bishop's Field than at the factory. She grasps her hat, pulls her muffler tightly around her neck and makes her way with difficulty, through the gusting air, towards the Mosquito.

If Orville Loftus is so eager to fly, where is he?

Just as she begins doing the walk-around inspection herself, two men emerge from the office building and head towards the plane's nose cone, where she pauses. Jimmy Petrik and the airstrip boys still huddle in the shelter of the maintenance shed, one of the boys hopping from foot to foot as the cold do. The two men coming towards her appear similar in age, both past youth's prime. Obviously the test pilot is the wiry, grizzled, limping one wearing a flying suit and aviation helmet, a second helmet under his arm, for her, she assumes. He reminds Muriel of a tramp she used to see on her childhood streets near Stanley Park. Despite the pilot's sore foot, he reaches the nose cone before the other man, and calls out to Muriel, "Ho, there, lady, let's go for a ride." He pumps her gloved hand and says, "Orville Loftus." He smells like red oxide primer; this strikes Muriel as odd, since the Mosquitoes are painted back at the plant. The smell is far from unpleasant, though. Orville Loftus acts as if the other chap isn't even there. How rude. Manners matter on an airstrip as much as anywhere. What's wrong with these northerners?

The other man wears a fine wool coat. He's thickset, but his weight is well distributed. Muriel extends her hand to shake his and, even through her gloves, she feels a tremor in his palm. He stares at her intently, and introduces himself as Lieutenant Colonel McLaughlin, adding that he's been sent by a subcommittee of the British Intelligence Division, to Fort William. It all comes back to Muriel. He's so pleased to meet her. He has heard much about her. To hide her pinkened face, Muriel continues her walk-around inspection of the Mosquito. They follow her. Orville Loftus harrumphs and says, "our *lieutenant colonel* is worried we're going to fly away and give this Skeeter to Hitler's boys – or *some*body. Must be *some* reason he's here."

"If Mr. McLaughlin thinks he should be here, he *should* be – he has a *right* to be here," Muriel declares, admiring the plane's rudder. A gust slams against them, sending a shudder through the Mosquito. Buffeted by wind, Muriel hears a sound emanating from Loftus like "*paaaa*," and she sees what she's up against with this test pilot. She asks him if he's quite sure his ankle is sufficiently healed for a test flight. Roper McLaughlin echoes her concern. All they get from Loftus is another "*paaaa*" which Muriel can only take as yes.

Jimmy Petrik and the airstrip boys have traipsed over to them. The test pilot tosses Muriel the helmet he's toted to the Mosquito. She catches it. He scrambles, surprisingly agile for someone rickety and recovering from a broken ankle, up the steps and into the cockpit. Muriel completes the inspection. She gives Jimmy Petrik her cane. She won't need it up there. Then she removes her hat (the wind ripples her hair), and tugs on the helmet. She asks the lieutenant colonel if he'd be so good as to keep her hat for her during the test flight. He tells her he'd be *honoured.* 'How gallant,' she thinks.

As she pulls herself up the wooden stairway to the cockpit, she can only hope Orville Loftus is less churlish in the sky than on the ground. She settles into the navigator's seat, set slightly back from the pilot's seat. It's cold in the cockpit, and their breaths hover above the control panel. Muriel pulls her fox collar around her throat, and settles her reporting form, secured to its clipboard, on her knee.

The airstrip boys get busy de-icing. Orville Loftus scowls at the sight of Muriel's test-flight form. He switches on the magnetos. She ticks "normal" in the box beside *magnetos.* Through the window she sees Lieutenant Colonel McLaugh-lin; he's stroking her hat, of all things. Orville Loftus activates the throttle. He moves the Mosquito ahead a few hundred feet. He checks the brakes. Muriel ticks inside the "normal" boxes for *brakes, tachometer, manifold pressure gauge, throttle valve, oil-temperature gauge.* She writes "run-up test suc-cessful" in the margin. Orville opens the throttle for takeoff. A crosswind slams the plane as it lifts from the runway; it wobbles at low altitudes. Loftus cusses the gust envelope. It's only wind. Muriel wishes he would loosen up. She ticks "normal" beside *throttle function, flaps, pitch control,* and *climb rate.* They make a turn that takes them over the airstrip, the men below already tiny.

Loftus' manners *do* improve with altitude, even though the plane shakes enough on ascent to make Muriel write "mod-erate" beside the box marked *flutter and vibration.* They rise two, three, then four thousand feet. Orville gives Muriel a thumbs-up. A creaky smile. "Plant," he hollers above the engine's bumble, pointing to the roofs of the three production sheds below. Muriel thinks of the Voutilainen girl riveting, and the hundreds of other aviation workers. She remembers the snack-wagon girl's reverence for flight. If only the workers could be up here where she is – wait, why *can't* they be up here, at least a couple of chosen ones? Some of Muriel's brightest ideas have come to her high above the earth. Orville

Loftus banks the Mosquito, follows the Kam River to where it spools into Lake Superior. Muriel scrawls in the margin, "*Let the Workers Fly! – Incentive Scheme – Revisit later.*"

Muriel can't deny that the wild country below has its own peculiar beauty – in the river's tango into twin white meanders. The islands, Mission and McKellar, snowy symmetrical lungs. A winter hawk dips, briefly, beside them. Nor can she deny the strange peace that has come over Orville Loftus. At last he breaks his silence, calls over to her that he's glad to be back in the saddle. His smile is less creaky.

Winds drub them, but the plane continues to rise. The workers' hands have built it well – so far. Loftus banks the Mosquito this way and that, to test controllability traits. Longitudinal, lateral and normal axes all seem fine. Angular displacements within range. Muriel marks her report form.

☑ Roll Satisfactory (pending stall/spin test)
☑ Pitch Satisfactory (pending stall/spin test)
☑ Yaw Satisfactory (pending stall/spin test)

Having reached their service ceiling, they chop over the vast lake, frozen a mile or so from shore. Open water at last. Orville Loftus apologizes for the bumpy ride. "Not – your – fault," Muriel returns. The grain elevators of Port Arthur are children's playing blocks. "Sleeping Giant" – the test pilot points to the huge rock with its uncanny resemblance to a human form, resting beneath a snow quilt.

Loftus tilts the plane towards the McIntyre River, and an area bordered by a boreal expanse. Muriel knows what this means. They'll test stall and spin capabilities next, not something to be carried out near residential areas. The western edges of Port Arthur and Fort William are abrupt. Houses. Then bush. As the clouds thicken, Muriel turns the page of her report form. They'll test for spin last, closest to Bishop's Field, where firefighting equipment is stored and the airstrip boys wait ready with hoses.

"I'm going to cut the power," Orville Loftus calls to her.

"Yes," she returns.

He stalls the engine. Now there's only the soundness of the plane, the test pilot's skill, and grace, between them and a crash landing. Muriel takes a deep breath. Clasps her clipboard. It's so quiet in the cockpit, the eeriest kind of lull. They hang suspended. The plane begins to lose altitude. Its wings must have picked up some ice because the stall speed is higher than Muriel reckons it should be. She silently brings to mind everything she recalls about stalls from her university notes, her flight manuals – *the airplane shall have sufficient directional and lateral control so that, when the plane is stalled, the downward pitching motion following the stall shall occur prior to any uncontrollable roll or yaw. Any such pitching motion shall not be excessive and recovery to regular flight shall be possible by normal use of the controls after the pitching motion is unmistakably developed, without excessive loss of altitude –*

It all sounds so clinical. The fact is, they're plummeting.

"*– loss of altitude – and why didn't I have time to smoke one last Camel?*"

"What?" Loftus shouts as they continue to lose altitude.

Goodness, she's been jabbering to herself, out loud. "Nothing," she returns.

The pitching motion is severe now; Muriel's stomach starts to heave and churn.

Orville Loftus lowers the plane's nose and decreases the angle of attack. The pitching diminishes as the air flows more smoothly over the wings now. He refires the engine. They're heading upwards. Muriel clasps her clipboard, hoping doing so will provide some purchase for her shaking hands. She hears Orville Loftus say something – either "no mere piece of cake" or "damned-near a mistake." She's too rattled to ask. The main thing is, they're alive.

One final test remains. Spin recovery. They fly south, towards Bishop's Field. If they come out of the spin, all that remains is to land in one piece. Gusts jounce the plane. It has clouded over more, but between white bundles they catch a glimpse of the airstrip, the tiny men.

"Brace yourself," Loftus warns. "I'm going to put her into a spin." He doesn't wait for her response before setting the rudder and elevator in the full pro-spin position. He places the ailerons in the neutral position. He cuts the power. The spin feels wrong to Muriel; its back-pressure nauseates her. She knows that the test pilot should be able to spin for six turns, then recover by applying the elevator and trimming the rudder controls. She knows, too, the spinning should stop and control should be gained in not more than one and a half turns after applying the controls. She also remembers that the spin can be corrected with the flaps and landing gear extended.

None of this happens. Loftus trims the rudder controls. He extends the landing gear. They spin. The earth looms close. They've made six, maybe seven, revolutions. Why aren't the controls more responsive? Muriel is dizzy. She clutches her seat. Loftus curses – something about the controls being stiff, then, "Son of a Pagan Dog-Bitch," followed by some profanity she can't translate in her sick, panicked state.

A white outcropping rises from below to meet them. This is it, then. Her mother will read about her death in the newspaper. Muriel hasn't even decided about God. For some reason, she thinks about Audrey and her snack wagon, and is glad that she'd begun to show kindness to the kid, considering, in all likelihood, she herself will die with no further chance to atone, down the road, for her earlier brusqueness – there'd *be* no road –

Orville Loftus yanks on the rudder controls with all his might. Suddenly, the landing gear extends fully; within a sliver from the earth, the plane shoots upwards like a bird scooping a worm, its booty in its beak. So there *is* a God. Muriel had been so sure it was over. Somehow, the test pilot rescued them from disaster.

Because of the spin, their pitch altitude is out of kilter, their approach speed too fast. Loftus is still scrambling to control the plane, but they're coming in for some kind of landing. The undercarriage indicator lights are blinking – not normal. The cockpit vibrates badly. Loftus extends the flaps. They can only hope the shock absorber cords on the landing gear have been properly installed. The airstrip isn't overly long. They can see the men, trailing fire hoses, sprinting towards the Mosquito.

The plane weaves crazily, then thunks down hard. Every ball joint shrieks in protest. They swerve on the ice, this way then that, before rocketing forward the full length of the airstrip, past the men, helpless with their hoses. At last, the Mosquito slows and comes to a stop, part on, part off, the runway. The airstrip mechanics shout and run towards them, McLaughlin ahead of the others. Even in her shocked state, Muriel notices the surprising speed at which he moves, given his age and blocky stature. One of the airstrip boys falls, splayed on the ice, then scrambles to his feet. Another mechanic wheels the wooden step-way ahead of him. Orville and Muriel sit, paralyzed, in the cockpit, breathing hard.

"Did you read the book I sent you?" Loftus asks.

"No," she admits weakly.

"You should," he says.

"I will." Because she didn't die, she'll read every word written from now on, even poetry.

Orville Loftus yanks his helmet from his head. He plants his eyes squarely on her face. "You weren't afraid, were you, Miss McGregor?"

She lies. "No, Mr. Loftus."

"Did you get your damned form filled out?"

Of course. He's back on earth. He *would* be churlish. Before Muriel can formulate an answer, two of the airstrip boys scurry up the wooden steps onto the small platform and open the cockpit door. Jimmy Petrik stands, smoking, at the bottom of the steps. The lieutenant colonel is there, too, holding her floppy felt hat. His face is white, his expression, shaken. The chap who fell on the ice extends his hand to help Muriel out of the plane. They're all talking at once – "Are you all right?" "We thought you were goners." "We saw that spin." Muriel tells another fib; she's fine. Loftus follows her silently out of the cockpit, down the steps. She loses her footing on the second-to-bottom step, and the ground-crew boys hoist her up in a single, grabbing motion, barely rescue her from falling.

"Be careful with her!" Roper McLaughlin shouts.

Jimmy Petrik rolls his eyes. He hands Muriel her cane. "Here's your stick."

"Your hat, Miss McGregor," Roper McLaughlin says in his lieutenant colonel voice.

She thanks him – she never thought she'd live to *wear* that hat again. She removes her helmet and lets the wind have full play with her hair. Cold, for once, feels good. Even *dry cold.*

Roper McLaughlin huffs he's so thankful she is – they are – the plane is – back in one piece. He strangely confesses that he'd *prayed* through those last minutes of the test flight. Muriel doesn't miss the unsteady quake in his voice. How considerate he is, but goodness, what a nervous Nellie. She wonders how he can work in intelligence, being high-strung like that. She dons her hat. Orville Loftus limps, scowling, around the Mosquito, scanning it from stem to stern.

"Looks like you were having some trouble up there, Loftus," Roper McLaughlin says when the test pilot has completed his circle.

"Trouble?" Loftus volleys back. "I flew through the Great War. *That* was trouble."

"Is that a fact?" McLaughlin asks. "So did I."

"Sometime when we're not freezing our hides, we should wax nostalgic. Right now I need a drink."

Loftus tells Muriel they'll debrief later. He's got a few notions about that Skeeter they just tested, but that can wait. He hobbles off in the direction of his office with no further words for Roper McLaughlin, or anyone else.

The Factory Voice
Fort William Aviation
March 3, 1942
Human Interest Feature – by Ruby Frances Kozak

REGGIE, OUR BOY OF THE WIRES

reetings, workers! March has arrived lamblike, but don't pack your toques in mothballs just yet, for surely the lion isn't far behind. In the absence of any news of genuine moment, your Voice *brings you a serving of light fare, a trifle akin to last December's sketch of the factory's snack-wagon girl. If you should ever find yourselves in the far corner of Sub-Assembly, you'll see a thin, dark-haired chap cutting wires. There he sits alone on his bench, pliers in hand. Your* Voice, *in her other capacity as employee recruitment officer, confesses she'd forgotten she'd hired him. He'd been one of the great unwashed, the faceless, nameless newcomers who've signed on at the factory over the past few months. In her desperation to find a story, any story, for your reading edification, your* Voice *cornered the wire cutter. His name is Reggie Hatch. He hails from Rainy River. But he could as easily have stepped from the pages of Dickens, such a Dickensian waif, an Oliver Twist figure is he. Never has a more timid lad set foot in this factory. He could hardly look into the eyes of the* Voice. *When he spoke at last, his speech proved heavily inflected with the parochial tones of rural life. He speaks in palsied quakes and nervous twitches. Yet his lowly task of cutting wires holds together our planes as surely as each rivet and weld seam. Next time you consider our glorious flying men, think of all the little people like this boy Reggie Hatch, who buoys up our Mosquitoes. Hail to Reggie!*

Reggie decides
it's High Time

*P*ayday. March's cold snap is over. Snow softens to slush, and at Fort William Aviation, the Sub-Assembly girls descend on the snack wagon, grab their refreshments and dash outside to the plant courtyard during coffee breaks. They tug their yellow scarves off their heads. Shake their hair. They squeeze onto the benches, their faces turned to the sun. Reggie Hatch leaves the plant during breaks, too. He leans against the courtyard wall and smokes and thinks. It has been sixty-four days since his deal with Jimmy, and Reggie hasn't had a single date. That day back in his garage, Jimmy had tooted about how the plant *oozed with sex*, but had Reg reaped any of that? Not even a drop of ooze. Eight Friday meetings in the plant parking lot, during which Reggie has slipped Jim the wires he required, and smuggled the ones Jimmy has given him into the plant. Reggie has kept up *his* end of the bargain, but whenever he's seen an attractive girl in the factory and flagged Jimmy down to remind him of his promise to ask this girl, on Reggie's behalf, for a date, Jimmy has swatted him away with words like, "not now, Rainy, I'm busy on important plant-constable business," or more prickly, "for crikey sake, Reg, can't it wait until after

119

work?" No, Reggie has been steady as rain, and what has Jim offered in return? Nothing. A nettle-thought has been jabbing at Reggie more and more – Jimmy Petrik is taking him for a ride.

This nettle itches hardest during times like this – coffee breaks – when the factory girls swarm and laugh and are *girls* instead of riveters or sorters or grinders or rubber-press operators. Reggie pushes his back against the courtyard wall and studies them as they chatter and munch apples and muffins under the winter sun and don't even notice him. Some of them aren't bad looking and, at an earlier time, Reggie would have found a few downright attractive – but ever since he's seen *her*, no one can come close. *Ruby.* And the other day she'd turned up at his workbench to *interview* him for that newspaper of hers, *The Factory Voice.* He'd just about keeled over from the shock, the sheer *wonder* of her, standing *right there,* over his wires – and he'd forgotten how pretty she was (flowing hair and perfect lips and tiny waist and yet curves) – that he hadn't been able to speak at first. She'd come smelling of lilacs. She was there so suddenly, with her sweet whiff, it was like she'd been lowered, on silk cables, from the roof, the very sky. Reggie was supremely relieved he hadn't been mixing wires for Jimmy Petrik at the moment of her descent. She might have asked him about it (though she hadn't, in the end, asked about what he actually did; she seemed more interested in him as a *person*, and hadn't *that* made his clock tick!). After she'd finished her interview (all too brief), she'd left, trailing her lilac scent. Reggie decided then and there it was high time for Jimmy Petrik to make good on his promise of a date. If Reggie is going to be fit for the likes of Ruby Kozak, he needs to be a gentleman, and there is no time to start like the present – so instead of buffaloing Jimmy in the men's locker room or the security office or the plant parking lot, Reggie will do the right thing and buy Jimmy a few glasses of beer on payday and ask him then.

Six and a half hours later, Reggie sits, waiting for Jimmy, at a small, round table in the men's taproom at the Royal

Edward Hotel. Reggie isn't about to stall his drink order until Jim arrives. He's thirsty. The taproom is sparsely populated except for a few old men at tables across the large room and, seated at the bar, several soldiers home on leave. Reggie doesn't wait for the bartender to amble over and ask what he wants. He goes to the bar, buys beer. One of the soldiers plays some frenzied polka on the jukebox, as if to make up for the room's heaviness. Across the hall, through the open door leading to the "Ladies and Escorts" section, it's a different story – laughter tumbles like water from Kakabecka Falls, in there. Well, Reggie won't be stuck here in the Lonely Hearts' Club much longer, once he's brought Jimmy Petrik to rights.

Reggie quaffs three beers and admires how his empty glasses resemble the hourglass figures of pretty girls at the factory. *No* woman's shape can measure up to Ruby Kozak's movie-star lines, though. Reggie lights into a new frothy golden brew, and just as he's wondering why beer tastes best on payday, Jimmy Petrik ambles into the taproom and flops down onto a chair across from Reggie. Brushing lint off his plant-constable's uniform, Jimmy says what he always says, that he's been busier than a cat watching nine mouse holes. Reg orders three glasses of ale for Jimmy along with a few pickled eggs from the big jar on the bar. He tells the bartender to "run a tab," just because it feels so good to say that. The two men chew their eggs and work through their beer and jaw about the mild weather, how it won't last, they'll pay for it. Reggie decides enough breeze has been shot. He reaches into the pocket of his jacket and retrieves a rolled newspaper. *The Factory Voice.* He opens it at the page containing Ruby Kozak's feature about him.

"You musta read this, Jim?"

Jimmy shakes his head. He doesn't read that rag. He doesn't have time. He'll skim the story Rainy now waves around under his nose, though. He scans it with skeptical eyes. He tosses the paper aside, and Reggie must rescue it from the table's damp residue left by the occupation of thirst.

"She's making fun of you, Reggie."

"What?"

"Miss Kozak-Stuck-Up-Stenographer who wrote this. Can't you see that?"

Reggie joggles his head back and forth, and presses Jim for his meaning.

Jimmy reaches for the *Voice,* and reads bits of the story out loud: "One of the great unwashed, Dickensian waif, palsied quakes and nervous twitches, parochial tones." Jim flicks the paper tableward and sends Reggie a high and mighty *told-you-so* look.

"I don't see no 'fun' in there, Jim."

Jimmy drains his glass and waves to the bartender, the universal "another round" signal. Six more hourglasses appear on their table.

Jim inhales the head off his beer. "She's saying you're a bumpkin, Reg."

"She likes the way I talk."

"Do you even know what 'parochial' means, Reggie?"

"No. Do you?"

"No. But it's not good."

Reggie Hatch takes a long sip of ale. "Hey!" he shouts to the bartender, "you got a dictionary?"

The bartender calls back, "What do you boys think this is, some kind of Ernest Hemingway watering hole? Of course I don't got a dictionary."

Reggie retrenches, pulls his beer closer. "I don't believe Ruby would run me down, Jim. Besides, she was *nice* to me. If I weren't so blasted shy, I'd have asked her out right then and there. But I am, so that's why *you're* going to get me a date with her, Jim. Tomorrow."

Alarm chases across Jimmy's face. "She didn't ask you nothing about the wires, did she Reg?"

Reggie can't believe that after sixty-one days Jimmy still stalls. An unfulfilled promise starts to stick in a chap's craw after a while. "She didn't *write* about them, *did* she Jim, and she didn't *ask* me, neither. Now, since I've been

122

helping you out with the wires, it's time to fill your end of the bargain."

"Sure, Reg, but Ruby Kozak's nose is stuck so high in the air, even those Skeeters can't reach it. Can't you pick some other girl?"

"*Other* girl? Like who?"

Jimmy takes a hard swallow. "I seen you talking to that *person* who pushes the snack wagon. Lots of times. Jawing away in the cafeteria, on the shop floor. If you like *her* so much, and a bit of cradle robbing strikes your fancy, why don't I set it up?"

Reggie laughs. "She's just *that,* Jim, a kid. I'm not using up my favour on a *child.* Besides, Audrey's my pal."

"What about the stout girl who rivets and welds? Florence? She's slimmed down lots lately."

"Sorry, Jim. Only Ruby fills the bill. Ruby. This is about more than wires, Jim. You know what this is about?"

Jimmy has no idea.

Reggie Hatch rises, raises his glass, turning in a half-circle as the beer teeters precariously near its brim. "*Love! Zats* what zis-is about, boys!*"

The old men stare at him with unimpressed eyes. One of the soldiers at the bar raises his glass in a sad, desultory toast. The bartender ignores Reggie.

"You better put the brakes on that beer," Jimmy says.

Reggie sits down. He keeps drinking. "It's payday, Jim. In more ways than one. I've got wires for you in my pocket. What've you got for *me?*"

"Ruby Kozak doesn't like me. I already told you that once. Little slip back in high school. I'll try, but no promises."

Reggie Hatch holds his glass so far out in front of his face it almost reaches Jimmy's mouth. "I need to smell her lilacs, Jim."

"You're corked, Reggie. Drunk."

"You know what, Jim? I *am* drunk. On love."

Jimmy rolls his eyes, lights a Lucky Strike. "Hate to burst your bubble, Reg, but Ruby Kozak isn't even interested in men. All she does is write her stupid stories."

"I don't care. *Do* it, Jim, and *soon*. It's high time. Who knows what Hitler's got up his swastika for us? You've seen the factory signs. All this could end tomorrow."

Jimmy glowers. Reggie asks if he'd like the latest install-ment of wires. Jimmy would. Then Reggie guesses they've got a *deal*, and he'll await further details of the time and place of his date with the *angel from Head Office*.

"All right all right all right all *right*," Jimmy rumbles, rising and smoothing his blue jacket.

Reggie jostles coins from his pocket to pay for their ales and eggs. As for the wires, he'll meet Jimmy outside.

Jimmy Petrik is almost at the exit door. As Reggie fumbles with his coins, he calls across the taproom to Jimmy's back, "If Ruby Kozak asks what I've got, you tell her, tell her, I'm going to *be* somebody."

Jimmy doesn't bother to turn. He makes a thumbs-up sign, but not high enough in the air to suit Reggie Hatch, nor with enough gusto to signify true belief.

Cow-Kicked

*H*ssst – over here!

That's right, behind the big sack of flour in the far corner of the storage room. What am I *doing* here? Stagger me, what do you *think* I'm doing? Hiding. I'm crouching on a crate because the mice scurry and there's flour on the floor tiles, like light snow. I don't want flour on my boots. You'd never see flour on Wonder Woman's high red boots. Stagger me, though, I've fallen far from wonder. You saw the snack wagon parked outside the cafeteria door, the sign on it – *Breaking! Come Back Much Later.*

I'm hiding from Ruby Kozak. I'm pretty sure she won't venture into the storage room; she might get flour on her dress, or grease. She doesn't even eat in the cafeteria. She brings her own sandwich and sits at her desk and chews it with her pearly teeth while she types *Factory Voice* stories over lunch hour. She told me Mr. Parks only lets her write the *Voice* if she doesn't do it during her regular work hours, that one day he'll see his mistake in holding back a talented writer like her.

For the past couple of weeks I haven't gone for my Wednesday report. I got Florence Voutilainen to deliver notes to Ruby in Head Office. I'll tell you about the notes in a jiffy. You remember Florence, the riveter whose red scarf I yanked off when the crane crone almost mowed us down? Since that fateful day, Florence calls me her liberator. She said because of me, she got to feel what it was like to be on that shop floor without the red scarf, and how that was the best feeling in the world. Besides, she and I had survived *a near-death moment,* which means we're destined to be friends. Florence is swell. You should see her! She's slimming down. Doesn't buy snacks anymore, but she waves my wagon over to her work-station anyway, and asks about me – not prying things, but sweet questions, like, do I enjoy Churchill Ladies' Residence, would I fancy going for a milkshake with the Sub-Assembly girls some night, do I know how to dance the lindy hop (I sure don't), have I seen *The Wizard of Oz?* (I sure have) and didn't I laugh when the Tin Man creaked and creaked until Dorothy understood him at last, *"Oil Can"* (I really did). Florence is kind, and when I asked if she'd do me a favour and deliver a note to Ruby in Head Office, she said she would, gladly. She'd be happy for a chance to visit Ruby, if even for a few minutes at lunch. The first note I gave to Florence to give to Ruby said, *"Audrey's Wednesday Report, Feb/42 – Have flu, don't wish to spread germs in Head Office, A.F."* My second note said, *"Audrey's Wednesday Report, Mar/42 – Flu gone. Nothing to Report, A.F."*

I've missed seeing Ruby's beautiful face and sniffing her lilacs, but ever since the lipstick day, something hasn't sat right with me. And I didn't like what she said about my pal, Reggie, in her story at the beginning of the month, either – she called him *unwashed* and *palsied.* Reggie is the cleanest person I know! And he may be beanpole thin but he doesn't shake.

No, when it comes to Ruby, I'm living on borrowed time. Ever since March and this darned heat wave, they've made me push my snack wagon an extra lap and park right beside the exit door so all the hungry girls who want to eat their muffins and drink their drinks outdoors in the courtyard don't have to traipse through the production sheds and leave trails of crumbs and such. The exit door is right near Head Office, and yesterday, after all the girls had finished descending on me, I felt this *hand* on the scruff of my neck – it clamped down hard like an *iron jaw*, then kind of yanked upwards on my blouse collar like it was going to drag me off. I knew it wasn't Reggie the wire cutter. He wouldn't pounce. He's shy. I thought it might be Jimmy Petrik, who never has forgiven me for grilling him about muffins. Then the worst horror struck – what if Clabber-Face had somehow found me and was going to haul me back to Spruce Grove and stuff me inside that white wedding dress? Finally I wiggled far enough around to see it was *Ruby Kozak* who'd seized me by the scruff. She was wearing a mauve beret. Her lips matched. She looked so pretty it made me *ache*. Stagger me if I could understand how such a graceful hand could be this grim vise, and I sure didn't take the time to figure it out just then.

"I'm *hungry*, Miss Audrey Foley."

I'd never heard this clenched-teeth sound come from Ruby Kozak before. She'd said my name like I was some Nazi vermin. I thought about hollering,

"SNACKS – hard drinks   soft drinks   fried gopher hearts" to get the attention of the girls larking away on the benches. Ruby must have sensed this – she's so terribly smart – because she grabbed the back of my collar even harder, and said, "Keep quiet and listen good, Audrey. You're going to tell me who got those tarts a few weeks ago, and you're going to make your Wednesday report to me *directly* and your next report will contain real substance as I think you'd like to keep your job and your nice room in Churchill Ladies' Residence and, am I not the one who got you both of these things?"

She'd thrown so much at me at once I couldn't sort it all out fast enough and she kept yanking me up by the collar, saying, "Am I *not?*," "Am I *not?*" All I could do was squeak, "Yes, Miss Kozak."

"That's better." Ruby eased her grip on my collar. "Now about the tarts. Who received them?"

I was cow-kicked, for I'd promised Miss McGregor I wouldn't tell anyone. And I'd been back to her office a few times *since* the tarts, and she was saintly and made tea and let me see more of her drawings of the little house she called a ski pedestal. Stagger me, Miss McGregor is –

A real live *Heroine.*

And she'd said I could come back whenever I wanted, and true to her word, she never again posted the *Do not disturb – No snacks wanted* sign on her door. One day, the same man who was in the meeting-room with Ruby Kozak was in Miss McGregor's office when I went to visit her, and she wasn't mean and didn't order me to leave. And the man was also kind. His name is Lieutenant Colonel Roper McLaughlin, and he was decent enough not to mention the day I'd made a jackdaw of myself by barging into the boardroom. And over the past few weeks, Miss McGregor's office had become the place I liked to go best. I sure didn't want to ruin that.

"I don't have all day, Audrey. *Spit it out.* Who got the tarts?"

"I don't know! I don't remember her name. Just some *yellow scarf* in Final Assembly."

Ruby released my collar. She thumped her forehead with the palm of her hand as if she was trying to chase a migraine out the back of her skull. She told me how disappointed she was, how I'd not risen to the *glamour of my job.* The high hopes she'd had for me would crumble to dust if I didn't soon pull myself together. I'd better have the tart-woman's name on the tip of my tongue next Wednesday, and it'd be dandy if I brought some *other* useful material for her, too, and if I sent some *lame excuse of a note* instead, that would be –

THE END OF ME!

She kind of hissed this in my ear.

Suddenly the bell sounded. Break over. Its merciful clang stopped Ruby's hissing, and she beelined for the double doors leading into Head Office. The assembly-line girls tied their yellow scarves back on, and shoved themselves off their benches. I didn't want them to see how rattled I was, so I left the snack wagon parked right there by the exit door, and I tore through the plant to my cower-spot behind the sack of flour, where you found me skulking. And to make matters worse, when I went back to the snack wagon, some louse had stolen all the cigarettes, some of the sandwiches and all of the tips from the Victory Bond jar. I had to tell Lucy Fell, the head dish. She wasn't rowing her bloody boat down the stream when she heard *this* news. Lucy Fell gave me hell and who knew hell had such fury east of Alberta? So here I am again, in the cafeteria storage room corner, flour on my boots and egg on my face. I'm cow-kicked, and out eighty-five cents from the stolen items, and pretty darned certain Wednesday will come as sure as the industrious moon will rise.

*A*s of yesterday, March 16, 1942, Florence Voutilainen weighed in at 170 pounds. Her overalls hang loose as she walks home from the factory after her shift. She has to thank hundreds of carrots for this – carrots she's chomped during breaks and lunch hours instead of the things she loves, like Butterfingers candy bars, meatloaf slathered in gravy. Muffins. Bread pudding laced with caramel sauce. She misses these tastes, no question, and the comfort they bring, but they're nothing compared to what the mirror now reflects back, a girl who just might live to have only one chin. A girl who can rivet and weld with the cream at Fort William Aviation. Who soon, with any luck, will be issued a yellow head scarf like everyone else, for her three-month probation will be over.

The new brouhaha at the factory – something about bad wires, ten-dollar reward offered for information (she'd heard only snatches during her anxious departure for the dentist's office) – had nothing to do with her. And happily, her mother hasn't for the longest time demonstrated in front of the Fort William Town Hall, parading with her megaphone and wearing her sandwich board with "Mounties are Murderers!"

painted on the front and "Voutilainen was Killed in COLD BLOOD in '29 we don't forget" on the back. No, her mother has laid low all winter and, best of all, has hardly been home to sew for the dead-eyed veterans or sit on the woodbox and drink too much dandelion wine and rant sobbingly about her brother, Florence's Uncle Janni, gone for more than ten years.

As of today, Florence can smile without covering her mouth. And the first person she's going to smile at is the stranger. If her good luck keeps jitterbugging along the way it has been lately, he'll be pottering around her house, especially during this mild spell. Her mouth is still stiff. She'd left Dr. Wishart's office almost two hours ago, but she can smile, hey, maybe the way a *rock* can, and she waves and sends her sincere, paralyzed grin to the Gruff rock as she passes it now. The rock, awash in late-day winter sun, smiles back.

Florence had spread her frozen lips in the dentist's bathroom mirror and, while her smile is full of mercury, the fillings large, they beat decay hollow. She wonders if maybe she'll be able to pick up radio signals. This is the first funny thought she's had about herself in ages. Before this, she'd been so cross with herself, and for good reason. Her piggish hungers had stretched the elastic bands on her underpants and she'd had to jerry-rig them with safety pins. She'd put too much bluing in her white blouse, and turned it grey, and that's only *one* of the scatterbrained things she'd done.

Today, March 17, 1942, Florence has new underpants three sizes smaller and a fresh white blouse she's bought at Chapples Department Store. The blouse is the cat's meow. It has the new, notched collar. And to make the cat meow loudest of all, she has a date with the swishiest man in the factory, Jimmy Petrik, a plant constable! She still can hardly believe it. He'd sprung the question yesterday, the moment she'd raised her safety visor in the Welding Department. "How about a ride in my De Soto, Voutie, next weekend or the weekend after that – we can call it a date if you want." The fact that Jimmy had been scant on details didn't bother Florence. He was a plant constable. Only a certain kind of person can land a job like that.

Besides, the date being down the road a ways gives her time to eat more carrots, shed further pounds. Wait 'til Jimmy sees her new mouth and, if it comes to it, her bright underpants without safety pins (not that he'd seen the ones *with* safety pins, but still, she imagines, it's surely better luck to date in superior undergarments).

Florence walks on air. Feels hardly there in the best possible sense. The days of trudging in her heavy boots, hauling her over-two-hundred pounds of flesh and her aching teeth, along Rosslyn Road are over. Hail to carrots. She reaches her laneway and marvels how spruced-up home has become since the stranger started coming around a couple of months ago. She hopes his debt is far from paid. She loves making tea for him and scrambling eggs and hearing him sing his odd little songs he calls "protest anthems." He's such good company for someone who protests. Today the mailbox has been painted a bright blue, and "H. + F. Voutilainen" restenciled in fresh letters. She notices that the *Veteran Seamstress of the Lakehead* sign has been left untouched, but that doesn't bother her. The stranger probably just didn't want to put his oar in when it came to the sign, not until he asked her mother about it. He's thoughtful like that.

She sails down the laneway. The veering weather vane has been straightened and resecured to the house's roof. The splintered, rotting newel post on the front steps has been replaced, and she admires the new, hand-carved newel as she floats to the front door and enters the kitchen. She's not surprised to see him drinking tea at the kitchen table, tapping his fingers in time to some nifty Duke Ellington playing on the radio. He's wearing his paisley neckerchief. He's been helping out so much, he hardly seems like a stranger anymore.

Florence's mouth is almost thawed. She leaves the bag containing her new blouse and underpants on the woodbox (she'll admire her lovely purchases later, alone in her bedroom). He pours her a cup of tea, except it's not tea. It's dandelion wine in a teacup, and *green*. To honour St. Patrick, he says. He'd fished around in the cupboards, found some food coloring and added a few green drops to the wine and cubes of ice. He'd wanted to surprise the daughter, and hadn't he ever? Florence had been so nervous about her teeth, she'd forgotten St. Patrick's Day. She's tickled, and for the first time since stepping into the room, she sends the stranger a *wide-open smile,* not one of her earlier, lipped-over ashamed ones.

"The daughter has been filled," he says, fingers still tapping along with Duke.

She can't stop smiling. The green wine tastes delicious, and her stomach hasn't had any visitors except carrots since breakfast. It's so much easier to talk, too, with her dental repairs. Florence takes happy green swallows and tells him the mailbox looks swell, so does the weather vane. He's one heck of a carver, she chirrups, and isn't modern dentistry a marvel? She knows his feelings about the war, and the aviation plant where she works, but her job saved her teeth, so the factory can't be *all* bad, can it?

He drinks and asks her to continue her thoughts.

"See, the funny thing is, that since I got on at the plant, thanks to my friend Ruby, I've felt free for the first time in my whole lousy life. It feels so good. If I weren't a factory girl, I'd lose that feeling. I'd lose *everything.*" Florence takes a triumphant swallow.

"There's the illusion of freedom," the stranger says. "And there's *true* freedom."

Florence figures he's caught the cloud that's scudded across her face, for he puts the brakes on his riddle. He's thoughtful like that.

"But I'm glad the daughter is happy. In fact, she's *glowing.* And I don't think it's just the wine."

More Duke on the radio, never enough Duke. This isn't the first time Florence has felt the stranger looking right through her. She tells him she has a *real date* with a *real man* who's well into his twenties. The stranger asks if he's a decent sort of chap. *Decent?* He's a *dream.* Florence willows forth this word, and his *automobile* is a dream, too. She joggles the ice cubes in her glass; they tinkle like small bells.

The stranger says he'd *better* be decent, that being "well into his twenties" doesn't make him a man, either. Duke ends, and an announcer's voice thuds from the radio. News. *Plant officials at Fort William Aviation are investigating production protocols after a test-flight probe just released by Bishop's Field cited faulty wires as the reason for a recent malfunction. Lieutenant Colonel Roper McLaughlin, sent by British Intelligence to monitor security issues, told Sleeping Giant Radio, "we won't rest until this wire issue has been solved." Plant manager Frank Parks was unavailable for comment.*

"So the imperial war machine's in trouble," the stranger says, draining his glass. He remembers he has a meeting he forgot earlier. He wishes the daughter top o' the evening. He trucks off, leaving Florence disappointed. He was gone before she could protest his leaving. She'd been looking forward to boiling some turnips for him, opening a couple of cans of sardines, having some herself (she allowed herself supper and how sublime even boiled turnips tasted after cold carrots). Still, Florence is too happy with how things are going her way to feel sad for long. She dines alone on turnips and sardines, and even dances the broom around the kitchen to divine Tommy Dorsey on the radio until, as is wont to happen, she is suddenly tired. She brushes her new teeth, being careful so the mercury won't fall out and she'll be back where she started, almost, and it doesn't. Florence takes a little notepad to bed with her, reclines on her pillow and writes: *Florence Petrik. Mrs. Florence Petrik. Mrs. James Petrik. Jimmy and Flo melt the snow (oh ho ho). Florence and James request the honour of your presence.* This pleases her so much she fills the whole page. She reaches over to her night table where she's kept the blue grey toque since Jimmy so thoughtfully tossed it to her that night on the road. She keeps his gift there, and often sleeps wearing it (her house being cold, it helps). She pulls it over her head now, and lays back and admires her handiwork on the page and understands, for the first time, why her friend Ruby Kozak is so crazy about writing, how the shapes and sounds of words can launch a whole new world. Florence sleeps, then. Sleeps in the toque's grey blue warmth. Some things are falling, in a gentle way, from the sky. Underpants. Underpants like big, white snowy petals.

Albatross

A Smoke of Luck
(Audrey – *cough*)

I smoke now.

The snack-wagon theft drove me to it. It made me so blue – what kind of swill-bucket worm would steal Victory Bond tips? – and they make *Florence,* honest as the month of March is long, wear the red scarf when meanwhile, tip stealers and skunky dealers and wagon peelers are robbing me blind. I'll tell you what – this factory has become

Husky-eat-husky!

And what about me?

It was rotten enough being in the bad books of *one* person (Ruby) but *two* (Ruby *and* Dish) snapped me like a twig in a dust bowl. After Dish yelled at me about leaving the wagon, I figured I was in so much trouble already a bit more wouldn't matter, so I took a package of Lucky Strikes for myself. It was one of those moment-spur things, yet not altogether. I was fed up with catching the dickens even though I hadn't really done anything wrong. Add to that Ontario, province of glamour and smoke – a place rubs off on a girl. The factory is filled with puffers (I've seen Miss McGregor partake in her office, too). Even the moon smokes. You've seen it those nights with that hazed-over look; it's having a puff.

Anyway, I took my cigarettes out to the factory parking lot after my shift. The mild weather had held on, so I crouched down behind a Studebaker, and lit a Strike. I coughed. After a few minutes I could take little puffs without my lungs somersaulting out of my chest. So I'm behind the car, smoking, and I hear two chaps' voices. I poke my head up over the Studebaker's hood, and I see Jimmy Petrik slouching against a fancy green car, and my pal Reggie. They're standing like two men who have a bone to pick with each other. And also smoking, and at first I think, *poor Rainy Reg is getting the dickens, too* – but it's the other way around. I stub my Strike and grind it in the dirt; I don't want them to notice my small stream of smoke and catch me eavesdropping. Anyway, Rainy Reg is the most steamed I've ever seen him.

Suddenly, just then

BURR   RARK   RUMBLE

from the open doors of the final assembly shed. This racket drowns out their words. But I still hear bits – Reggie is saying, "yeah, well, I kept my mouth *shut*, Jim. They grilled me good, Frank Parks *and* that snooping Scot, and I *could* have told them, but I *didn't* –" and Jimmy is barking back, "but if you had, we'd *both* be out of a job, wouldn't we, Rainy, so why *would* you blab about the wires?" And I can tell Reggie is stumped on this one. I know him. When he's stuck over something, he twitches his head and his face rips out in red and those acne things stick out like little white muffins, and that's happening right now. And he's stubbing his boot toe into the dirt, and smoking harder than I've ever seen him smoke. I'm worried he's going to swallow his cigarette. I'm fretting for Reggie's health, when he says, grandlike, in a way that also surprises me, "I could *blab* in the name of *something higher,* but I'm going to give you one more chance to fill your end of the deal, Jim. You've been stalling, but now you're going to get me a –

CLANK   ROAR

darn those machines, I can't hear, you'd think there were lions
rutting in that factory, not airplanes getting born –

BURR   RUMBLE

I can't catch Reggie's drift, then I hear him again – "and if you
don't, I'm going to tell them about the wires and you can kiss
your" – more lion ruts, ROARS

Jimmy glares at the hood of the shiny green car, then at
Reggie, and finally he says, "Saturday. Seven sharp, Rainy. Be
ready at your rooming house. We'll make it a double since
(industrial noise) is more likely to fall in line with (lost in the
lions, the screaming roars). Reggie stomps away, back into the
factory, and Jimmy Petrik makes a "kiss my armpit" signal,
and I'm so riled that this stuffed-shirt plant constable would
make that sign behind my friend's back, I almost blast out
from behind the Studebaker and give Jimmy a piece of my
mind. But I think it through, for once, and suddenly I realize
that the answer to the mess those plant brass have been trying
to untangle – the bad wire business, I mean (I heard about it
on the radio) – has fallen right into my lap, MINE. Jimmy
Petrik, without knowing, just spilled big beans about the
wires. This means that what I just witnessed is *supreme
skunky dealing* – a *real juicy story* bound to land me back in
Miss Kozak's good books so I won't feel like a louse every
minute and she won't hiss or grab my collar when I'm not
looking.

Best of all, I won't have to leave town in shame, which
would mean I'd never see my friend Florence again, or Miss
McGregor either, and who knew that, around here, Wonder
Woman is a lady who has polio and walks with a cane, and is
no less wondrous for that.

So the STORY – I have a *live one* on my hands here, a
winner yarn, a regular barn buster! Stagger me, did I get lucky
or *what?* Good thing I started smoking, wouldn't you say?

Now if I can only find a way to deliver this big-dilly item about the wires to Ruby without spoiling it for Reggie. I've got it – I'll just pluck Reg from the story for a short while. Take him out for an ice cream sundae, why don't you, while I tell Ruby that Jimmy Petrik knows about the wires. Reggie said they'd already grilled him and so he's out of it. Likely they'll leave him alone. Still, it'd be better for Reggie's sake if he was kept from harm's way, for a bit, which makes ice cream a dandy plan, don't you think?

Imagine – a *plant constable* playing with bad wires. Oh, this is going to be *ripe*. I already know what I'll say when I first walk into Head Office – I'll say, "Miss Kozak, I hope you're sitting down." She *will* be. She's always typing and slamming the carriage in that cranky way of hers, but it'll be a swell thing to say anyway. *I hope you're sitting down.* Then what joy I'll lay at her slender feet when she receives my offering –

For the first time in ages, I wish Wednesday had wings, and would land smack on my shoulders.

Ruby
The Things a Girl
Must Do for Her Career,
It Seems

The icicles of Fort William have been *drib-drib-dribbing* for days. Why such a fully un-spectacular event as the melting of frozen water makes everyone at the factory so zippy, Ruby can't fathom. It's only going to get cold again anyway. Ah, well, she *does* know why; simple things amuse simple people. The workers are content to be cogs, pin-sized whirligigs in destiny's vast spin, something Ruby's never been. Besides, no one at the factory bears the burden *she* bears. She is their *Voice*, their entry point into production (*Apply in Person to...*). She's the stenographic handmaiden for two reigning drones, Frank Parks and, more recently, that lieutenant colonel from British Intelligence (what he *does* with himself all day, she can't imagine). As for her, she types, types, types and wears her new sailor dress that no one even bothers to notice. And now she's been ordered to send letters of condolence on behalf of management at Fort William Aviation to the families of lost boys. Her dreariest detail yet. Frank Parks continues to heap work on her with no pay raise. She should have been gone from the Narrow Writing System and the Swamp ages ago.

But here she is, typing. *Deaf Mr. and Mrs. Deaf! Drat,* another spoiled sheet of stationery. Ruby rips the paper from her typewriter, but not before her fingers pound out a telegram to the perverse gods of the Narrow Writing System.

QWERTY YOU WAIT – ONE DAY I'LL WALK OUT OF HERE @#^&%*

She crumples the deaf letter into a ball and tosses it into the waste bin. She rolls a fresh sheet into her typewriter. *Dear Mr. and Mrs. Hardwith; We extend our deepest condolences to you on the loss of your son, Private Jerome Hardwith,* and on it goes. These days, she's farther than ever from the sort of writing she was *born* to do. And her running girl, Audrey Foley, has been nothing but a disappointment. Not to mention embarrassment. Fickle as the day is long. The kid hadn't brought her any real newsworthy material, much less the Big Story that would free Ruby from the Narrow Writing System. Still, the thought needles Ruby, the very real possibility that she used the girl too roughly the other day by the snack wagon. She'd scared the daylights out of Audrey who might, after all, still prove useful (one never knew). But minutes before the snack wagon affair, Ruby had received the results of a writing competition she'd entered; *The Fort William Daily Times Journal* had solicited submissions on the topic, "What small things do you do for the war effort in your daily life?" Ruby couldn't believe her own eloquent entry had been trumped by: "Confessions of a Rubber Salvager" (First prize! Ten dollars); "How I Learned to Stretch Butter" (Second prize, Five dollars); and "Lux Your Stockings for Twice the Life" (Third prize, Three dollars – for *that* drivel). But it had. She'd won nothing, and the appalling lack of imagination that had always epitomized the Swamp came home to her, and the Foley girl had taken it by the scruff.

Ruby continues to tap out the Hardwith condolences. Courage. Valour. She has typed this script so often her fingers move but her brain camps outside the page. Never mind, Ruby reflects, the snack-wagon girl could be pressed back into service without much trouble. The kid is easily swayed by glamour. Ruby would buy Audrey a trinket, or some ice cream. She might even let her use her lipstick.

Tap, tap. The end. Ruby rolls the finished letter from her typewriter. She checks the clock above the door leading to the switchboard foyer. Still not lunch. She glances at the ALL THIS COULD END TOMORROW banner tacked over the cabinets filled with shorthand pads, typewriter ribbons, plant stationery, and Gestetner fluid. Just then, the person Ruby least wants to see in the whole western hemisphere slithers into Head Office, right to her desk. Jimmy Petrik stands before her, jamming his hands into his blue pockets, his peaked constable's cap pulled low over his forehead, but not so low that Ruby doesn't see his weasel eyes scanning her sailor dress. She doesn't ask him to sit down. He does anyway. She informs him she's got a mountain of typing, he'd better not beat around the birches. He'll tell her what he wants *forthwith.* Jimmy lights a Lucky Strike. Oh yes, he can just sit there and blow smoke in her face despite what he did to her after the graduation dance. (When she'd told him what had happened, he'd wished her good luck. Were two more useless words ever spoken?)

Jimmy exhales. "I need a favour, Kozak."

Ruby chuffs forth a whopping, derisive laugh at this ludicrous request, then, remembering where she is, curls its edges with a more musical trill. Not that she cares what Jimmy Petrik thinks, but there are others around her, stenographic minions. The intermittent pecks of their keys betray their greedy ears.

Ruby makes rapid downward-patting flutters with her hand, a signal for Jimmy to lower his voice, as she now drops hers, "Why on God's green earth would I do *you,* of all people, a favour?"

Jimmy leans far forward, forcing her to wave his smoke aside. "Because I'll pay you."

"What makes you think I'd stoop that low, *Mr. Plant Constable?*"

She hates his smirking mug, his whiney parrot voice pitched to mock her literary talents. "I glance at your little news sheet once in a while, Kozak, when I'm bored. I believe you wrote, in your very first *Voice*, '*Dear Readers, I know not how long I will grace these pages. Greener pastures call, and my career as a reporter will soon soar me beyond these industrial walls, away from here.*'"

"Yes, I wrote that. Bravo to your good memory. So what?"

"So *what*? 'Away from here' costs money, that's what."

She slices her eyes at him. "When am I supposed to grant you this 'favour'?"

"It'll only take a couple of hours this Saturday night."

"Saturday night? That's after hours, mister. What do I have to do?"

"All you have to do is throw some bowling balls, Kozak. And make nice with the wire cutter. You know, Reggie, the fellow you wrote the story about."

She forgets greedy ears, lobs a walloping laugh through Head Office. "You don't mean that scrawny grass rake with the acne, that hick who can hardly talk, *do* you?"

Jimmy flicks his ashes onto his boot. "Reggie's not so bad. And just to make sure you're nice to him, I'll be there myself, with your friend Florence, if they can find bowling shoes to fit her clodhopper feet. Men's maybe? But she's lost a lot of beef. She might even be able to fit onto a bowling lane." It's Jimmy's turn to laugh.

"*Florence?* What makes you think Florence would go with you?"

"Are you off your cob, Kozak? If *Jack the Ripper* skated into the factory and asked her for a date, she'd go."

"You're right," Ruby says. "How much?"

"Five dollars."

She flicks her long bang aside so he can see fully her serious green eyes. "Considering it's after hours and considering the company, I wouldn't do it for less than fifteen."

"Ten." Jimmy calls this his final offer.

The writing-contest money that should have gone to Ruby storms through her mind. "So all I have to do is bowl and be nice to Acne-Face and I get ten big ones at the end of the game?"

Jimmy butts his cigarette on his boot. "That's it. You'd be the dizziest dame I ever met not to take it. But act like it's a *date,* for crikey sake, or I'll have to adjust the fee."

Ruby sighs. The things a girl must do for her career. "All right, but for ten I don't kiss those pimples."

"*Don't,* then. Just be ready a little after seven o'clock."

"Give me five bucks now," she says. "The other half on Saturday night."

"Don't you trust me, Kozak?"

"*Never.*"

Jimmy Petrik bucks the ashes and the butt from his boot onto the floor. "Oh, one other thing, I almost forgot, Reggie Hatch wants you to know that he's going to 'be someone.'"

"Is that so?"

"'Parently," Jimmy says.

Ruby sniffs. "And *what,* dare I ask, are the aspirations of a *wire cutter?*"

"You might as well ask the wild blue yonder, Kozak, 'cause *I* don't have a clue. But who knows? *I* was once a wire cutter and look at *me.*"

Yes, look at him. Mr. Wheelie-Dealie Plant Constable. Big frog in a small swamp. The lunch bell rings.

"I'll take my half now," Ruby says, peeved at having to press like this, to draw blood from such a bone-headed stone.

Jimmy rams his hand into his pocket, fishes for his billfold, and removes five one-dollar bills. He slides the money along the desk to Ruby. He snarls *Saturday,* and trucks out of Head Office in no time flat. She takes the money and deplores the ashy mess he's left on her floor. Some day she won't have to endure such gauche barbarians. That day can't come soon enough. She calls a steno-minion at one of the desks to sweep up the ashes left by *that plant official.* The minion obeys and, while sweeping, says to Ruby, "I saw you talking to Jimmy Petrik. He's *so* swish, but everyone says you don't *like* him."

"I *don't*," Ruby snaps, rummaging in her raffia handbag for her sandwich in its brown butcher paper wrapping. Rummaging and wishing one sandwich could be two, or even *three*, for suddenly Ruby Kozak is so hungry she could eat the snack wagon, wheels and all.

Picture the Swankiest Neon Sign You Can
Picture: **Stardust Bowling**

lorence scorches her new white blouse with the iron. She breaks out in hives for the first time in weeks, her nerves are *that bad.* Today is Saturday. The Date, and just as Jimmy Petrik's De Soto joggles along the potholed laneway to her front door (she's been watching out the kitchen window for him), her arms and neck sprout itchy, red welts. She'd agreed to let Jimmy pick her up at home instead of meeting him in Fort William since she'd have had to walk several miles, then take the trolley, and the temperature had nosedived the night before to nasty depths after weeks of mild weather, and *stayed* at nasty depths. She'd have *done* it, though, at an earlier time, rather than let Jimmy see where she lived. But there's less need for shame, now, in the realm of *houses* at least. Since the stranger began paying his debt to her mother the Voutilainens' place is so spruced up that, thanks to his handiwork, Florence can bear to let a man – a plant constable, a *Date* – come to her home (though she *will* apologize for the potholes: the stranger has been meaning to dump gravel in them, but hasn't gotten to it yet). Florence's mother is sitting at the kitchen table, drinking dandelion wine and hemming for an amputee.

Florence will dash to Jimmy's car; there'll be no need for him to come inside and witness Henni with her blizzard of grey-flecked auburn hair, her fierce face bent, now, over a pair of tragic mutant trousers. Florence had thought everything through; it's just that the hives and the scorched blouse threw last-minute spanners into her plan.

Jimmy's beautiful green De Soto floats to a stop in front of her house, and Florence checks the mirror above the pump by the kitchen sink. Seeing the red welts on her arms and neck, she sends out a groan. Jimmy honks his horn. She'll have to think fast. She darts into her bedroom and grabs her old green sweater (matches his car!). It's pilling badly, but it covers the blouse's scorch mark. Flo also snatches the blue grey toque Jimmy tossed her that night long ago; she's always thought it good breeding to show someone you're *using* a gift they've given you (even though she's had little opportunity to test this notion, having received precious few gifts in her short life). Today is so cold that the toque extends beyond manners. She *needs* it, no longer wanting to freeze her ears. Florence is going on *dates* now, and can't afford to tempt the gods of ugliness any further.

Jimmy bleats his horn again. She's got to sprint out there lickety-split, or he'll come in and see her mother, who's the reason for the red probation scarf Florence must wear at work. Florence *still* can't believe Jimmy's compassion, his willingness to overlook her *status,* at least long enough to take her on a date. She wonders if it couldn't land him in hot water, a plant constable dating an employee on probation, but he must know what he's doing, and far be it from *her* to spoil her own crack at happiness.

"Have a good time, Florrie," Henni smiles wanly, hoisting her worn red eyes from her sewing. So her mother has been crying again, for the millionth time, over her brother Janni. Suddenly, a rare insight wallops Florence hard in her stomach. If only the brass at the factory could see her mother sitting there like that, they might remove the ugly label of "dangerous subversive" they'd stuck on Henni and, instead, know her for who she *really* is, a sister unstrung by grief. For the first time, Florence grasps her mother's core, and unfortunately hasn't a second to do anything *about* it, for a boy waits outside. Her very *life* hovers, on four wheels, beyond the door of her small house. Still, maybe if Jimmy came inside and witnessed Henni like that, sewing and crying, perhaps if he glimpsed Henni's true, *utterly harmless* self, he could persuade the security bosses at the plant to take Florence off probation and issue her a yellow scarf. But Florence hasn't had time to think this through. She is slow on her feet, and what if her mother suddenly went haywire in Jimmy's presence? Henni was unpredictable, and if she didn't act normal in front of Jimmy it could *worsen* things for Florence at the factory; they might even *extend* her probation.

No, Florence can't take the chance. She must walk through the door (a more insistent honk outside). She kisses the top of Henni's scalp and pulls the toque over her own head. She hates the itchy red welts on her arms but can do nothing about them. She bolts out into the bitter cold, and clambers into the seat of Jimmy's warm De Soto; the inside of that car is every bit as dreamy as she'd imagined, cream upholstery with burgundy piping. The notes of "Boogie Woogie Bugle Boy" scamper from the radio, perfect ditty for a date. Jimmy wears his swell plaid shirt, the same one he wore the night he came upon her on the road. She smiles broadly at him for the first time, broadly and with pride, flashing her new dental fillings. Jimmy throws the De Soto into reverse and bumps backwards out of the Voutilainens' laneway, and Florence is quivering so hard with excitement she forgets to apologize for the potholes. She sings "Boogie Woogie Bugle Boy" along with the radio. She's glad she's wearing the toque, not only because it's a gift from Jimmy, but because right now she's so happy the top of her head might blow off, and the toque helps hold it down.

As they drive towards the lights of Fort William, Jimmy tells Florence that with a mouthful of metal like hers she might be able to pick up telegraph signals, maybe even intercept German spies. She'd liked to have heard she looks nice, but even with her lost weight, she knows that's a stretch.

Florence decides to take Jimmy's quip as a compliment, for there are lots of ways to pay compliments, aren't there? Sure there are. She can feel her hives subside. They itch less.

They turn onto Arthur Street, skidding on ice for a moment. Jimmy corrects the skid easily, and says, "I've got a surprise for you, Voutie." Flo can only chirrup, "What?" Jimmy springs it, "*Bowling.*" And, how about *this?* Her *old pal* Ruby Kozak is coming too, along with an acquaintance of his, Reggie Hatch, the wire cutter from the plant. Florence must have seen him? She had. Cafeteria. Jimmy fiddles a cigarette from his shirt pocket and announces that they're on their way to pick up Kozak and the cutter. After that, they'll make like jackrabbits for Stardust Lanes, and won't that be swell?

"Sure, swell," Florence says weakly. She pulls the toque lower over her forehead to keep her disappointment from bursting through her skull. Her hives flare up again. She's confused as the dickens, and itchy. Why is Ruby going bowling? Ruby doesn't like Jimmy. A couple of weeks ago, when Florence delivered Audrey Foley's note to Head Office, she had a hurried chat with Ruby. When Ruby asked if Flo had found a "fellow" out there in the production sheds, Florence confessed *no,* but there *was* a chap she was sweet on, and after Ruby pried his name from her lips, *Jimmy Petrik,* Ruby made these awful gagging sounds. She'd hurt Florence's feelings. Ruby then warned Florence that Jimmy was a sneak and a boor, and she should be careful. And now Ruby is going *out* with them? And the *wire cutter?* Florence didn't know much about Reggie Hatch, but enough to peg him as being far below Ruby's type. He was skittery, shy and shadowy, working away, as he did, in the corner of Sub-Assembly. Not to mention bone thin, a face full of acne. Florence is completely flummoxed. Is this some kind of April Fool's gag? Is *she* an April Fool?

Jimmy Petrik motors along, and sings *deet deet deet* to a new radio song Florence can't place. All she knows is, she won't have him to herself. As she scratches her midriff through her coat, Florence can't help feeling hoodwinked. She shoves this inkling away, though, for surely the only approach now is to be a good sport, the *best sport* she knows how to be. Jimmy says today is the coldest April 1 on record. 1942, isn't *that* something? He asks Florence if she's liking her ride in his De Soto, and before she can answer, he tells her he's going to expand his Autobody shop, that there's nothing he can't do when it comes to cars. He's just replaced the rocker panels on Frank Parks' Chevy sedan. He's installed a new Budnick steering wheel on a Buick Streetrod. He's helped a fellow in the factory's paint shop cobble together a Crosley kit from '39. The chap couldn't crack the twelve-horsepower Wankeshaw that ran the thing.

Jimmy stops on Syndicate Avenue, in front of a large house with a sign in its front yard.

Rooms For Rent
Telephone South 73021

He gives his De Soto's horn a quick knead with the heel of his hand. Realizing that if she's ever going to say anything of a *personal nature* to him while they're still alone, she'd better *say* it now, Florence declares Jimmy a *genius* in the autobody department. He shrugs in a manner that indicates she hasn't overstated the case one iota.

The wire cutter, Reggie Hatch, strides out of his rooming house and slides into the back seat. He looks jittery and skittery, the way Florence remembers him from the plant cafeteria. Rawboned as ever. His hair is pomaded. She can see between the lapels of his threadbare coat that he's wearing a necktie. Jimmy bounces Flo's name into the back seat by way of introduction, and Reg says *everyone* knows Florence, the plant's star riveter. She blushes.

Fort William's downtown streets are a mass of frozen ruts. "Might as well be corduroy roads," Jimmy grumbles. They joggle and sledge towards Ruby Kozak's big, booming house on Marks Street.

"Hey, how come you're wearing my toque?" Reggie calls out to Florence.

"It's *my* toque," she says, not knowing how much more confusion her throbbing skull can take. "Jimmy gave it to me."

"April Fool, Rainy," Jimmy barks.

Florence wonders why someone would give a girl a gift he took from someone else. She's a good sport, so she drops the subject.

As they twist and turn through town, Florence can *smell* Reggie's jitters, shave lather and rooming-house sweat and boy nerves. Fear. It's there in his prattle, too. Reggie chatters about yesterday's cold. He wore three pairs of pants and still got frostbitten testicles while walking to work, and he had to see the factory nurse. A moose's hind end looked better than that nurse, he says.

"You want to hear about *cold,*" Jimmy carps, yesterday he went to his *garage* and found Einstein, the crow, frozen stiff as a two-by-four in his cage. Florence won't heap on more gloom, so she doesn't mention the man she'd read about in *The Fort William Daily Times Journal,* found dead behind a grain elevator in Port Arthur. No, this is a date. She's a good sport. A dead crow is enough. Frozen testicles are *too much.*

Marks Street. Ruby Kozak flounces out of her house. She wears a lavender wool coat with stylish darts and carries a fur muff. A white wool beret perches rakishly over her long, wavy hair. Ice crystals shimmer in a wake around her, and Reggie Hatch emits a gasp. Ruby stakes out the corner of the back seat farthest from Reggie, and slams the door. Jimmy churns the De Soto's tires, and they peel off for Stardust Lanes.

"Don't you just *love* bowling?" Florence croons, flipping her face towards the back seat.

Reggie calls the sport the cat's pajamas with the *right company.* Ruby's never seen any sense in rolling silly balls down a hallway and *normally,* on a night like this, she'd be making better use of her time than riding in automobiles – she'd be home, *writing journalism* in her bedroom. Jimmy says, "*Enough,* Killjoy Kozak," and Reggie remarks that maybe they can change her mind about bowling. Ruby *highly, highly doubts it.*

Stardust is the most stylish – the peachiest – place Florence Voutilainen has ever been. They walk into laughter and music and lights – shiny wooden lanes running right off the horizon line. Five pin *and* ten pin. Who'd even guess it's winter outside in a place like this? Happy brigades of chaps and girls are bowling like gangbusters and the pin-boys way down at the other end scramble like fury and sometimes holler and curse at the bowlers. In the beverage lounge behind the lanes, a *live band* is playing swing, and Florence can't help bouncing to the beat as Jimmy rents their shoes at a nearby wicket. Ruby stands still as a statue. Reggie's eyes are sponges soaking in her presence, and when he asks Ruby if she sewed her bowling skirt with its dandy felt poodles and that row of gewgaws, Ruby answers, "Of *course* not. I've got better things to do and why *would* I. Didn't you hear me say I don't care for bowling – and by the way, that 'row of gewgaws' is called *rickrack.*"

Jimmy trucks over with an armful of shoes. "Let's bowl," he brays. As they lace on their rented shoes (maroon with cream Vs stitched in the front) under the *Victory Bond Tournament* billboard, Reggie asks Ruby if a big, bustling spot like this gives her the *reporter's itch.* Does she want to cover it? He tells her he's read every *Voice* she's ever written. Ruby looks pleased, Reggie, tickled, and Florence thinks maybe this date won't be so bad until Jimmy pipes in, "Yeah, Kozak, if you're such a big-shot reporter on the beat, why don't you cover our little bowling adventure?"

"Because, Mr. Jimmy, it's not *important enough,*" Ruby says.

"Well, it's important to *me!*" Florence blurts, surprised by her bold move. Hell's bells, she's not herself. A brush fire ambushes her cheeks as Jim, Ruby and Reg gawk at her. For the first time in her life, Florence sees her beautiful, talented friend, Ruby, in light less shot through with worship. Ruby always had everything. Why does she have to spoil things with her vinegar tongue and her high-and-mighty manners?

They begin to bowl.

Florence tries to submerge her pique at Ruby, but she can't chase it away. As Flo thrusts her fingers into the bowling ball, she thinks that if God had seen fit to bestow a single gift on *her,* an ounce of *reporter's talent,* say, she'd have covered this monumental outing, this game's highlights, the best she could. She'd call it as she saw it, through the only eyes she has, *hers,* and she would call it something like this –

FIRST FRAME: Florence is so relieved to have found a pair of men's bowling shoes that fit her feet (she'd worried about that), guttering doesn't bother her. Ruby chips a fingernail, sulks. Reggie bowls a strike, Jimmy a spare. He hollers to them that Reg is a regular Andy Varipapa, isn't he? Reggie says *hardly,* but he'd sure love to master Varipapa's famous boomerang ball.

SECOND FRAME: Flo gutters again, but is a good sport. Ruby gutters too, mutters, "Fiddlesticks!" Jimmy throws a dazzling strike, Reggie a spare. Florence can't follow all the bowling words the boys bandy about, words like *cranker* and *turkey.* They are so worldly. She hears turkey most often in relation to her own throws. They can say cockadoodle, for all she cares, she's just glad to *be* there.

THIRD FRAME: "*Hey!* Jimmy overstepped the fault line," Ruby sings out. He advises her to go drizzle her Dixie. Reggie saw the throw, says Ruby's right. Jimmy *did* step over the line. Florence, huzzah, a strike! Same goes for Reggie. Jimmy has to go and see a man about a horse and they can just *wait* for him.

FOURTH FRAME: Jimmy is back. He gutters. He bellows at the pin-boy to, for crikey sake, get out of the way down there, and stop distracting the bowlers. The pin-boy makes the universal hand sign to indicate what Jimmy can do with *that* opinion. Florence, distracted by wondering why everyone can't just be *decent,* misses the rest of the frame.

FIFTH FRAME: Strike for Ruby. She leaps high into the air. Her poodles hurtle with her, and clever britches that she is, she's wearing special sports bloomers. Seeing them, Reggie whistles with both fingers in his mouth. Jimmy hollers, "About time you threw a decent shot, Kozak." Ruby sticks her tongue out at him. Florence knocks out the corner pins. That's it.

SIXTH FRAME: Between balls, Ruby asks Reg if he *always*

intends to be a wire cutter. "Absolutely not." Didn't Jim mention to her that Reggie is going to *be* someone? (Florence stands fully outside the frame here; she hasn't the foggiest notion what Reggie is talking about.) Ruby says sure, Jimmy said that, but what does "being someone" *mean*? Reggie asks, what does Ruby *want* it to mean? She replies: "A *soldier*, now *that* would be something." Reggie returns with *himff*, then "maybe I will, maybe I *just will*." Jimmy barks did they come to bowl or *what*?

SEVENTH AND EIGHTH FRAMES: They bowl. Florence stumbles over her own feet in the eighth.

NINTH (and, as it turns out, final) FRAME: Jimmy drops a ball on Ruby's foot, and she howls so loud and long the other Stardust bowlers freeze in their frames and shout their concerns across the hardwood lanes. Reggie drops to his knees and unlaces Ruby's bowling shoe. She leans on him, cringing with pain, whimpering, and sputtering something through her teeth that sounds like, "it better not be *broken*, or you owe me extra for damages, Petrik." Flo can't quite decipher Ruby's anguished words, though, and even if she *has* heard Ruby right, what sense does *owing for damages* make? They're on a *date*, aren't they? What's money got to do with it? Florence starts to whimper and then take in low gulps of cry-full air, and Jimmy says, in a crosspatch voice, "For crikey sake, dry up, Voutie, there's no *bawling* in bowling," and that looses Florence into full-flood tears.

Reggie loops Ruby's arm over his thin shoulder and leads her, limping, to the bench by the score table. He gently removes her bowling shoes and sends Jimmy for ice in the beverage lounge. Jimmy tramps back with cubes inside a knotted tea towel. Reggie applies the ice. Ruby (*ouch*) *told* them from the *get-go* that this was a stupid game. She calls Jimmy the *clumsiest oaf ever*, and Florence bawls, "For pity's sake, it was an *accident!*"

Ruby glowers at Jimmy. "*Was* it?"

Reggie makes Ruby wiggle her toes this way and that. She winces, but does it. He's pretty sure her foot isn't broken. Jimmy wants to know how Rainy can be so sure? Because he took a first-aid course back home, Reggie says. Florence calls that a nice, useful thing to do.

"Since you've got the healing touch, Rainy," Jimmy taunts, "maybe you should be a *nurse* instead of a wire cutter."

"I'm going to be much more than a wire cutter soon enough, Jim," Reggie says, "and a lot more than a *plant constable.*" His sudden intensity hushes the others.

Jimmy reminds them that *he's* the one who fetched them and drove them around on his gasoline rations so they wouldn't freeze and now they, *the three stooges,* stand there hurling insults at him. He looks hardest at Ruby and Reg.

"*I* didn't insult you," Florence whimpers, "And I'm not a *stooge!*"

"No, *you're* not," Jimmy says. "You're a good girl. But you *other* two," he jerks his thumb at Ruby and Reg, "are a couple of *in-grades.*"

Reggie helps Ruby to her feet. She can stand, shakily, now. She tells them to go finish their silly game, just as a managerial voice from the Stardust office booms in their direction, "Hey, Lane Twelve, are ya *through,* or *what?*"

"We're through all right," Jimmy gruffs back.

They return their rented shoes, bundle into their coats. Reggie helps Ruby across the icy parking lot to the De Soto, and she tells him if he wasn't so *hopelessly homely,* so bony, with no muscles, and if he didn't have all *that wretched acne,* she might just *fall* for him.

They drive. Reggie broods in the back seat, his bow tie askew as they bump their way back over the dark, icy streets. Everyone's so grim, Florence, to lighten herself up, starts singing, "Boogie Woogie Bugle Boy" until Jimmy says, "Not now, Voutie." But he doesn't say it mean, more in a worn-out way.

When Jimmy reaches Ruby's house, he announces that he'll walk her to her front door, that Reggie needn't trouble himself. Florence reckons Jimmy's assisting Ruby is his way of making amends about the bowling ball. Reggie mutters, "Why don't you *do* that, Jim," and sits there like a lump of coal. The driver's door is left open long enough for Florence to hear Ruby, halfway out of the car, say, in a hissing voice, to

Jimmy, "*Pay up*, Petrik. Remember, this was no date. This was a *deal*, and it would never have happened without me." Jimmy hisses back at her, "*Monday.*"

A sickening notion swamps Florence. Ruby Kozak's words are a flock of poisonous messenger pigeons flying into Florence's ears. She'd heard right what she'd thought she didn't hear. *This was no date, this was a deal.* What a fool she's been to imagine that Jimmy saw enough in her to take things beyond *dealing.* A fool in April and every *other* month, that's Florence. She should have seen things for what they *were* the minute Jimmy sprang his surprise about the double date earlier that night. Should have faced the fact that she's only ever been a fat, plain girl on probation at the plant, a worker whose skill at riveting and welding has gone to her head. She tells Jimmy she'll take a taxicab home from Reggie's rooming house. Jimmy can drop her off there. Florence knows it'll cost her plenty, but she can't ride around in that beautiful green car anymore like some kind of hopeful, deluded princess itching with hives (they're back). Jimmy says, "Whatever creams your corn, Voutie." He drops her and Reggie on Syndicate Avenue, and spins off into the night.

Reggie asks Florence if she'd like to come inside. She wouldn't, but if he'd call a taxi, she'd be grateful. She'll wait outside by the front door. She *wants* to feel the cold, she informs Reggie. She *welcomes* numbness. He lobs her a worried, puzzled look before slipping into the telephone booth in the rooming-house lobby to phone a taxi. Then he returns to Florence, who stands shivering beneath the lone light bulb over the door, the toque pulled low over her forehead. He asks if she'd care for a cigarette. Not now. Reggie lights a smoke, puffs hard on it, and eyes Florence in a sideways way.

"Do *you* think I'm homely?" he asks cautiously.

"No, Reg, I don't," she replies, and she means it.

"Honest?"

"Honest."

"You can keep the toque," he says.

Three Badly Drawn Men

*M*uriel McGregor can't make head or tail out of *The Rime of the Ancient Mariner,* the strange ballad Orville Loftus had given her. Whenever they were on a test flight, he kept asking if she'd finished reading it. Lately and luckily, these test flights had met required standards. Before switching on the magnetos he would ask about the book, and Muriel, strapped beside him, began to feel badly about saying no. Over the past couple of weeks, she'd plowed through the poem's queer medieval phrases, its ghostly, lugubrious ravelings. She didn't like it much, but being a determined woman, she kept returning to those brittle pages in search of some hidden charm that might have eluded her earlier perusals. She'd been plodding through the *Rime* again, the other day in her flat, Sleeping Giant Radio playing softly, when she'd heard the news. A man had been found frozen behind a grain elevator in Port Arthur. She'd dropped the book, poured a glass of sherry and lit a French cigarette. She'd prayed the frozen man wasn't who she feared it was.

It wasn't. A couple of mornings after that news report, and a few days into April, she'd found a note slipped under her back-porch door.

It wasn't me, Muriel. Somebody else froze, one of our people, though. A bad blow for us. If it was me, I wouldn't be writing this, would I? If you care. T.B.

She skims her fingers over Brink's words now, before folding his note and tucking it in her night-table drawer.

She cares. She must hurry, though. Brush her hair. Orville Loftus is picking her up in a few minutes. He'd been hounding her to see his project and it's Sunday, so she finally said yes. Though Loftus had made much of his project over the past weeks, he never elaborated on it, and Muriel's curiosity simply got the better of her. She has always been a curious woman.

Yes, she's glad that Thaddeus Brink didn't freeze in that wilderness. But she'd inked a red, recent truth in her diary. *Sometimes I almost forget that Thaddeus haunts this place. So many other, more alive, more present, pleasures. Like Lieutenant Colonel McLaughlin's visits to the office. His intellect is thrilling, his aeronautical knowledge gained through his British Air Ministry work and his earlier days as a flier. He knows almost as much as I do! And such courtesy, such charm. The other day he had the Foley girl deliver a package of fine chocolate powder to my office. Roper McLaughlin is, simply, the best kind of company. I'm increasingly inclined to think he sent the tarts on Valentine's Day; when the moment is right, I'll press him.*

She'd added, in red – *Orville Loftus, the test pilot, has become much more tolerable of late, though I still dislike his gloomy mariner book.* Below that, she'd scribbled yet another afterthought. *Must do something for workers, ensure morale equalization after business with bad wires; word on the shop floor is, that rattled them (according to the snack wagon girl).*

Muriel sets her hairbrush down, still only a couple of grey strands. She checks the outside thermometer attached to the frame of the kitchen window. The temperature has risen in spades overnight. It's raining lightly, but she's sure it won't last. She spies a blue patch in the sky. She dons her navy travelling suit, and, on one frivolous whim, applies a bit of rouge to her cheeks, her personal strike against the wanness brought on by the long winter. She expects Orville Loftus any minute. While scrubbing her teeth with baking soda, Muriel recalls their last test flight a few days ago; the fact was, Loftus had taken her breath away. The sure-handedness with which he'd soared over Lake Superior, its ice melting into a cobalt blue expanse, above miles of budding bush veiled with the mauve cast of early spring. Despite the season's late cold, the earth was returning to life. Loftus had executed a perfectly controlled spin, landing them as if on silk. Muriel had checkmarked all remaining boxes on her report form: *approach speed, trimming characteristics, throttling, range of stabilizer (elevator tab), touchdown tendency (to float, to settle – all fine)*. No, check marks in boxes weren't the full story of that flight. The truth was, Loftus had been magic. After they'd landed, he'd told her that whatever she'd been working on in her office, she was doing something right; those birds were handling a hundred times better than before. Muriel asked Orville if he'd just paid her a compliment. He'd come back with, *you bet your boots he had.* Then he gave the undercarriage indicator a tap, went earnest on her and asked her to visit his farm on Sunday, to see his project.

Sunday. Orville Loftus holds the passenger door of his panel truck open for Muriel, and her cane. He remarks how spring has touched down, almost overnight, and she agrees. The light rain has stopped. Today is the first time Muriel has seen Loftus not wearing his baggy flying suit. He wears relatively clean, poorly pressed trousers (their iron marks reveal a great deal – he'd tackled them above the knees, abandoned them below), and a wool shirt that smells faintly of mothballs. He has carried the scent of red oxide primer since the day she met him, and still does (she'd miss it if he didn't!). He'd actually picked up a razor. They lurch along Arthur Street. Orville Loftus seems less content driving a truck than flying a plane; he bears a grudge against the gearshift in particular. As they reach the open road beyond Fort William, his sullen, laborious manner of driving smooths out. A few miles after Kakabecka

Falls, they turn off the main road and jounce over muddy pot-holes along a narrow, slushy one. Because the temperature had moderated drastically overnight, the shrinking snow banks are now dun ribbons flanking this road. A whiskey jack flashes between the trees. Loftus jokes that he lives out so far, they have to pump daylight in. She can see that.

At last they reach a haggard mailbox, "O Loftus" sprinting across it in crooked letters. Muriel stares down his laneway at the tangle of busted-up barns and sheds. The farmhouse with its peeling gingerbread trim. The house's wraparound porch, though in a state of disrepair, suggests how stately this home-stead must have been, once. But now everything speaks a for-lorn language. The largest barn looks halfway solid at least.

Loftus brakes his truck in front of the house. He goes round to Muriel's side to help her out. Just as her feet settle into the brown, spongy earth, a large dog of dubious pedigree tears out of nowhere. Startling her. It bounds right up, barking, making like it will jump on her.

"Down, Sancho," Orville says.

The dog stops barking and shunts its tail back and forth. It would still like to jump on Muriel, so Loftus clutches its collar.

"So this is your farm," she says.

He closes the passenger door and nods. "Not much grows up here. She's fallow anyway, long as we got this war." He tells Muriel he'll rustle up some coffee, but he wants to show her his project first, if that's okay. It's fine.

Loftus leads her to the largest barn. It's a dark, neglected, mangy edifice, and when he undoes the door's padlock, it takes Muriel's eyes a minute to adjust to the dim light inside. Sancho squeezes past them; his bark shatters pigeons on an overhead rafter. A bat hurtles out of nowhere. The dog scur-ries off to explore the rest of the barn. There's nothing in it except ancient bales of hay that lean askew from a once-tidier stack, a pile of wooden crates that have been emptied, their lids strewn about, and a large object under an enormous canvas tarp. Orville Loftus drags two bales of hay into an open area in the middle of the barn, to a spot that affords a view of the thing that hulks under the tarp. He points to one of the bales, hoping Miss McGregor will not be offended by the rustic seating. His sudden formality doesn't bother her. She would not. She takes the bale.

Loftus' eyes shine like a boy's, it strikes Muriel, as he bounces on the balls of his feet beside the canvas-covered hulk. He peels away the tarp covering the object; his unveiling reveals a small airplane, old model, clearly in mint condition. The test pilot looks at Muriel expectantly.

"My project," he says.

"It's beautiful. What is it?"

"An airplane."

He sounds so earnest, she laughs. They both laugh. "I *know*," she replies. "What kind?"

"A genuine Sopwith Grasshopper. Two-seater."

"Did you build it yourself?"

"Piece by piece," Loftus says.

"So *this* is why you smell like red oxide primer? Not that I've minded."

"Must be."

"Have you ever flown it, Orville?"

"Nope. I'm waiting."

"Waiting? For what?" Muriel asks.

"The right time."

Orville Loftus is a puzzle. When she'd first met him, Muriel had been taken aback by his gruff manners, his oddness. She'd honestly wondered if he was several tomatoes short of a sauce. She knows better now. His manners have improved. And she sees that he has to reveal things in his own way.

"How did you come by this, Orville?"

He lowers himself onto the other bale. Sancho settles at his feet. "It came from a chap who would have walked through hell in a gasoline suit for me. His name is Harry Hawkes. He was a test pilot for Sopwith Aviation in England. I was serving over there. I'd flown Sopwith fighters in '16 and lived to tell the tale. Those birds weren't even ten feet high and they held one lousy machine gun, but I can't tell you how swell it was, flying them. Those people up in Fort William," he gestures roundly, as if Fort William is right there, around them, in the barn, "they brag about their spiffy modern planes. They haven't flown Sops. I landed one on the Royal Navy's HMS Furious in 1917. That's when I met Harry. He was so much more than a test pilot. He was an artist. Harry designed this Grasshopper Two-seater."

Muriel shifts on her hay bale. "Go on," she says.

"Sopwith Aviation bought the design, but Harry masterminded it. I told him I'd give anything for one of those blissful birds. And you know what Harry said?"

Muriel has no idea.

"Harry said, 'Orville, you shall have one if I have to send it to you piece by piece across the Atlantic, and that's a promise.' After my tour of duty I trucked around with Harry. Those were the best days of my life. I was even younger than you are now. I can't count how many grog shops Harry and I closed down together. The only kick was, Harry had a wife. Redhead. Oh, she was a looker, make no mistake. And her talk, smooth as custard. She could charm the fleas off a dog. She came between Harry and me."

He stops speaking for a moment. Muriel knows enough not to stir a muscle. The test pilot's eyes glitter, but his tongue takes on wormwood.

"I was so green I couldn't see it coming. She had a sweet tooth. She'd send Harry out for Bassett's Jelly Babies and, while he was gone, she'd ask me to help her lift something off a high shelf, or place some heavy object on a low shelf, anything to force me closer to her. Dang it, she *ravished* me."

The word "ravished" sounds to Muriel so odd, coming from a man more likely to say things like "dang it." She longs to laugh, but she suppresses the urge.

"She ruined me," he goes on. "It wasn't long before the ravisher and I were taking a room at an inn across town a couple of times a week, or whenever she could get away. And all this time, Harry's in his shop, sanding and lathing and welding parts for my Sopwith Grasshopper. I partook of this nefarious stew for many weeks. I was drunk with depravity even though guilt gnawed my heart out, ripped it from my chest cavity with no laudanum to ease the ripping. Have you ever had a major, life-sustaining organ gnawed out with guilt, Muriel?"

She can't say she has.

"Pray you never do. The agony of betraying Harry was swallowing me whole. I had to tell him. I told him one night in his shop. The pain of telling him far exceeded the shrapnel I took in my leg in the war. I wanted Harry to make several knuckle sandwiches on my face. I wanted him to grab the Sop prop on the bench and bludgeon me until I fell unconscious. I begged him to take the pound of flesh he had coming to him. Harry never lifted a finger. All he said was, 'Orville, I don't want to see you anymore, but I'll send you the Grasshopper as promised.' Have you ever heard of such a chap?"

Muriel shakes her head. Shifts her weight on the bale.

"Soon after that, I left England. I caught an ocean freighter. For ten years I wandered the North American continent, did odd bits of work. I kept a hand in flying. If you'd seen me, you'd have written me off as a tramp. I lived in rented rooms. I read books. Collected guns. I've been in every taproom, ale-house, and honky-tonk from Mississippi to Maine. My elbow's got a permanent crook in it. I picked up some flight work in Columbus, Ohio, lived there for a couple of years. The chaps there were always trying to draw me out, hook me up with some she-wolf. No dice. I kept to myself. I *deserved* exile. Then the war, lots of flying work in Canada. I came home. Looked like an old boot and felt like hammered snot. I'm sorry," he says, somehow jarred back into the moment. "I hope my language doesn't offend you."

She tells Orville Loftus not to give it another thought. He takes a deep breath suffused with relief. He continues. "I didn't think even the National Salvage Committee would take me, so I was pretty flabbergasted to get the call from Fort William Aviation."

"And then?"

He points to the stack of empty crates piled along one side of the barn. "About eight months ago, back in '41, these crates started coming, addressed to me c/o Bishop's Field. They were stuffed with Sopwith parts. The chaps were some curious, I can tell you. The first crate was crammed with an 80-horsepower Le Rhone engine and a note: *Your Grasshopper, as promised. Took years to track you down. You'll figure out how she goes together, I'm sure. Harry Hawkes.* You could have hung bats from my eyes. I was that surprised. The parts kept coming; no more notes, though. No 'I forgive you, Orville,' only parts, parts, parts. I was able to work on assembling the plane the whole time my ankle was busted. Good thing, or the boredom would've unravelled me. I've got her all together, but she's never been flown."

"Why don't you? Fly her, I mean?"

"I won't feel right about flying her unless I'm forgiven."

"How will you know?"

"I wrote Harry. Asked him."

"When?"

"Back when the parts started coming."

"And you've heard nothing?"

Loftus shakes his head. "That's life in the putty factory, I guess."

"So you're just going to let that plane sit and rust while you wait for a letter that might not come?"

Orville Loftus sends Muriel his heaviest look. "That's my albatross, it seems."

She returns an enlightened expression. "So *that's* why you fancy that book so much, the one you gave me to read, that *Ancient Mariner* yarn."

"Yes. There's some comfort in knowing it has happened to someone else."

"*What's* happened, Orville?"

"Remorse. Guilt. Unpaid debts. Unfinished business that hangs like an iron bird around a person's neck."

"I've got two of those birds around mine," Muriel confesses glumly.

"Must be heavy. Are you at liberty to say what they are?"

"*One* of them. My mother."

"You owe her, or she owes you?"

"Both."

"Must pull you way down," Orville Loftus says.

"Sometimes, yes," Muriel sighs.

"What's the other one?"

How quickly he'd forgotten her qualification; his uncharacteristically gentle tone prompts her to lift her own prohibition. "The other one is a man I can't speak about."

"I see. Does he hail from these parts? *Wait,* it's that lieutenant colonel, isn't it? Is he *bothering* you?"

"*Orville.*"

"Right, then. Let's go into the house. I'll make coffee. C'mon, Sancho."

The dog bounds happily towards the barn's entrance. Muriel rises from her bale with difficulty; she brushes the hay off her navy travelling suit (hardly barn clothes!) and uses her cane to propel her way to the heavy door Orville holds open for her.

They make their way across the muddy yard to the derelict farmhouse. Sancho trails them and, once inside, flops down by the stove. The kitchen is damp, so Orville makes a fire in short order, boils water for coffee. Muriel sits gingerly on a chair that looks none too steady. She looks around the room, at the ancient fly-sticker suspended from the ceiling, laden with brittle victims, the snapper-rigged curtain over a doorway that leads to, she can only guess, a pantry. A tiny panel of light the size of a peppermint stick fights its way in through the only window, coated in a thick film of dust, and lands on the floor near her feet. Loftus fossicks around for cups, then brings her coffee in a china one. His only, he says. He parks a wooden folding chair a few feet away from where she sits, and drinks his coffee from a tin cup. He apologizes for the room's uproar. He's not much of a housekeeper. Neither is she, Muriel remarks.

They sip coffee in silence, sip through a long gap in April. Finally, Muriel says, "Orville, do you *really* think the absolution you're waiting for will arrive by post?"

"I can only keep hoping, Muriel."

"Of course."

The peppermint stick of light is gone. Muriel tells Orville she'd still like to work on the ski pedestal; if he could ferry her back to town, it would be grand. As Loftus' panel truck slogs through the mud to Fort William, they discuss factory matters. Neither of them can explain the deficient wire gauge problem; they can only hope the investigators get to the bottom of it soon. Nor can they fathom what anyone would gain from sticking below-standard wires in those Mosquitoes. "If anyone can crack the wire debacle, Lieutenant Colonel Roper McLaughlin can," Muriel declares (the truck succumbs to a particularly craterlike pothole, sinks). "Good thing they've intensified security since the report from our near-disastrous test flight," she adds, once they're back on course. Muriel tells Orville that she remains convinced of the wire cutter's innocence. She knows an honest boy's face when she sees one, and Reggie Hatch has an honest face. Besides, he'd gone through rigorous questioning and no one had doubted his word. *How* does she know an honest boy's face, Orville Loftus probes, and, realizing how utterly she's out of her depth, Muriel clams up until they reach her flat on Brodie Street. As she climbs out of the truck, she frees an errant piece of dried clover from the woof of her skirt, while thanking Orville for the pleasure of letting her see his project.

Loftus brightens to full capacity for the first time since the barn. "I figured you'd like it," he says. "I was waiting to show it to someone who'd have the *proper appreciation.*"

Later that night, Muriel smokes at her kitchen table, working through some equations for landing skis. She hears wet flakes of snow lash against the dark window behind her. 'Spring snow, won't last,' she reflects, sadly. She'd hoped to be ready to test her landing skis that winter, but with the wire fracas, her centre-of-gravity adjustments and the cold season winding down, it's unlikely she'll reach her goal. High above the earth on her recent test flight with Orville Loftus, Muriel had thrilled at the promise of spring. Her elation now crumbles into gnawing anxiety as she scribbles furiously – aspect ratios, widths, gross weights, lengths. Her equations swim before her eyes. She can't focus. She keeps picturing the glitter in Orville Loftus' eyes when he pulled the tarp away to reveal that Sopwith. Keeps thinking about the story he'd told her. His tale had moved Muriel, and the anguished way he still awaits words from an old friend that might never arrive.

Oddly, what moved Muriel *most,* though, was Orville's appalling attempt at pressing his trousers.

She abandons her aspect ratios. She begins to doodle, a frivolous schoolgirl activity she rarely permits herself. Before many more wet flakes dive, then trickle, down her window, she's drawn (badly) a small, antique airplane. The heads of three men protrude, propeller-like, from its nose. Thaddeus Brink, Roper McLaughlin, Orville Loftus. She's elongated their necks to form propeller blades. A stranger trio could hardly be imagined, Muriel muses: a hunted enemy of the state; a courtly gentleman with intelligence expertise; a crack flier with, all too often, rough manners (that day, being Sunday, had proved the *exception,* not the rule). Muriel stares at her crude sketch. She writes at the top of her doodle-page: Let M = Muriel. She slides her hand down the page, to the human propeller she's drawn. She proceeds to annotate above each head.

Let B = Brink, someone I loved in a previous life;

Let R = Roper, someone I increasingly feel I could love in *this* life;

Let O = Orville, someone whose brilliance inside a cockpit notwithstanding, I couldn't love in *any* life –

Could I?

Sunday's Trumpet

*I*t's raining the best kind of rain, spring rain, but that doesn't raise Florence Voutilainen's spirits one droplet. Neither does the fact that her mother has just left for a sewing convention in Bemidji, Minnesota – "Radical Seamstresses of America" – or that the stranger brewed tea and now sits, sipping, kitty-corner from Flo at the kitchen table, cracking jokes (in vain) to ignite a smile on her downcast face. He can crack away until doomsday. His efforts won't help Florence forget the bowling date that wasn't *real*, and her lonely taxi ride home that had emptied her wallet. But that was *nothing* compared to being duped by Jimmy Petrik who, it seemed, had to be *paid* to go out with her. Florence had been a buffoon to think her lost weight and dental fillings would make someone care for her. A bit earlier that morning, she'd told the stranger, between mouthfuls of miserable porridge without sugar (rations, diet), about the nine-frame washout. The retelling made her cry all over again, tears plopping into her porridge.

The stranger reaches across the table's corner and squeezes her shoulder quickly, in a comforting way. He's never seen the daughter like this. She can't be brought *that* low over a boy, *can* she? She *can.* She tells him the boy, Jimmy, turned out to be a sneak and a boor. And she has to wonder what her best friend, Ruby Kozak, is about, making *deals* behind her back. The stranger says it's just a matter of the daughter taking her mind off *all that business.* He unhooks the crokinole board from the wall, clears away Florence's empty porridge bowl and moves aside the teapot, the cups. They start a game of crokinole, but Florence can't concentrate. She keeps hitting the pegs. She says her stomach feels like a lump of mock duck.

He knows a duck joke. "A duck walks into a candy store and buys twenty pounds of licorice. The clerk asks the duck, 'Will that be cash or cheque?' How do you suppose the duck answers, Florence?"

This is the first time the stranger has used her real name, but she's too sad to make much note of it. Florence shakes her head sadly. No idea.

"The duck says" – dramatic sip of tea – "'just put it on my *bill!*'" The stranger chuckles until he sees Florence's new-sprung tears, then goes quiet, but only for a minute. Is the daughter aware that ducks prefer fowl weather? She isn't. She sits, unmoved. He soldiers on – "So this fellow has a tiff with his mistress. The mistress yells at him, 'if you were my husband, I'd give you poison.' And the chap, what do you suppose *he* says to *this,* Florence?"

Flo doesn't have the foggiest; her eyes pool again.

The stranger adopts a W.C. Fields voice that, even in Florence's determinedly sorrowful depths, surprises her; she's never seen him clown – she's seen the serious, zealous singer of protest anthems. But here he is, flicking an invisible cigar in the air to punctuate his punchline (*flick, flick*) – "The fellow says, 'Lady, if *you* were my wife, I'd gladly *take* poison!'" Despite being smack in the middle of a morgue, the stranger bursts into *a-ar-ar* cackles.

"No more jokes," Florence pleads. Somehow, they worsen things. She feels glummer than ever. She assumes the stranger has never had his heart broken. He goes sullen – says the daughter assumes wrong. His heart is broken every day of the week and twice on Sunday.

"Dear me, *today* is Sunday," Florence murmurs, then adds, incredulously, "Surely not by my *mother?*"

He shakes his head. "Your mother helped save me. She burnt my yellow coat and got me regular clothes, and that's a lot – I was a walking target before that. But she's too sad to break a man's heart. No, the breaking is done by someone who works for the imperial war machine."

"Is there no hope?"

He grows so gloomy Flo wishes she'd tried harder at the crokinole.

"Precious little," he says. "Listen, Florence, about this boy, Jimmy. If he made things right with you, would you give him another chance?"

"I might."

"I thought as much."

"But that doesn't make me feel less rotten *now!*" Flo laments.

The stranger knows. That's why he's got just the thing for *now.* He rises and ducks behind the beaded doorway, into her mother's bedroom. He returns with a dirt-smeared suitcase with rusty hinges at the back and muddy snap hinges at the front.

"That's not a *gun,* is it?" Florence gasps.

The man laughs. No gun – gift, for her. He was going to wait until her birthday, which she'd told him while watching him split wood one day is in August. But this seems like the moment, and just the ticket to boost the daughter's spirits. He's sorry it's not wrapped better. He hangs the crokinole board back on its hook, and lays the case on the kitchen table. "Open it," he urges. "It won't bite." He pulls a small jack-knife from his pocket and gives it to Florence, telling her that she might need it to clear away the mud caked around the front snap hinges.

Florence scrapes at the hinges. "Why is it so dirty? It looks like it was buried."

"You could say that. It has been in storage – *underground,* in a certain sense."

She blows dust off a small metal plate between the hinges. The initials T.B. are engraved on the plate. "Is this you?"

"Well, it's not Terrace Bay," he says. "And it's not tuberculosis."

More of his larks. Florence unsnaps the hinges, lifts the lid. Lined with rich blue material like velvet, the case's interior is all grooves. Resting in the grooves, a shiny trumpet. The horn fits its blue bed perfectly. There's a special hutch for its mouthpiece. The trumpet is the most beautiful thing Florence has ever seen. Gold poured into a labyrinth.

She lifts the instrument from its grooves, and slides on the mouthpiece – where some things (like this mouthpiece) fit, is obvious to anyone, even to her, the butt of a dating joke, a frump.

"Try it," the stranger urges.

She blows. Nothing but air rushes through the golden coils. She tries a few more times, her cheeks heating with exertion.

The man says playing a brass instrument is a bit like spitting. Does she know anyone she'd like to spit at? Oh yes. He shows her how to form her mouth into a tiny opening and force air through it until she feels her lips vibrate. Florence follows his method. She raises the horn to her buzzing lips. She sounds a note. Not music, more like foul, rushing air, passed wind. But something. The stranger explains how to change her mouth to control pitch – loose for lower notes, a primmer jaw for higher notes. She makes more sour noises, and asks the man how long it might take a person to learn *real* music. "A few weeks with the right teacher," he says, "but you must practice every day."

Florence hands him the trumpet. He flexes the valves, blows a few wild scraps of scales. He warns her he's rusty. He plays in earnest, then, and for the first time since the bowling fiasco, she brightens. As far as she's concerned, he's such a dandy player that Roy Eldridge himself could have been filling the kitchen with "It Don't Mean a Thing (If it Ain't Got that Swing)." Despite her lingering sadness, her feet tap to the music. When his song ends, she applauds. He passes her the golden trumpet. Florence asks him the obvious. Will he teach her to play?

"On one condition."

She says anything.

"That you not breathe a word about where you got this trumpet."

"What trumpet?" Florence laughs for the first time that day. Then she does something she's never done before. She winds her arms around the man's neck for a brief instant. "You give the best gifts in the world," she says, "but you tell the worst jokes."

She Can't Be
Just Another Former
~~Beauty Queen Lost in Oblivion!~~
(*can* she?)

uby Kozak's foot isn't broken. But it's swollen and tender and throbbing and blue, and a ghastly galosh covers a knitted slipper on her stricken foot as she types, each keystroke a small drum of doom. The only way Ruby can account for the recent nose-dive her life has taken is that she had too much good fortune too early (her nightmare after high-school graduation, and her subsequent visit to the secret doctor in Toronto had been, of course, an enormous exception, but she'd *taken care of it*). She stops typing long enough to wonder if *other* girls who've borne the crown of Miss Fort William have found *their* lives spiralling listlessly into disappointment after the glittering heights of beauty pageantry. Ruby can't bear to think of herself as just another former beauty queen lost in oblivion. She *won't* follow this morbid line of thought – she'll keep the zest keen *somehow.*

At least she's nearly caught up with her work. Ruby lets this small stenographic mercy pass for cheer; it's all she's got. She pegs the last black period into place, in the final memorandum from that morning's stack. (From the chief engineer, Muriel McGregor – something about a contest, but not a *writing* contest, so Ruby had barely read the words she'd typed. The engineer had also telephoned and asked her to compose a piece for the *Voice* about this contest. Things have reached a sorry pass when plant officials start telling *her, Ruby Kozak,* what to write!)

There. She's finished for now. She dashes on some lipstick. She gropes in her desk drawer for the small bottle of Dorothy Gray White Lilac Cologne. Dabs Dorothy on both wrists. This divine whiff, and the knowledge that in a few weeks *real* lilacs will bloom, comforts her. Heaven knows she can use cheer. The morning has been rotten. She'd rung Jimmy Petrik in Plant Security, and ordered him to see her in Head Office *forthwith.* She'd reminded him of his promise, the night of the lousy bowling, to pay her the other five dollars on *Monday.* It's Wednesday. He, in turn, refreshed Ruby's memory on "the chain of command." He didn't take his orders from *her* – he took them from her *father.* She hissed into the phone that Jimmy could stash his chain of command where the sun never shines, and that she'd long suspected he *lacked business scruples* and this last lapse of his, the five dollars he still owes her, *confirms her view fully.*

Late in the morning, Jimmy had trotted grudgingly into Head Office at last. "Well, and where is the money?" Ruby pressed. (The truth was, Jimmy owed her *much* more than five dollars – the secret doctor in Toronto had cost Ruby plenty, her whole life savings, in fact, but she'll only peel back the most recent layer of her grievous history with Jimmy Petrik. The rest is too painful.) He'd slouched in the chair before her desk and smoked, and wondered aloud why he *should* pay Ruby the other five dollars, considering they hadn't finished the bowling game, and she had not demonstrated *date behaviour* at all – she'd only ended up insulting his friend, Reggie Hatch, and Rainy was sensitive, Jimmy said, and strung tighter than Gene Krupa's drum, and, when it came right down to it, *flimsy as eggshells.*

Ruby started to sweat then, and she *hated* sweating; it spoiled her clothes. Jimmy Petrik sure knew how to make lilacs turn to skunkweed. They didn't finish the game, Ruby told him through her teeth, because he – Jimmy – had dropped a bowling ball on her *foot,* as he – Jimmy – might recall. And she *had,* in fact, paid Reggie a compliment, the *highest* – she'd told him she could fall for him under the right conditions. And Jimmy had been standing right there and heard her say it and there were *other* witnesses, too – Florence Voutilainen – so Jimmy could just pay up and get out of her office *forthwith* or – or – Ruby might have to tell her father, head of plant security, that Jimmy had no business scruples.

"Are you *done,* Kozak?" Jimmy had asked in a flat tone.

She was. The starch in her blouse, under her arms, was stuggy. Just then Fraudena poked her frizzled head into the office. "Security check in Sub-Assembly pronto, Jim!" Too bad he couldn't chat longer, he told Ruby, but since she was *done* anyway, and he'd just been called to duty, he'd have to skedaddle out of there. The thought blazed across Ruby's mind that if there was any justice in the world, *no* former Miss Fort William should have to endure slovenly manners like these. He left her office without paying. Slipped away like an oiled weasel, leaving her to stew in his low ruses, her own stenographic juices. She'd dabbed on more lilac cologne. Then Ruby typed, feeling all the while, with her club-foot-like foot and swampy underarms, about as feminine as a moose.

Now she's caught up with her work, but still out five dollars. She's cross as a wet hen. When will those boors and ingrates – these Swamp people – pay her the respect afforded a former beauty queen? While Ruby wonders this, Audrey Foley careens into her office. Ah, Audrey, her running girl, for once, *running* – *and* bothering to materialize for her Wednesday report, instead of sending some trumped-up note. A cameo appearance. Isn't Little Miss Audrey looking jazzy these days in her porkpie hat and – what, is the kid *smoking?* The snack-wagon girl jogs towards Ruby's desk (speed surely bodes well). Sure enough, Audrey holds a cigarette in one hand, a muffin in the other. She's rather breathless. She sets the muffin on Ruby's desk in a single, grand flourish – maybe, for once, some due deference will be shown to a head stenographer and former Miss Fort William.

The cigarette shakes in the girl's fingers. Ruby attributes the kid's nerves to their debacle at the snack wagon awhile back; Audrey had taken a royal dressing-down that day. Ruby's hand had clinched the girl's collar. Tightened it around her small neck. Ruby had meant to smooth that over, and here's the moment to set the girl at ease.

"Thanks for the muffin, Audrey. Now, sit down." Ruby flips her hand towards the chair Jimmy Petrik slouched in not long ago. Audrey lowers her small body gingerly onto the chair.

"Aren't you looking smart these days?" Ruby points to the hat. Audrey says it had been in the plant's "Lost and Found" for weeks. Some fellow must have left it behind when he joined the Lake Superior Regiment. He must have been small, like her – maybe the army needed a snack-wagon boy. They'd finally said Audrey could take the hat for herself, and –

Enough of the girl's prattle. Clearly Ruby had loosened her up – time to get down to business. "Tell me what you've got for me *this* week. You *have* something, I hope?"

Audrey smooths her apron over her knees. Heavens, the girl's face is white as school chalk. Her lower lip quivers. The cigarette jumps in her hand. The kid is a tangle of nerves. She nods tentatively in response to Ruby's question. Announces that *this* Wednesday, she brings bad *and* good news.

"It's all right, Audrey," Ruby says. "I'm not going to *bite* – spit it out – bad first."

The running girl reports that the tart story is dead in the water. She can hardly look Ruby squarely in the eyes. The girl in the yellow scarf who got the tarts is gone, gone, gone, Audrey laments, stubbing out her cigarette. The *good* news, Audrey whispers to Ruby across the desk, is this–

"Jimmy Petrik knows about the wires!"

Ruby's red lips open into an O – "O – *really?*"

"Uh- *huh,* he sure does."

Ruby grills the girl. "This is the kind of story that can't have any mistakes," she warns. Audrey spills what she knows. Even though Audrey admits she couldn't hear the whole conversation in the plant parking lot, between Jimmy and the other chap (who Audrey says she couldn't place), it strikes Ruby that the snack-wagon kid *has* heard enough, has caught the important parts. So hanging on to this running girl has paid off at last. And *better.* Ruby suddenly recalls the ten-dollar reward offered for information about the nonregulation wires. Oh, this is *prime.* Soon enough, Jimmy Petrik *will* pay Ruby back, by hook or crook.

Ruby wheels her office chair round her desk and parks close to Audrey, their knees almost touching. Despite the kid's charade of smoke, she's still such a *child.* Ruby takes Audrey's shaking hands, and the girl asks, in her childish way, if she did *good.* Ruby releases those young fingers and replies that Audrey has finally, after all these months, brought something useful. Audrey asks if she's still the snack-wagon girl. Everything in life is so very *extreme* for the kid that Ruby must laugh before shutting down her smile and turning serious. Ruby warns the snack-wagon girl that she's set the bar very high for herself, and must continue her *new and improved Wednesday reports.* Audrey nods, equally solemn. She asks about Ruby's bound foot and, when Ruby recounts Jimmy Petrik's vile ball, is suitably moved.

The break bell rings. Ruby tosses Audrey five cents, a tip just for *her.* "No need to drop it into the Victory Bonds jar," Ruby breezes. The kid beams, and must dash to her snack wagon. As her boots tat-a-tat out of Head Office, Ruby thinks about how little it takes to make her running girl happy. Then she turns her attention towards much more important matters, the story already forming in her rampant mind, the scathing feature that will expose Jimmy Petrik. She'll have to peg down some facts, of course, talk to her father, Frank Parks and the intelligence man from Britain, make everything official – they'll have to get Jimmy's confession – but Ruby will be the one to spring the story on the industrial world, tell the people. She's their *Voice*, after all. And she'll soon be frying much bigger literary fish than Muriel McGregor's silly contest story.

Since Audrey's tip about the wires, the throbbing in Ruby's injured foot has subsided. Cranking a fresh sheet of paper into her typewriter, she thinks about the ten-dollar reward that will land right inside the pocket of her own brilliant investigative skirt. She thinks about the maroon chesterfield set that she'll lounge on, perhaps even sooner than she'd dared to hope. The long-awaited respect and recognition of her journalistic talents that will, finally, be hers.

*I*t's almost May. The only worthwhile thing Florence Voutilainen has to show for April, besides her pay from riveting and welding, is her marked improvement on the trumpet. Each day after work, she takes the horn and a small, three-legged stool out to the chicken shed and practices the fingering positions and the scale the stranger taught her. She can even play a rickety version of "When the Saints Come Marching In." She practices and the chickens cower in the corner, and the rooster tries to out-crow her, but can't, and she gets some grim satisfaction from that. She practices in the chicken shed because her mother complained that Flo's terrible trumpet was worsening her bad nerves. The spring weather is cool (lake ice), and the shed shelters Florence from the wind. Every few days, or whenever the stranger graces Florence and her mother with his appearance, she plays what she's been practicing. He says she's doing dandy.

Despite the music at home, and the muffins Audrey Foley juggles at the factory in an attempt to cheer Florence, she's miserable. Most days, like today, she cries behind her welding visor. It has been three weeks since the bad bowling date that wasn't a real date, and she hasn't been able to forget Jimmy. Oh, he's sailed past her when she rivets, as always, but she's turned her face away from him. She has her pride, despite the red probation scarf she still wears. He'd asked her if he could sit at her table in the cafeteria one day about a week ago, and she'd told him there wasn't room. "I don't see anyone else," Jimmy had countered, and Florence had assured him they were coming, yes, her *many friends* would be along *any minute now.* She'd eaten lunch alone (meatloaf with gravy; she'd quit her diet), and had wondered if maybe she'd missed the moment to forgive Jimmy. Maybe there wouldn't be another chance. Maybe no boy would ever take an interest – even a *dubious* interest – in her again.

There *is* another chance. It's happening right now, in the Welding Department. The bell rings for lunch and Florence raises her visor. She sees a man's shape out of the corner of her eye. 'Jimmy,' she thinks. 'Yes, I forgive you.' But she's wrong. She doesn't recognize the fellow at first. He's well built, dark-haired. Handsome. For crying out loud, it's Reggie Hatch, the wire cutter who'd gone on the skunky date with them. He looks like day and night from the scrawny, pimpled boy Ruby Kozak insulted at the bowling alley. Florence had heard through the rivet-vine that Reggie didn't work in the factory anymore, and now he stands before her in, she notices for the first time (his new good looks, so much to take in), a military uniform. He has biceps. Muscles. Posture. Clear skin. How someone could change so much so quickly is beyond Florence, but then look at *her.* She plays the trumpet. She sickens the chickens like the dickens.

Reggie Hatch wonders if she has "lunch plans." It sounds so queer to Flo's ears, she almost laughs. No one ever asks her that. She doesn't. In that case, he's going to treat her to lunch at McKellar Diner. They board the Neebing streetcar, and before Florence can say Fibber McGee, they're seated across from one another at a booth, ordering hot pork sandwiches. She shoves her shyness aside and asks Reggie about the change that's come over him since he left the plant.

"Chin-ups. Weights. The taskmasters at Lake Superior Regiment, they don't waste any time toughening up new recruits," he says.

"I thought you might have an older brother," she jokes.

Reggie grins and this grinning man in his private's uniform sends a flutter through Florence's chest cavity, a flutter she's not felt since the day Jimmy asked her on the date. Private Reggie Hatch has something to tell her. More flutters, shudders, between her bones.

"I owe you a big thanks, Florence. That lousy night, you know, in the cold, in front of my rooming house after bowling, when you told me I had *potential* – that *saved* me. Your words gave me the courage to go on and –"

"Yes, Reggie?" (she can hardly still the flutter) –

He pushes his spine against the back of the booth. "– go on and *improve* myself, make myself worthy of the Woman of my Dreams." He sinks his dark eyes fully into her incredulous gaze. "Ruby Kozak."

An invisible gyro wheel bangs Florence squarely on the head. Of course it would be Ruby. The flutters have flown. "That's nice, Reggie."

As he pays for their hot pork sandwiches, he tells Florence again that he never would have had the courage to *become someone* if not for her encouraging words that night. Flo says, "Oh *sure*, you would. You'd have done it without me." But Reg insists that Florence had bucked him up. She was like his good fairy, or something. She waves his words away.

Florence walks with Reggie to the Neebing streetcar, tugging her heavy wool sweater around herself until the front buttons overlap their holes. Reggie's taking a different streetcar to Port Arthur; he's due at the Armory. Flo asks him when he'll be shipping out for service. He doesn't know, but he's going to give Ruby a ring before he leaves, and he'd appreciate it if Florence didn't say anything. He wanted to tell *Flo*, though, because she'd been his *good fairy*.

Flo shoots Reggie a puzzled, concerned look. He offers a penny for her thoughts.

"I'm just surprised," Florence admits, "that you can still have *designs* on Ruby after the way she treated you that night at bowling. She *insulted* you, Reggie."

"No, she *challenged* me, Florence. And *you* helped to convince me that I was up to it. Besides, I've got Ruby figured out, now – she's hard on the outside, soft on the inside."

Reggie's face suddenly reddens. Flo's follows suit. He tells her to rest assured – he'll make Ruby Kozak sweat a little, now that *the tables have turned.* Reggie swears Florence to secrecy on the subject of the ring. She promises him, mum's the word – she never sees Ruby these days anyway, she says. Ruby has moved beyond her. Sad, considering what good friends they once were, but even when they were small girls, Florence tells Reggie, her own dull horse followed Ruby's bright pony on the carousel at Chippewa Park. What Flo means is, she's always known she was out of Ruby's league.

As Florence boards the streetcar, she thanks Reggie for the lunch. The trolley clanks her back to the factory, and she's never felt worse. 'Good fairy my clodhopper foot,' she thinks crossly, as she pulls the red scarf on her head and takes up her rivet gun.

At the end of her shift, Jimmy Petrik is waiting for Florence in front of the women's locker room. She's about to breeze past him when he steps in front of her, almost like he's been served a warrant to arrest her. Jimmy announces that the two of them should take a ride. He has something to tell her. Florence must go home to sicken the chickens, she replies, trying to duck past him.

"*What?*" Jimmy asks.

"Practice the trumpet – nothing better to do these days."

"Look Florence, I know I was rotten to you at the bowling alley," Jimmy says. "That's why I want to take you for a drive now, to set things right. Your trumpet can wait."

"You *were* rotten, Jimmy. I never did anything to you."

Several girls in yellow scarves skitter past them with curious eyes as they hurry into the women's locker room.

"Please, just go for a drive with me, Florence. I can explain everything."

She gives him a hard look laced with suspicion. "Are you sure no one is *paying* you to go driving with me? This isn't some kind of *deal?*"

He sighs heavily. "I'm sure. This is *me*, Florence – and *you*. Two people going for a drive."

"All right," she says. "But this better be *real.*"

"It's as real as I am, standing before you now," Jimmy Petrik says earnestly.

They drive to the Hillcrest Park lookout in Port Arthur. Jimmy cuts the engine and they sit in his De Soto, gazing down at trees swaddled in that early-spring lemony green, at the Finnish Hall on Bay Street, directly below where they're parked, and beyond, Lake Superior and the Sleeping Giant. Florence has lived not so many miles down the road all her life, yet this is her first visit to Hillcrest. Her first time parking with a boy. It sure beats playing the trumpet. Jimmy Petrik lights a Lucky Strike, then slides his arm along the back of the bench seat, across her shoulders. He tells her she's slimmed right down, she'll soon be a real hotsie-totsie, if she's not careful. She's even starting to look a little like Deanna Durbin.

Florence slides his arm away, and would like to know what *happened* that night at the bowling alley. Why did it end up being about money when it was supposed to be – (her eyes well up) – about possibly, just maybe – *romance?*

"You've got a lot to learn, Voutie," Jimmy says, and when a testy cloud scuds across her round face, he adds that he just means in the *romance department.* He tells Florence that all that *transpired* that night was that he – Jimmy – was trying to help his friend, that poor sod, Reggie Hatch, get a little experience with dating since Rainy Reg, being so homely, wouldn't have a snowball's chance in hell with the feminine sex if someone more experienced like Jimmy didn't step in and give him some assistance. And Ruby Kozak had agreed to help if Jimmy made it worth her while, that was all.

"Reggie's not so homely *now*," Florence interjects. "I saw him earlier today. He treated me to lunch, and I must say he's looking positively dapper in his private's uniform."

"Oh, *hang* Rainy," Jimmy carps, sliding his arm across Flo's shoulders again. "We're not here to talk about *him*. What do you think, Florence? Can you give me another chance? Old Jimmy's not so bad, you'll see."

"I guess I will," Florence says. "But you'd better not do me wrong again. And you should drive me home now."

Jimmy starts his engine. As they motor south, towards Fort William, he turns on the radio – Artie Shaw's "Continental." He tells her that he'll never do her wrong; she's the cat's very pajamas. He was a bonehead to have learned *that* so slowly, but he knows it for good, now. As they drive south, towards Fort William, Jimmy asks Florence if they can go for a spin again tomorrow after she's finished work. She must practice the trumpet, she says.

"Oh yeah, the trumpet – then how about *after* the trumpet? It'll get your lips limbered up nicely." He unleashes a loud, cracking laugh as they enter Fort William, the kind of laugh that begs for company. But Florence holds back. She knows more about the *romance department* than Jimmy Petrik, plant constable, thinks, and one thing she knows, is that he hasn't earned the company of her laughter – *yet.*

ou saw what a scared hamster I was, cowering back there in Head Office, at the feet of Ruby Kozak. You witnessed my hands, those dumb shaking lumps. The fact is, this factory and my cozy room in Churchill Ladies' Residence, is *all I've got.* And though it's nerve-wracking, with all the darned security alerts and the crane crone and the noise and the sniping boys with their bits of wing, it's *home,* and Florence is a swell friend now, and so is Miss McGregor a.k.a. Wonder Woman. And if Ruby hadn't liked what I told her, I'd have been out on the soup line. Any money I've saved has gone to paying back the snack-wagon heist.

Isn't it funny how words can sink you or swim you?
You SAW ME   SWIM   back there
Oh I swam   I swam through

                                        my own smoke!

And it *did* go pretty swimmingly, didn't it? But in case you're still wondering why I was so skittish considering the *pure-cream* offering I had for Ruby – about Jimmy and the wires, I mean – it's just that the day Ruby came at me from behind, and grabbed my collar, I saw something that scared me more than Clabber-Face. If she could go like that all of a sudden *once,* there's no reason why she couldn't *again.* Maybe worse.

I'll tell you a secret. The thing that perked me along was Ruby's lipstick. I spied with my little eye her red upper-lip line – it ran *off-course.* That little craft paintbrush hadn't done the job, or rather, she hadn't held steady her stately, slender hand. Whatever happened, the red line ran too high on one side, and gave her mouth a slightly crooked look, something like this–

U

Un-art

Nart

Un-art   unart

Un-art

Gave her a very crooked mouth for sure! So I fixed my gaze on her cosmetic hitch, those un-artful lips of hers, and they bucked me up and bumped me ahead. Now Ruby wants *new and improved* Wednesday reports. Well, I've got a couple of fish swishing around in my little porkpie-hat pool on that score – just watch me –

The Factory Voice
Fort William Aviation
May 1, 1942
Special Feature by Ruby Frances Kozak

WIN WIN WIN! – "The Sky's the Limit" Talent Contest

*M*ay Day Salutations, Plant Workers. Here's a little quiz for you.

 You build our steadfast Mosquitoes, but have you ever flown in one?

If you answered "never," keep reading!

Do you ever wonder what home looks like from the sky? Do you long to see through the eyes of a bird? Yes? Then here's your big chance.

Our own chief engineer, Muriel McGregor (B.S.E., M.A.E.), will sponsor a talent contest right here at Fort William Aviation (plant cafeteria). The winner will receive a ride in a shining new, previously test-flown Mosquito! Read on.

We know you can rivet and weld. Sure, you've mastered the nozzle and grommet and flange. But can you yodel? Juggle? Tap dance? Mime? Play a musical instrument? Walk on stilts? Eat fire? If these feats seem too exotic for you homespun northerners, can you recite? Speechify? Imitate a farm animal? The sky's the limit when it comes to our gifted workforce!

The talent contest will take place on August 28 in order to give entrants "ample time to practice," says Chief Engineer McGregor. She fully expects competition to be "keen." All *entrants must register with ME, Ruby Kozak, at Head Office, by June 30 at 4:00 pm.*

Contest winner will be determined by audience ballot. Intermission music by Joe Turner's Orchestra.

Twenty-five cents admission to "The Sky's the Limit." Proceeds to Victory Bonds.

Stay tuned for more details from your faithful Factory Voice. *Even more important, your* Voice *will present a Shocking Story of Major Proportions, one likely to unravel the threads in your industrial socks IN THE NEAR FUTURE!*

Note to the Talent Contest: There is, regrettably, no literary component and will be none unless some diligent reader wishes to address this lamentable oversight.

Another Note to the Talent Contest: No bowling balls in cafeteria!

*T*he stranger has many talents, Florence muses, as she sits, cross-legged, on the hood of the old Model-T Ford in her back yard, watching him string twine along a row of corn seeds he's just sown. Music. Chopping wood. Painting. Patching. Now agriculture. He's dug a garden for them. When he's finished stringing, he grabs the watering can, soaks the corn. He works with such calm for someone whose life is a secret, Florence thinks. Such order. He takes a round, flat stone and hammers more short stakes into the ground, one at either end of a new row. "Peas," he proclaims. The daughter should pick them in July, and freeze them, since the war machine, it seems, won't be easing up on rations any time soon.

"I guess any garden *you* plant isn't a Victory Garden," Florence calls down to him, teasingly, from her perch on the junked car (it had belonged to her Uncle Janne and now its wheel axles sink a bit deeper into the earth every year).

"No indeed," he says, notching the soil for the pea seeds. "This is a protest garden."

Florence lets the May sunshine burnish her face. Just as she's about to tell him she's glad he's still coming around, he straightens from his planting, and says, "The daughter has been home so little these past few weeks."

Florence blushes. It's true. Since she'd given Jimmy Petrik another chance, they've gone driving after work almost every day. Flo officially has a fellow. She can still hardly believe it herself. The wheels turned quickly. A pattern is already in place. She waits at the factory's employee entrance until Jimmy's done driving the lady engineer home; then he picks her up and they tool around Fort William. Jimmy gets extra gas coupons, one perk for being *indispensable* at the factory. Often they park on old logging trails just off the bush road near Mount McKay. They kiss. Breathe heavily. Jimmy showed Florence his autobody shop the other day. She was the first girl he'd let in there. He spread a blanket on the cement floor. Flo complained it was hard, that floor. Jimmy said she'd forget about it soon enough, and she did. They lay there while the sign outside, "Petrik's Autobody" creaked on its hinges, rattled by wind. He had a *prophylactic device,* Jimmy said, and Florence told him she *was awful sorry to hear that,* and he howled at her innocence, which, happily, *left* her not long after darkness fell, but before they'd padlocked the garage door behind them and driven back to Flo's place at the edge of West Fort William. As they motored through the blissful, non-innocent night, Florence, snuggled against Jimmy as he steered and smoked, suggested that since he was a plant constable and all, couldn't he maybe see about getting her probation period ended? It had gone on for six months when it was only supposed to be three, and all she needed to make her life complete now, she crooned, was to be issued a yellow head scarf, since she was just an honest worker and, she joked, "pure as the driven snow." As they spun past the Gruff Rock, Jimmy tousled her hair and said, "Now, Voutie, you know the probation periods got extended because of that blowhard coming from England, that brass from intelligence, McLaughlin, and I can't do anything about it – I would if I *could.*" And Flo murmured that she knew, she *knew* he would if he could.

After that, Jimmy fell silent. They parked among the dark trees in Florence's front yard the way they always did, and she didn't think anything was wrong, at first. Jimmy smoked some more and stroked her knee, and she happily heard her body's inner purr, and walked her fingers, like little legs, along his forearm. Suddenly Jimmy turned to her and said, "Florence, would you still like me if I wasn't a plant constable?"

She laughed. "Sure, Jimmy. I like you for – *you.*"

He inhaled smoke deeply. "But what if I did something lots of people thought was wrong? Would you care for me supposing I was, say, almost part of the world's *underbelly?*"

His questions reminded Florence of the other gift in her life – the stranger. She peered out the De Soto's window into the spring night, the dark shape of her house and, even without light, all the improvements the stranger had made during the past months were evident to her. If this was underbelly, it was good enough for *her.* "Of course I'd still like you, Jimmy, but what are you talking about?"

He answered her question with another one. "What if I was thought by *some* people to be – bad – and if I had to go away to make myself better. Would you – *wait* for me, Voutie?"

Florence wondered why, after their divine moments on the garage floor, he now had to go and make her so sad. She'd never heard Jimmy talk like this before – all *if* and *if* and *if.* But since it looked like he wasn't going to be more direct, and since, given the red scarf she must wear at work because *some* people thought *she* might be bad, she could fully understand how someone decent and innocent could be mistaken for someone from the Underbelly, and she could only burrow her face against the taut chords of his neck and whisper down into his jacket, *yes* before she shoved herself out of his car, her bones in full rebellion.

She hears her name. The stranger is calling her back to the world. He stands, holding the watering can. He sets it on the fresh earth, its long, perforated snout pointed towards where she sits on the car's hood. He has planted peas while the daughter drifted into a faraway dream, he says, hoeing soil over the newly planted row. Her face has been flushed the whole time, he adds.

"Must have been a good dream," he remarks, looking at Florence intently.

"The best," she says. "And the briefest."

And then her tears begin.

Audrey–
Back on the beat, winging to the moon–
Swinging to beat the band–

*F*irst muffin – up!
  High in the air, like *zo*–
 Muffin two, up you go, now–
Muffin three, airborne – can I do it?–
   I DO it!

all by my lonesome – I can juggle three muffins – it's getting to be a cinch. By the time the talent contest rolls around in August, I'll be up to five muffins, maybe even a half-dozen. I'll wear my porkpie hat, fill the air with baking, wow the crowds. I'm going to win that ride in the Mosquito! I'll soar the skies. I've already put my name in with Ruby Kozak, Keeper of the Contest. I also told Miss McGregor, Patron of the Contest, my juggling act will *steal the show,* and, kind soul, that lady-genius said, "maybe you will, my dear, maybe you just *will.*"

  I'll let you in on a muffin secret. When I first started juggling, quite a few muffins landed on the floor. I notched the sides of the ones I dropped, and sold them to Jimmy Petrik. "*Ha,*" I thought – "let him catch the plague." Besides, he dropped a bowling ball on Ruby Kozak's foot. If she'd *broken* it and stayed away from work, a couple of things wouldn't have happened –

I'd never have got back in her good books –
I'd never have gotten a nickel –
(Good thing she has strong bones!)

But I *did* get out of the doghouse and into Ruby's good books again. Back into her lilac fold.

Jimmy Petrik doesn't work here anymore. After I laid the *Big Bone* at Ruby's feet, the wire story, didn't she write it up dandy! "A Rat in Our Constabulary Midst – Wire Scandal Blown Wide Open" – An Exclusive Feature by Ruby Frances Kozak Including One-Time-Only Interviews with her father, Conrad Kozak, Head of Plant Security and Lieutenant Colonel Roper McLaughlin, Special Intelligence Officer" (*The Factory Voice*, May 21, 1942). That story cooked Jimmy's goose. He got his walking ticket. They said army or jail. He said he had a game leg. "Not game *enough*," they said, so he took army. I guess he'll be off to fight Hitler's boys soon, though Florence told me that Jimmy promised her those Nazis aren't going to get *him*. Maybe. I've been hearing the lists of lost boys on the radio while I scrub pots, and they're getting longer. *Private Jerry Batho. Private so-and-so and so-and-so.* Maybe not, Private Petrik.

When Florence and I play double solitaire at lunch sometimes, I sure don't mention that Jimmy might not make it. And Flo doesn't know I squealed on him, either! If she knew, she'd probably drop me like a hot spud, and I couldn't bear that. She doesn't have any inkling, though, because Ruby Kozak never gave me any credit for the story, not a single ounce.

Everybody's heard all about the wires by now. Talk spreads like a brush fire in this plant, and of course everyone reads *The Factory Voice*. Turns out Jimmy was selling the stronger-gauge wires to some fellow named Mack, who smuggled them into the detainee camps at Red Rock and Magpie. Those chaps were trying to saw their way out, just like the men from Angler did at the end of last year. I never liked Jimmy Petrik, but he didn't squeal on Reggie Hatch, and I have to give him some credit for that. I'm blue that Reg doesn't work here anymore. He rings me at Churchill Ladies' Residence once a week or so and we have a good jaw on the telephone, and that's swell. I told Reggie he reminded me of one of those lizards that switches colours to suit what's around it. He asked what in blazes I meant, and I said, "well, *think* about it – first you were a taxi driver, then you cut wires, now you're in the army," and Reggie said "look who's *talking* Diana-Audrey," and he added that he never believed that Prince Edward Island hogwash I tried to pawn off on him that day in the cab back in '41. We lark around on the phone like that; we're both so much older, now.

Jimmy being gone is only one reason I'm happier than a mole on a golf course. I've paid off the snack-wagon heist. I'm saving like sixty and before long I'll be able to settle accounts with the cherry jar back in Spruce Grove. I'll send my parents the money I borrowed – all right, *took.* Reggie Hatch is going home to Rainy River to visit his mother in a couple of weeks; he'll mail my banknote from there so the envelope won't show a Fort William postmark.

I've been bringing Ruby Kozak regular Wednesday snippets. She seems happy enough with them. I didn't have the foggiest notion how to make them *new and improved.* Then I heard two girls talking in the bathroom – they were saying some slinker in Final Assembly was spooning two factory girls at once, a riveter and a stenographer – *well well well I can work with this,* I thought when they were gone and I got down from the toilet tank in the cubicle. Ruby clucked her tongue and said the story would make a nice light-interest piece, and I was off the reporting hook for another week.

"New and improved" – ha HA HAAA

Spring is here! Violets are popping their little purple faces open all over Fort William. The lilacs smell as swell as Ruby Kozak's perfume. There's a lilac tree right outside my window at Churchill Ladies' Residence. A few miles away, the Dominion ice-crushing boat has been shattering the cold white ledge of Lake Superior's shore. From the top floor of Chapples Department Store (Lingerie), your eyes can feast on the blue water, and the moving ships. You can see clear to Port Arthur, and all you have to do is ride the lift to Lingerie and pretend you're buying a girdle. When I win the talent contest and I'm flying in the plane, I'll be able to see the *whole lake*, I'll bet – maybe even across it, to the shores of America. Well, I've got to go practice my juggling, now. When it comes to muffins, all I can say is, "keep 'em flying!"

*R*uby's Veronica Lake bangs are melting as she sits, notepad and pen on the table, across from Reggie in a booth at the McKellar Diner. A fan whirrs on the sill of the rectangular opening in the wall that separates the diner from the kitchen. The waitress shouts her orders through this window, to the cook. Bing Crosby croons from the radio, but he isn't calming Ruby. She'd barely recognized Reggie at first, the pimply, stumbling boy who'd once cut wires at the plant. Ruby could have been toppled by a whiskey-jack feather when Reggie rang her at the factory that July morning to say he had a story for her. What about? "About me," he'd said. This striking young man in uniform had shaken her hand and sat down across from her, as she'd wondered who he was. It had taken Ruby a full minute to get her bearings. What a difference a few months can make. Reggie Hatch is all rippling muscle, his military hat dipping over his deep, earnest eyes that take her in. Ruby has gotten him very wrong.

"You look different," she says. "Besides the uniform, I mean. Better. Your face – it's clear." Ruby regrets her words right away.

He doesn't seem phased. "I got some dope for my skin."

She sends a silent prayer upwards, praising herself for choosing her pink percale sundress – it flatters her figure. She's looking swell, Reggie tells her. The waitress waits, perspiring, over their table. Reggie orders two hot pork sandwiches and two lemon phosphates. Ruby hardly hears the banter of lunching workers around them, the waitress braying orders into the kitchen, the fryer's sputter and whoosh.

Ruby pulls her pencil from her raffia handbag. She tests the lead on a corner of her notepad, a signal that her interview is about to begin. Their glasses of lemon phosphate are thunked down in front of them. Ruby tells Reggie that the earlier story she'd written about him, "Our Boy of the Wires" is sorely out of date, and so scanty on details that they should start from scratch.

"Scratch," he agrees.

First some basic facts. She questions. He answers. She writes: *Reginald Hatch. Date of birth: June 11, 1917. Place of Origin: Rainy River, Ontario.* Hardly the stuff of riveting human-interest copy. But his transformation into, 'this manly swan,' Ruby thinks, *is* astounding. For the first time, she's not sure how to write something. And he stares at her still. She pulls in a mouthful of phosphate through her straw in a frantic way.

The waitress clatters down their lunches. Two columns of steam wisp upwards between them. Neither of them picks up a fork. He takes a sip of his drink.

Scrambling to collect herself, Ruby shoves her plate aside (too hot to eat just now), and doodles on her pad to give her time to reclaim her reporter's aplomb. She sketches a perfect hummingbird in the corner of the page. Then some notes. *From Wire to Flier.* That might work. She regains a bit of her usual journalistic confidence. *A Soldier's Story* – that would be better. Yes, she can do this. She'll just get Reggie to talk. He compliments her hummingbird. She makes tropical eyes at him.

"Let's do the story, Reggie."

"Ah yes, the *story.*"

She can't tell if he's making fun of her. She straightens her spine against the hard, puritan wall of the booth. Reggie

Hatch is still watching her closely, admiringly, she thinks. Ideas rush into Ruby's head. She explains the thrust of "A Soldier's Story" – the scarecrow boy from Rainy River who no one would give a second look had risen from parochial ashes into a dashing soldier –

"What I want to know, Reggie," – Ruby pipes her voice down to a whisper so he must lean closer to hear, near enough to breathe in the scent of her Dorothy Gray White Lilac Cologne – "is, what can change a man so – *drastically* – in a few months? I'd like you to *search your heart* before answering."

She sends him her most significant look. He returns it with an expression so similar, she feels like she's been gazing into a mirror.

"Love," he says.

"Love?"

"Love. Write that down, Ruby."

She writes the word under the hummingbird. Chews on her pencil. She presses her back into the booth's severity again. He looks at her in that deep way of his.

"Why do you want to be a soldier?" she asks.

"Love," he repeats.

"Anything else?"

"End of story."

"You haven't said enough, Reggie."

"I've said too much, Ruby."

Neither of them has touched their plate. He signals the waitress for the cheque and puts his army jacket on. The waitress, eyeing their hot pork sandwiches, asks if something's wrong with the food. She passes Reggie the tab.

"The food looks hunky-dory," he tells her. "We ran out of conversation, is all."

"What can you do?" the waitress shrugs, removing their plates.

Reggie Hatch lays two dollars and fifty cents on the table. Ruby's eyes sting. She swipes at them. Her nose releases small, alarmed snuffles. Reggie bends to tie an errant shoelace, and she asks him how in the name of Roosevelt, is she supposed to make a story out of one word?

Reggie Hatch drums the table with his hand. He rises and lobs her an anguished look. "*Search your heart,* Ruby – and if *that* doesn't work, just read the newspapers. You'll find stories built on a whole lot less."

With those words, Reggie Hatch hurries out of McKellar Diner. Ruby watches him board the streetcar, and it's not until it lurches forward on its tracks that she catches sight of the small, velvet box on the table where his hand had been drumming.

Even in That Boreal Wasteland
Some Plants will Grow Robustly
August 17, 1942

*R*oper McLaughlin reclines far back in his chair while, on the fireplace mantle, the electric fan Ferris-wheels at breakneck speed. The August heat is surprisingly intense. He fights off the stupor it sends over him. He must keep his mind sharp. Country of extremes, he muses, scanning the Canadian map on his library wall. Fire and ice. Roper rises to turn off the radio, settles back into his chair. He needs to concentrate. His wife, Glynis, is downstairs arranging zinnias in a vase (she's been forced to admit that *some* plants will grow robustly even in "this boreal wasteland"). Soon she'll summon him downstairs to supper, though, and he must discover a solution to his dilemma before their evening meal, or he'll sit distant and distracted over his plate, and Glynis will start in with her accusations – that he's not really *there* even when he's *there*. She's right on the mark, that's the trouble.

The fact is that, for the past eight months, Roper has been making up his job as he goes along. Luckily, he's had convincing enough reasons to keep raising security alert levels. The foiled escape from Magpie Detainee Camp. The much more recent unpleasantness around one of their own plant constables getting caught smuggling non-regulation wires into the factory. He'd felt badly about extending the probation periods of several line workers – they were, no doubt, simply innocent kids – but he needed more time to devise a method for making himself known to Muriel McGregor. He'd been calling on his daughter for months. Had grown acquainted with her. Comfortable. She was a fine woman. Handsome (like her mother). Muriel was sensible. Muriel was logical. A woman of science. But she was also a human being, and she'd been increasingly, on Roper's visits to her office, looking over her wire spectacles at him and, undeniably – *flirting*. She was getting the *wrong idea* about him, and it needed to stop. A couple of weeks ago, she'd forced him to admit that, indeed, *he* had sent the tarts to her back in February (he questions the intelligence of *that* scheme, now, but of course it's too late). When, one day not so long ago, he'd suggested to Muriel that perhaps Orville Loftus, the test pilot, was not such a bad chap, she'd replied that while Orville had indeed "risen in her estimation," he lacked sophistication. Moreover, he had queer traits. He kept reading the same book over and over – that gloomy *Rime of the Ancient Mariner*. Muriel had also begun asking Roper how he spent his weekends. She struck him as thoroughly modern, his daughter – so ready to take the initiative.

Roper will simply have to tell Muriel the truth. And soon. Zinnias don't take long to arrange.

"Rope – *Supper!*" – Glynis from downstairs. She has a way of making the word sound like 'super.' 'Stupor,' he thinks. 'Must rise from this stupor. End stupor time.'

He goes downstairs. Over a cold supper, Glynis havers on about the big talent contest coming up at Fort William Aviation. She'd read about it in the newspaper, and it's all over Sleeping Giant Radio, she tells her husband. "Open to the public. Proceeds to Victory Bonds."

"Could we not *go*, Rope?" Glynis asks. "*Please?* Yave got to admit we haven't gone anywhere. I need to get *out*, Rope."

How can he deny her? She's right. In Roper's efforts to

know his daughter, he's neglected his wife. But Muriel McGregor will be at the talent show. She's *hosting* it, and suddenly there he'll be, in the front row, with his *wife.* He should have mentioned Glynis to Muriel long ago, but he'd so much enjoyed her bright company, he hadn't wanted to spoil things by being her father, or by bringing another presence into their companionable bubble.

He makes one last-ditch ploy to buy more time. He stabs his ham slice with his fork. "But Glynis, would you *really* want to watch a bunch of amateurs sing and recite and hula dance and do whatever they do? Surely you'd find it tiresome, provincial?"

"Not at *all!* Roper, after eight months in this Dominion backwater, a dancing *moose* would send me into raptures!"

That's that, then. Let the moose dance.

Muriel
Timing is Everything

*S*he is reading an article on flutter theory, her Detrola
Pee-Wee radio playing softly when the music stops.
Special news report – *Dieppe – heavy losses.* Nausea
swamps her as she listens. She swallows some Dr.
Chase's Nerve Food and wonders about Frank Parks' son.
Then she calls Fraudena at the plant switchboard to ask if
they've received any word. Fraudena rings Lake Superior
Regiment, and telephones Muriel back. Private F. Parks Jr. is
reported as *Missing in Action* – they might not have further
information for days. Then Muriel phones Frank Parks who,
Fraudena said, insisted on coming to work despite the news.
Was there anything she could do, Muriel asked the manager.
He told her they could only wait. She'd asked, too, if she
should cancel the talent show set for nine days down the road.
Frank Parks told her no matter what the outcome with his
boy, the show should go ahead. The workers' morale would
benefit from it.

Muriel hangs up the telephone. She is struck with panic.
She's done little about the show – her own "worker incentive
scheme" – other than have Ruby Kozak advertise it, and register entries. She must ring the Kozak girl and ask her to be

the mistress of ceremonies. The girl is fetching, loves the lime-light. Then dozens of other tasks tumble into Muriel's thoughts.

Balloons. Microphones. Voting forms. Refreshments. She's bitten off more than she can chew – these aren't the sorts of details to which she's accustomed. And now, in the middle of the awful worry about Frank Parks' son – not to mention all the other Canadian boys – Lieutenant Colonel Roper McLaughlin wishes to speak with her about a "deli-cate, rather urgent personal matter – something too sensitive to discuss by telephone." Fraudena had slipped a sealed enve-lope, the note inside it, under Muriel's office door. Until today, when it came to calling or visiting her, Roper McLaughlin had impeccable – no, *uncanny* – timing. His friendly knock on her office door always seemed to come when she needed a break from her aeronautical designs. Same with his telephone calls. Oh, *she's* wanted to talk with Roper about an *urgent personal matter,* too. Badly. She's been filling her diary with red ink lately –

Tell Roper the truth. Tell him your admiration for him extends beyond his intelligence and collegiality. Let him know you have little experience with men, but when it comes to him, you feel sure your sentiments are calibrated with absolute precision. No. Pass over the technical palaver for once. Tell him you love him. Pure and simple.

Muriel has been longing to speak these words. The need to say them has been filling her with ache. But she can't say them today. It's the wrong time. She's too distracted, too dis-traught. She can't afford to botch what she's so long wished to divulge. Her future depends on the clarity of her mind. She writes a reply; she'll ask Fraudena to have it delivered to Roper's house. *She's most eager to discuss this matter,* she writes, *but whatever it is, it will have to wait until after the talent show. She is sorry.* Signed. Sealed. Her.

A couple of hours later, she receives another note from Roper. Her busy schedule is very unfortunate news for him. He wonders if she wouldn't have even a *few* minutes, for lunch, perhaps, in the next week. If she *does* discover some unclaimed moments, perhaps she could ring him at his home library number – South 75301 (*not* the general house number) – to let him know? His note sounds so *put out*, Muriel dares to wonder if the delicate matter he had to speak to *her* about isn't, in fact, the very same sensitive subject she wishes to reveal to *him* – but only when the time is right. 'Surely that's *it*,' she thinks. There has always been a confluence of their minds, hers and Roper's.

Just then Audrey Foley's familiar knock strikes Muriel's door, the kid's bright, muffled voice –

"Muffin, Miss McGregor!"

Muriel calls "enter," and in waltzes Audrey, her head bobbing like a balloon. *Balloons!* Why didn't Muriel think of this sooner?

"I'm anointing you 'Balloon Girl' and 'Person in Charge of Decorations' for the talent show, Audrey."

The snack-wagon girl beams. "So long as I can still be *in* it, and juggle."

"Absolutely."

"And as long as I can still come and ask you airplane things...?"

"Goes without saying, my girl."

"Then *anoint away*," Audrey beams.

That night, Muriel, her diary open before her, inks Audrey as the one spot of cheer in that whole anxious day.

Where the Pots Soak and the Itch Itches
And the flag flies at half-mast in the factory courtyard

Have you ever had an itch that just would *not* go away? An itch that keeps clawing its way under your skin even *after* you've counted the many swell things about your life? Here's a for instance.

Listen while I scour these pots (soup today, it's a cinch) –

Things couldn't be better for me no matter which way you slice it. The cherry jar has been paid back. Snack wagon, too. I'm back to saving money, and I can juggle five muffins without dropping a single one. Unless Judy Garland herself waltzes in, I'm pretty sure I'll be cruising in that Mosquito soon. Twice a week I have tea with Miss McGregor in her office and she treats me like a real person, and the Scottish man still visits there too (though he hasn't come much lately, and when he does, I've a bone to pick with him – here it is – he extended all worker probation periods due to recent "heightened security alert procedures," and that means my friend Florence has to wear the red scarf longer and she hates it). But back to dilly things. I'm now the balloon girl for the talent show. I've got a three-foot geranium with red blooms in my window at Churchill Ladies' Residence, and a cat I call Marilla. We're not supposed to have pets, but Marilla was a stray. She kept mewling at my window, so I started to feed her (stagger me, I know how it is to look for a place!). The other girls in Churchill get a bang out of her antickle doings and they're not about to squeal about a kitten that leaps after paper airplanes and makes everybody laugh. Some of the girls have fellows overseas. They need to laugh.

I know every corner of the factory – where the stories are, and how to dig them up and serve them on a silver platter to Ruby Kozak in Head Office, and if there's nothing to dig

I MAKE THEM UP!

I pull word-snacks out of the air

(it started that day in the bathroom I heard the girls talking and I thought

WAIT – I could add spice to what they say – stagger me WAIT AGAIN – they don't even have to be *real*, do they? So I invented factory girls –

Mavis and Mabel – and plunked them into all sorts of scrapes
words   stories
and best of all

Ruby *believes* them!

Ruby will believe anything these days. If I told her the moon crash-landed on the roof of Sub-Assembly, she'd swallow it.

Why?

Because she's in CAPITAL-L *Love* –

With my friend Reggie, of all people! He gave her a ring and everything (I can sure see what he sees in her – she's still as much of a peach for the eyes as the first day I set my boots down in this factory, but when will he see beneath her furry peach skin, I wonder?). Ruby doesn't check any of the *"new and improved" dilly items* I bring her every Wednesday. She just feasts her starry eyes on me and smiles her new, woozy smile – a *Love smile,* I guess – and thanks me for my dandy little report (you'd never catch Wonder Woman with that vacant and witless kind of look!).

I don't cower at my Wednesday reports anymore, no sir! Hundreds of girls come and go through these industrial doors

faster than a spinning top. Ruby doesn't check. And *they* sure
don't. The workers, I mean. They read *The Factory Voice* at
lunch and titter and *tssk,* and I hear them say to each other,
"Do you know Mavis?" "No, I sure don't know Mavis!"
"Mabel?" "Which one? There are lots of them" – *"Well they*
must work here – this story's about them, but seeing the trouble
they're in, tsk, tsk, maybe they don't work here anymore."
"Small wonder, according to the Voice*!"* More titters, *tsks* –

So now you know –

~~There never *was* a Mavis.~~

And Mabel could be anyone.

And that suits me fine. Ruby Kozak gets fed. I keep my
plum job. No one gets hurt. The workers are entertained.
They clamour for the *Voice.* I dance into Head Office each
Wednesday.

So – you might imagine my life is perfect. But wait for the
other part. Here it is – the grouch in Wing Assembly told me
he'd let me watch them fasten a wing in exchange for a kiss. "I
don't kiss," I said (why everything in Ontario has to be a *deal,*
I'll never know). Then there's Florence. When Florence
started going around with Jimmy, I forgave her even though
you know how I feel about Jimmy. I've *never* seen a girl who
wanted a fellow as much as Flo did, so how could I *not* forgive her? Seems Florence has fallen into CAPITAL-L *love,*
just like Ruby Kozak. I just stuff tissues in my ears when Flo
starts mooning on about Jimmy, and finally I ask, "are you
finished?" and she gives me this woozy smile, just like
Ruby's, and says, "for the time being," and I unstuff my ears.
But after Jimmy got caught with the bad wires, and fired from
his job, poor Florence has slid deep into the dumps, she fell

FAR
     Down
into   Dumpland

The red scarf bothers her more than ever. She's been slowing
down with her rivet gun. Her weld pool is bad (I saw). She

never wants to play double solitaire anymore, or go for milk-shakes. She's been saddest this last little while, and these recent days have been lousy for everybody, with the newest mess overseas (I think it's called Dep?) and the Union Jack in the factory courtyard sagging at half-mast for the past week.

Florence was swell before love tumbled her into the dumps. We'd go to McKellar Diner for milkshakes, or she'd stroll over to Churchill and the girls down the hall would teach us dance steps, the Regina rumble and the turkey trot (Florence often tripped over her feet while we were cutting up the carpet, and wouldn't we laugh?). One day, Florence brought her trumpet and played it in the Ladies' Lounge. She was a wonder with that horn! Stagger me, Flo surprised us all and, to top it off, she told us she'd entered Miss McGregor's talent contest.

(Even though I like Florence plenty, it tugs hard at my hobnailed boots
  to think
she could win the talent contest
  instead of ME,
and I can't sort out that hitch just yet –
I want that plane ride bad, I've been feeling the air rush under me for weeks,
  yes, ME –
Me and my flying muffins).

I've had to push worry away, even though the contest is coming up furious. After all, Florence is pretty new at the trumpet. She still misses the odd note and gets flustered. And who's to say I won't drop a muffin (though I *haven't* in ages) when comes the moment of truth?

So I've shoved the contest deep into a gopher hole marked "Unknown" for the time being. Besides, the worse itch I still haven't told you about – the BIGGEST ITCH of all – Ruby Kozak. The thing is, stagger me, I've been Ruby Kozak's eyes for eight months. I brought her the big story about Jimmy, and what bites at me more and more is this – Ruby collected the ten-dollar reward from the wire information. Now, don't you think she might have sent a *little* of that my way? Instead, she gave me a nickel. You were there. You saw –

FIVE LOUSY CENTS   for all my trouble

That doesn't seem fair to me. Especially when most of what I told her was true; only the Reggie part I kept hidden. *This* is what has been gnawing at me bad, that someone like Ruby, a former Miss Fort William, someone so divinely beautiful with flawless skin with flowing hair and Gene Tierney eyes that look like they might eat you and sometimes *do* eat you, but who, despite the danger is still perfection on two legs that someone like this can be

A SKINFLINT –

This is what's eating me!
Now as I said, I'm doing pretty fair in the money arena. But who couldn't use a bit extra? After all, like the banner says, ALL THIS COULD END TOMORROW. We might lick Hitler one day – *then* what will I do? Where will I go? No, a few extra dollars tucked away never hurts. Besides, it's more than the money. It's the – what do you call it – *principle* of the thing. Let's say you picked up a scouring pad right now and helped me out with these dirty pots. I'd be flipping a lot more than a *nickel* your way. Why? Because:

I MAY NOT SMELL LIKE LILACS BUT SKINFLINT I AM NOT

There, I feel better having gotten that off my tiny chestless chest.
I'm done. Caught up with the pots. I'm going to have to sit on my sack of flour while I tell you the rest, because it's hard to tell. It happened yesterday.

A Place in France
August 26, 1942

ake a deep breath. You'll need it. Here's what happened. That awful mess with the Canadians lost in France killed everybody's appetite. Almost nobody was buying snacks. But I had to make my rounds as they still wanted smokes. I took a few of my usual wares up to Mr. Parks in Head Office. He often likes coffee or a Snickers bar, sometimes both. He's never paid much attention to me. Suits me dandy. Ruby Kozak is my boss, not him. He's been more or less harmless, which is more than I can say about *her.*

Usually I hear his boomy voice on the telephone behind the door, and I wait until he's done talking, then knock. No boomy voice. I clunk his door with my knuckle. Still nothing. Then I hear this sort of whimper. More whimpers; this isn't right. My stomach is one big twisted knot, I can tell you, but I tiptoe into his large office anyway. Stagger me, the place is topsy-turvy. Papers everywhere. A file cabinet has been pulled from its usual spot out into the middle of the room, its drawers flung open, files on the floor – paper birds, crash-landed.

Holy Fibber McGee, it's hot in there! And where is Frank Parks, and why doesn't he open a window? I smell whiskey.

"Coffee, Mr. Parks?" I call out.

The whimpers become sobs. I'd never heard a man cry in Alberta, and the sound of it wrenches me bad.

Then I see Mr. Parks. In the corner of his office. Sitting on the floor. That tornado that ripped through that big room spat him out and dumped him there. His face looks grey, and rumpled as his suit. He takes a swig from a flask of whiskey.

"Ah, there she is, the snail-wagon girl. I've been waiting for you." His voice is full of marbles and he ruffs out a gloomy laugh.

"Coffee?" I ask again, and raise my pot.

He's scaring me. All I can do is squeak again – "*Coffee,* sir?"

"Zoor, pour some of this whiskey into it, Missie – and have some yourself. Siddown, take a load off those cobblestone boots of yours."

"Are – alcoholic beverages allowed at Fort William Aviation?"

"Today's *different,*" he says, waving the flask. He tells me there are cups on his filing cabinet, right beside the picture of his son (a small boy swinging on a tire tied to a tree). Then he starts sobbing again and I hurry to the filing cabinet and get the cups – anything to make him stop. I pour myself, and him, some coffee. He splashes whiskey into his coffee. He pats the hardwood floor beside him. So I sit down. I'm pretty sure this isn't cricket – if only Mr. Kozak from Security would take a gander up here and sort Mr. Parks out.

The telephone rings. My eyes bounce towards possible rescue. "Would you like me to answer it?" I ask. He tells me to leave it, drink my coffee. Then he stares at me, scaring me again.

Mr. Parks takes a long swallow of his hot whiskey drink. "How old are you?"

"Eighteen – sir." I've been saying I'm eighteen for so long, I almost believe myself.

"*Eighteen,* eh? Well, well – only two years younger than my Frankie."

I can't think what to come back with, so I don't say anything.

He drinks some more. "Whas-zure name again, kid?"

"Audrey." I try to keep my cup-holding hand from shaking.

"Have you ever heard of Dieppe, *Audrey?*"

"That place in France?"

"Ri' on the money, kid. Do you know that the barbed wire the Germans strung along the wall they built on the beach at *that place in France,* would stretch right across Lake Superior and back?"

"Nope."

"The Royal Regiment of Canada landed at *that place,* on the beach – at that wall – at 5:06 in the morning. In broad daylight, *late* because of a foul-up on the channel."

"Some chaps were talking about it in the wing assembly area, uh-huh."

"The German snipers rained down bullets when our Canadian boys tried to scramble up the wall."

"Those chaps I overheard said there were losses."

Tears drip down his rumpled face. Stagger me, I sure wanted out of there. And for the first time, I wanted somebody *else* to be the eyes of the factory.

"*Losses,* kid?"

I'd have done anything to make this stop. Usually I can think fast on my feet, but I *wasn't* on my feet – I was cow-kicked and helpless on the floor – and I couldn't think of a single thing to say or do.

"I lost my son in that advance, Audrey."

He fumbles in his trousers pocket and brings out a folded piece of paper. He thrusts it at me. I've never seen a real telegram before.

Regret to advise Private Frank Parks Jr. killed in line of duty at Dieppe stop letter to follow stop deepest condolences stop Lake Superior Battalion Casualties Officer L. Norman Eckrods stop

I fold the telegram. Once again, his phone rings, and once again, he waves it away. I return the telegram. "I'm awful sorry, Mr. Parks."

He eyes me in a glowering sort of way, but his words

aren't mean. "You *are,* aren't you?"

"I truly am." And I *was.* And all the silly things I'd ever spun from fancy and air, about the made-up Mavis and other girls seemed foolish stacked against this awful thing. I wanted to stick my head in a gopher hole. Then things got worse. Mr. Parks curled up like a caterpillar on the floor and cried long gashes of sound, along with some of those earlier whimpers.

That was it. I flew out of his office, across the courtyard to Sub-Assembly, past the girls reaming and riveting and sorting and threading, past the spinning lathes, and up the steps to the eagle's-nest Security Office. Through the milky window in the door I saw the shape of Ruby Kozak's father at his desk. Heard the swishy strains of big band music coming from the radio. I rushed in and told Mr. Kozak he'd better get someone up to Mr. Parks' office, it was *bad,* and Mr. Kozak flipped on his blue cap and hightailed it out of there.

And then what do you think happened? I was shaking so bad, I headed for my sack of sorrows in the storage room behind the cafeteria kitchen where I keep my cigarettes. I hoped they might steady my nerves. Just as I was about to spin into the cafeteria, I heard my name –

"Audrey Foley!"

Ruby Kozak was right behind me. Ruby the Skinflint, holding back the sound of her footsteps so I couldn't hear them.

She stared at me with her gluttonous eyes and hands on her hips, and she was *not* wearing her woozy in-love smile. "It's *Wednesday,* Audrey. Report day. Dilly items. Remember? News. What've you got?"

"I've got *news* all right," I blurted. "Men cry. And they do it lying on the floor!"

Ruby looked at me like I was cracked. She asked, what was she supposed to do with *that?*

"Do whatever blows your dress up," I said.

And then, she fired me.

Exit Procedures

Where O Where is the Balloon Girl
when You need Her?

*M*uriel McGregor is frantic. The talent show is tomorrow, and where's Audrey Foley? The girl has vanished. She was supposed to report to the office after her morning snack-wagon round. There was no snack wagon this morning, Florence Voutilainen and the other workers griped when Muriel went down to investigate. They were none too pleased. If not for the industrial noise, they bet Miss McGregor could hear their stomachs growl. The fellows in Final Assembly were even crankier. They were starving and blast it, they needed cigarettes too – where *was* that kid? Muriel hadn't walked among the workers often enough to witness their primal needs. She hobbled on her cane into the cafeteria where Lucy Fell, the chief dishwasher, shook her head sadly. No, she hadn't seen hide nor hair of Audrey. The pots were piled to the moon, and who was going to wash them, Lucy had lamented.

This is strange. Audrey Foley is the factory's most chipper employee. She never gets sick, not even in the midst of the sniffles and sneezes and other rampant germs her wagon work takes her through every day (the girl had recently boasted this to Muriel, apropos of nothing, laughingly calling herself a "tiny Jesus walking among the lepers"). The kid can't simply vanish – not *now* when everyone needs her, Muriel most of all.

Something must be done. Lately, Muriel has begun to listen to her bones more intently than to science, and her bones are telling her something is very amiss. She hangs her *Gone Flying* sign on her office door and takes a taxicab to Churchill Ladies' Residence. Perhaps the girl *isn't* Jesus, and has been stricken with leprosy, or worse.

Muriel has never been to the residence and she sees, for the first time, how all these hundreds of young women who've blown in from across the Dominion live, cheek by jowl in their tiny rooms. She thinks of her own commodious flat. The lady at the residence's reception desk tells Muriel that Audrey Foley lives in Room 101. Muriel pokes her cane along the hallway, past the Victory Bonds posters, and stops in front of Audrey's door. It's open a crack, and Muriel, keeping herself hidden, hears Audrey muttering. Muriel peeks in through the crack – the kid, whose back is turned from the door, is clearly distraught. She's sitting on the floor beside a pile of clothes, stuffing blouses and slacks and underwear into a carpet bag, while a cat mewls at her side. Audrey is jabbering, an anguished babble bubbling forth. This is what Muriel hears –

> *Stagger me I'm supposed to be "a very important person in this factory," Ruby said so, and then she (sniff) fries me out of the blue, fries me in her frying pan – it's worse than: "she's no one she's only the snack-wagon girl" (sniff, sniff) – now I'm less than the snack-wagon girl, how much do her words weigh anyway?*
>
> POOF –
>
> *About as much as a hen's feather, that's how much – and HER A REPORTER can you figure that? – I guess that's really it for me (sniffle) – they'll have to find their own snacks I bet they're darned hungry down there right now good thing I saved a bit of money (she*

turns to the cat) *oh Marilla it stabs my gizzard to leave my home here, what will happen to you?*
(sob)
and what about the talent show and the ride I woulda won in the Mosquito, I can keep five muffins flying but that's not even the thing anymore – I told Miss McGregor I'd help with the balloons
(louder sob)
and here I am packing my suitcase instead and I don't even know where I'm bound and what will she think? – I wouldn't have let her down for the world –

Muriel enters Audrey's room. "I *know* you wouldn't, Audrey."

The cat scuttles under the bed, and Muriel is sorry she didn't knock, for she's frightened the poor animal, and the girl, half out of their senses (and the kid was a considerable way out of them already).

"I'm sorry, sorry, *sorry* – about the balloons," Audrey gasps "but I got *fried* – I mean *fired."*

Muriel's bones are screaming, yes, something's wrong here. "Ruby Kozak fired you?"

Audrey nods tragically. She tries for several long minutes to explain what happened – *whiskey, coffee, a place in France, telegrams, men cry on floors, Ruby's skinflint heels.*

Muriel can't make much sense of the girl's whirl of words. She only knows there was some kind of misunderstanding between the head stenographer, and the snack-wagon girl. Well, this tempest in a teapot can be sorted out easily.

"Put those clothes back in your dresser drawer, Audrey. You're not going anywhere – except to work. Hurry. Make an unscheduled snack-wagon round since you're quite right, they're "darned hungry" in those production sheds. And I've got three hundred balloons in my office that need inflating and stringing up by tomorrow night. You can take a taxicab with me back to the plant."

"But I got *fired,"* Audrey protests, but she's already

unpacking the carpet bag.

"Well, you just got *un*fired," Muriel says. "And you can unpack later."

The girl's eyes are incandescent stars. "Can I still be in the talent show?"

Muriel assures her she can. Audrey Foley rises, a small streak of joy. "You are the luckiest cat in the *world*," she calls to Marilla, still in retreat under the bed. "And *I* am the luckiest girl."

"More like the *pluckiest*," Muriel smiles. "Now, for heaven's sake, let's *go*."

They go. One dances, one hobbles.

And the Winner is . . .

*R*uby Kozak stands before the mirror in the ladies' bathroom in Sub-Assembly, her hand trembling as she grasps the red tube of lipstick – a hand made even more beautiful by the sparkling white-sapphire engagement ring. This night, of all nights, she'd like to look perfect, but she's unable to apply her lipstick with the usual precision. In thirty minutes she'll be in the spotlight, Mistress of Ceremonies. Already the plant parking lot is crammed with Ford Phaetons, Packards, Studebakers – and other tin lizzies that will still roll along on their patched and repatched tires.

Ruby's hand won't stop shaking. Her lips are a mess. Earlier in the day, Muriel McGregor had marched (in her limping way) right up to Ruby's desk, demanding to know why the Foley girl had been sacked (as the chief engineer put it). Ruby said, "I thought *my* department was hiring and *yours* was flying planes, Miss McGregor." Talk about a misstep – Ruby sees that now as she stands before the mirror, her deodorant cream doing *nothing* on a night surprisingly hot for late summer. The engineer had a lot of fire, for a cripple, and someone so *methodical,* so *mathematical.* Muriel McGregor wasn't satisfied until she'd wrenched the truth from Ruby – that Reggie Hatch had shipped out, and Ruby had been more upset than she'd expected to be, and yes, she'd probably taken it out on the snack-wagon girl and *had* fired her.

"Well, I'm *re*hiring her," Muriel said. "Audrey will decorate the cafeteria under my supervision. And she'll do whatever trick she intends to do in the talent show. And she'll resume her snack-wagon rounds as per usual – I want the workers well fed. They *need* to be, to build planes." And then the engineer had gone on about the war effort, and how Ruby wouldn't want to hold up progress, would she? Oh jeepers, no.

Their huffy exchange had ended. Ruby Kozak had been nailed to the wall, and all because of some silly girl in hob-nailed boots from Prince Edward Island. She takes her comb from her raffia handbag to tidy her hair, when who clomps into the bathroom but her old friend, Florence Voutilainen, wearing a mauve summer dress, her hair pinned up in a pass-able roll, looking almost *feminine.* Ruby had been floored when Florence entered the talent show. 'What talents could Flo possibly have?' she'd wondered. Music apparently. Florence, on seeing Ruby, suddenly looks distraught. She's carrying a case. 'Trumpet,' Ruby thinks, remembering the information on Florence's entry form. 'Flo never had any musical talents' – this also crosses Ruby's mind as she glances at the case, the initials engraved on a scuffed-up metal plate – *T.B.* A used trumpet, of course.

Flo says a cool hello, Ruby a strained, but warmer, one.

"I'm surprised you're still working here, Ruby," Florence says, her voice as chilly as last fall's frost.

Ruby stares at her, the comb suspended in her hair. "Why?"

Florence looks hard at Ruby in the mirror. There are four women in the bathroom now, as they each have a reflected twin. "Your big story that got Jimmy fired and now" – (here Flo grows tearful) – "he's been sent *overseas*. Hasn't your *big story* sailed you right out of here, like you wanted?"

"I have a fellow overseas, *too*," Ruby snaps (she won't

tackle Flo's question here, now). "It's not easy for me, either."

Florence glances at the ring sparkling on Ruby's finger. She reaches above the sink and rips a paper towel down from the roll, pulls with such force, the dispenser rattles. "Nonsense, Ruby – things have *always* been easy for you." Flo swipes at her dripping hands, crumples the towel into a ball and tosses it into the trash bin.

Before Ruby can wish her old friend good luck in the talent show, Florence grabs the trumpet case and tramps out of the bathroom.

Minutes later, when Ruby enters the cafeteria, she's astonished at the sight of hundreds of white balloons dangling in huge clusters from the rafters. The wainscoting around the massive room is festooned with bunting, bows and crêpe-paper streamers. A wooden platform has been built from, Ruby assumes, airplane-crate wood, since *Fort William Aviation* is stencilled on some boards. A maroon curtain on a heavy wire backdrops the platform. Large amplifiers and microphones are positioned, ready, on the stage. A table near the rear of the room has signs above it: "Talent Ballots," "Victory Bond Donations." Hundreds of chairs in rows, most of them already filled, and more people are filing into the cafeteria. Everyone Ruby has ever *seen* is in that room – her parents, Mr. Parks, her boss, even her high-school English teacher, Miss Izza Sawb (of *keep the zest keen* fame). The stenographers who work under her. Fraudena the plant switchboard operator. Some mucky-mucks she doesn't know, but who must have come down from Lake Superior Regiment, given their medals and uniforms. The waitress at McKellar Diner. The cranky old test pilot, Orville Loftus. Ruby notices reporters from Fort William and Port Arthur; they're bouncing around the room as if their shoes are made from rubber, and before Ruby knows it, a flashbulb pops in her face, and she already knows the photograph won't capture her beauty at *all*.

Just then Ruby sees Lieutenant Colonel Roper McLaughlin enter the cafeteria with – oh jeepers – a *woman* – maybe the one who received the tarts! (how long ago that seems). He wears a doleful look, and Ruby hasn't time to think *why* he would look so glum – the woman is fairly young and, Ruby must admit, striking in appearance, and her clothes don't look like she bought them in Fort William. The first two rows of seats have been cordoned off, marked *Reserved for Contestants*. They pour in, now, Girls. Women. A few men. A boy with a bearded dog.

Ruby steps up onto the stage and Muriel McGregor, dressed in a navy travelling suit, bustles, as best she can, out from the wings, a clipboard in her hand. The lady engineer doesn't appear to hold any grudge over their earlier exchange. She gives Ruby the clipboard – "talent roster" – but first, the national anthem, a moment of silence for the boys lost at Dieppe, then Muriel McGregor's welcome speech.

The show begins. Chairs clatter. Hundreds rise for the anthem. The fierce moment of silence for the boys that nearly breaks everyone. Then Muriel McGregor approaches the microphone and explains the contest. Ruby has to admit that the engineer is well spoken as she praises the diligent workers of Fort William Aviation; because of them, a hundred Mosquitoes have, in the past eight months, been sent flying. Cheers from the crowd. She announces that tonight's winner will receive a flight in one of these planes, flown by their very own highly skilled test pilot (she gestures to Orville Loftus who, hearing the audience's appreciative bumble, sinks lower in his chair, and flicks his hand into an acknowledging wave). She continues. The audience will cast votes to choose the lucky passenger. But then, they're *all* winners, aren't they? Warm applause. The chief engineer pauses to scan the crowd, and then thanks Miss Ruby Kozak, head stenographer, a former Miss Fort William, and *famed author of The Factory Voice* for acting as mistress of ceremonies ('decent of her,' Ruby thinks). But Muriel McGregor would also like to thank, *above everyone else*, one *very special person* without whom no one would eat or drink during breaks in these industrial sheds, and without whom this artfully decorated room they now enjoy would simply be a plain cafeteria. She speaks of their *very own Audrey Foley,* the snack-wagon girl (terrific applause) who is now hiding behind the curtain, but whose talents will soon become apparent to them all.

('All right, *enough,*' Ruby thinks. The engineer will bias the vote if she insists on touting Audrey like this –)

Suddenly, in midsentence, Muriel McGregor stops speaking. Her face goes stiff. Her cane shakes slightly. Ruby can't fathom what's come over her, and she sees that the engineer is staring intently into the audience at someone. *Who,* though? Ruby can't tell – it's darker there, though clearly *Muriel* has penetrated the dimness. Despite their thorny relationship, Ruby bites her lip anxiously on the engineer's behalf – she's shaken, obviously, has turned pale, and lost her train of thought. Nervousness riffles through the audience as Muriel steps unsteadily away from the microphone and pushes her way backstage through the curtain.

Ruby zooms into the spotlight, takes over the microphone. "All *right* – let the show begin!" The audience is back. To kick things off, a girl from Salvaging plays a Scottish ballad on a reed pipe. Then Lucy Fell sways her way through a Hawaiian hula dance. The bearded dog walks on its hind legs. A stout woman yodels an Alpine air. A girl in a fluffy chiffon dress drops a needle on a gramophone, a cornet *ditty dits-dits* and the girl is something, all right – her shoes have big pink bows just like Pauline Ward's, and she can make those long sideways leaps like Pauline, though she can't manage the cartwheels. She almost loses her balance in the attempt, but the audience lets her know there was courage in the trying. A fellow from Wing Assembly saws a girl in half and the audience goes wild when the girl emerges from the box uncut. The Sleeping Giant's Own Houdini! On it goes. Cheers for all the contestants.

Then it's Audrey Foley's turn. She looks almost as pale as Muriel McGregor did earlier. The kid wears a full apron with a huge front pocket, and walks onto the stage as if she's scared her hobnailed boots will break the boards beneath her. She carries a pan of muffins. The room grows quiet. Audrey takes five muffins from the pan. "I'm now going to keep all five of these in the air at once," she says. That nervous riffle runs through the room again, and Ruby suspects that the girl is too rattled to pull it off.

Audrey tosses the first muffin high into the air, way up where the light bulb dangles over the stage.

The second (her small hand a blur) –

Someone hollers, "Keep 'em flying, Audrey!"

There goes the third, soaring into the light –

(split-second-near-fumble) – the fourth – her knees swivel, her hand reaches into the crook of her arm –

– And the FIFTH!

By now everyone's hooting and hollering, "Keep 'em flying," or "C'mon, Audrey!" or "Don't muff it now, kid!" Ruby hears even herself cheering. The muffins are a blur as Audrey flips them high for several more rounds, faster, faster, without a single crumb dropping. Audrey Foley has cast a spell with muffins. Then she makes a cradle with her arm against her slight rib cage, and one after another the muffins land safely. She gently drops the unscathed muffins into the apron's big pocket. Then she takes a small bow as the audience hurrahs and claps vociferously.

"Thank you," Audrey says. "Ladies and Gentlemen, now that I have your ears, you need to hear about one of tonight's contestants who'll soon show her face."

Ruby scowls. Where's the vaudeville hook when she needs it?

A hush descends on the room. Audrey steps forward, her pocket bulging with muffins, until she's teetering, almost, at the edge of the stage. "This is the kind of dilly item that *should* be printed in the *Voice*."

('The *ingrate*, the little *brat*,' Ruby thinks.)

"So I'm going to tell you while I've got you all here. There's a gal in this factory, riveter and welder, Florence Voutilainen. She's my friend. I bet lots of you know her, too. Soon she'll play for you. Well, and what *about* Florence?"

"Tell your story some *other* time, kid!" someone shouts. The audience hisses at the heckler. Even Ruby thinks, 'how rude!' Somebody hollers, "Aw, stuff a *muffin* in it, Tommy!"

"*Now* is the time for my story, Ladies and Gopher Holes – now!" Audrey shouts.

I've created a monster, Ruby Kozak muses glumly, yet makes no move to send Audrey off the stage.

"Listen to me. Florence has been on probation for *eight months* – wearing the red scarf while, stagger me, gunning those rivets and welding those seams even faster than I can juggle muffins."

Tongue-cluckings at the injustice sound from the rows of chairs, cluckings which, it's clear to Ruby, buoy up the snack-wagon girl as she sweeps her arm broadly across the audience.

"The scarf makes her cry," Audrey says. "I know so. I found her bawling in the bathroom once, from shame. It makes her cry every day, but she can't run away from it. What did Florence ever do, except work hard? She's just trying to help the war effort. Should she have to wear this red rag?"

"Off with the rag!" a voice rings out. Then the entire audience shouts: "No more red! No more red!"

Ruby Kozak could throttle the kid's scrawny neck.

"So –" Audrey ballyhoos. "If you think this scarf is just *wrong,* free Florence. Sign the petition at the back of the room, right beside the ballot box – at intermission, which is" – the girl glances at Ruby nodding resolutely – "right about *now!*"

Ruby hopes Audrey is pleased with her *little Good Samaritan act.* During intermission Joe Turner's Orchestra plays swell swing tunes; the lineup to sign the petition snakes all the way through the cafeteria and then loops around it once more. Hundreds of people are signing, except for those who've snuck outside to sip from flasks or spoon or take some air as the cafeteria has grown very warm.

Intermission extends past its allotted time, thanks to Audrey upsetting the apple cart. People finally return to their seats, pencils and ballots in hand. Just as the show is about to resume, Frank Parks waves Ruby over to his chair, where he'd been talking with Lieutenant Colonel Roper McLaughlin during the intermission. Mr. Parks slips a note into Ruby's hand and asks her to read it after she announces the results of the ballots at the end of the show.

The second half of the concert kicks off with a Charlie Chaplin impersonator. Then a pained-looking woman wearing feathers in her hair recites Pauline Johnson's, "The Song My Paddle Sings." A mime tries to work her way out of a glass box, followed by another tap dancer, this one tripping over her feet halfway through the number. Finally, Florence Voutilainen, trumpet in hand, flaps across the stage on her platypus feet. She jokes about having drawn the shortest lot, which means she performs at the tail end of all that talent, and she hopes everyone can stay awake for a few more minutes. Laughter.

Florence raises the trumpet. From her spot at the side of the stage, Ruby sees Audrey, tucked behind the maroon curtain, but not *so* far behind that she can't peek out. Clearly she has the jitters on Florence's behalf. The kid always was transparent. A moment later Muriel McGregor also pokes her face out from behind the curtain. After all the fuss the Foley girl has made over Florence, the audience, it's obvious to Ruby, desperately does *not* wish Flo a flawed song. Audrey has turned the heat *way* high.

And Florence could hardly have chosen a more difficult piece, Ruby thinks, aghast. "Somewhere Over the Rainbow." Lord, the leaps. Flo must have practiced her heart out, as she hits the highs with no apparent strain. Her ear is right on key. It's almost miraculous. The trumpet catches the light, a golden star flashing in the air. Standing there under all the balloons, Florence's face shines like Dorothy Gale's as she stood at the entrance to Oz. But there's still that awful high note to come, the song's last. Ruby has heard more than one singer and horn player duff it mightily. She sees Florence take a gulp of air for the moment of musical truth. Up go her sounds – *"why, oh, why can't –"* (she wavers for a split second, oh dear), but then it's there, fully there *"– I?"*

Florence lowers the horn. She bobs her flushed face, an

embarrassed bob. The audience breaks loose, vast applause. As Flo ducks off the stage, Ruby announces that everyone should now cast their votes and says thank you to Joe Turner and his boys for the songs they're going to play during the voting. The Turner boys blast off with "In the Mood," and some chaps and girls from the audience jump out of their seats and jitterbug and lindy hop and swing in the open area between the front row and the stage.

Finally, the votes are counted and Ruby, grasping a piece of paper, steps behind the microphone. Lush hush. The contestants must take their places in the reserved front-row seats. They do. Greater hush. Ruby reads the results (smatterings of votes) for:

the bearded dog

the yodeller

the feather-haired reciter

the magician with the saw.

More votes for the hula dancer. This and that for so-and-so – some tally, if small, for almost everyone. Honourable Mention goes to the first-half's tap dancer with the pink bows.

Then –

"Audrey Foley and her Flying Muffins: 491 votes!" (Even Ruby can't help but sound *somewhat* enthusiastic – it's a huge number, after all –)

Great cheers – Audrey sends her boots into a victory dance, rodeos her tousled hair –

"And –

Florence Voutilainen and her golden trumpet: 491 votes!"

As the other contestants crowd about Florence, smacking her shoulders and hooting congratulations, she blushes. Then there's a stunned silence. Someone in the audience bellows, "Tie! Fly them both!" And almost instantly the room fills with echoes – "Take them *both* up! They *both* win!" and "Here! Here!"

Ruby Kozak is, unusually, at a loss. She considers asking for a recount or a final showdown performance, muffins versus trumpet. Just as Ruby is mulling this, Muriel

McGregor steps up to the microphone. 'She still looks distraught,' Ruby thinks.

"We do *indeed* appear to have a tie," the chief engineer announces. "If Mr. Orville Loftus, our test pilot, will agree to two flights – one for Miss Foley and one for Miss Voutilainen – we will officially declare *two* winners tonight!"

All faces turn towards Orville Loftus. He hoists his thumb high. Everyone goes off their nuts, whistling, cheering. Ruby summons Florence and Audrey up to the stage. Florence dips an odd curtsey, Audrey a slow, sweeping bow. The reporters explode flashbulbs in their faces. Ruby trills into the microphone: "Pardon me, but there's one final announcement." She unfolds the piece of paper Frank Parks had given her. She reads – *"Due to an exemplary employee record and a groundswell of support here tonight, Miss Florence Voutilainen, riveter and welder, is officially off probation and starting tomorrow, shall be issued a yellow head scarf."* Whoops and applause.

Hearing these words, Flo's eyes fill with tears. Audrey hollers *"whoo-hoo,"* and dances Florence around. 'Quite the night for the workers of the Swamp,' Ruby thinks as she takes it in. She supposes she'll have to write something about this in the *Voice.* She thanks all the contestants for their talents, reminds everyone to donate more to the Victory Bonds jar at the back of the room and wishes the assembly good night, thinking they *might* have set aside a bit of special applause for *her.* She'd kept things moving as swimmingly as she could – but no, the evening's accolades must go to muffins and a trumpet, it seems. Audrey and Florence had only been hired in the first place due to *Ruby's* kindness. They were pretty *marginal cases,* after all – one underage and queer, and the other a member of a family of local subversives. It had been *Ruby* who'd fashioned their entry into the industrial world.

But the oblivious audience files out of the cafeteria, leaving Ruby alone on the stage. Just then she sees the trumpet case lying near the edge of the platform. Florence, in her glory-fog, had forgotten it. Ruby examines the case, its carved initials.

T.B. Wait just a minute. Then it comes to her – one of her own *Voice* pieces, from months ago, last December. *T.B. Yes!* Florence Voutilainen's trumpet was stolen from the Angler Detainee camp last December. If people should find out, wouldn't *that* be a scandal?

Oh, jeepers – *another* big story.

Ruby snatches her raffia handbag and the trumpet case. She dashes out of the cafeteria into the warm August night. At first she can't find Florence among the throngs of people shuffling towards the Neebing streetcar stop. But once her eyes adjust to the darkness, Flo's broad back emerges among the walkers, her fingers curled around the trumpet.

"Florence!" Ruby calls out. "I know where you got that trumpet!"

Suddenly Florence, her old friend, breaks into a run. Ruby can race like a panther and easily outrun Flo who, despite having lost weight, is still heavy and awkward, and never did have feet suitable for anything but plodding. The people leaving the concert are in the way, and Ruby must duck and swerve between them. Just as Florence is about to squeeze onto the crowded streetcar, its doors close, and the car shudders down the track without her.

Ruby catches up, panting – "Flo, you heard me – I *know.*" She holds up the trumpet case.

Florence is panting harder, her eyes wide. "I've no inkling what you're talking about, Ruby."

Well, just because Flo's some big celebrity in the plant now, that doesn't place her above the law. Ruby considers pointing this out, but decides to keep things simple. "Your trumpet was taken from Angler Camp. *T.B.* stands for Tom Bee, which puts you in possession of stolen goods." Ruby jabs at the engraved brass plate above the clasp to punctuate her words.

Ruby expects flustered confession. Contrition. Instead, what Florence does – and the lightning speed with which she does it astounds her – is Flo's hand flies up to her hair and, before Ruby can pull it away, to the trumpet case. A quick, neat flick of a hairpin, and *T.B.* is gone. It's as if some vacuum lodged in the sleeve of Flo's mauve dress had sucked the brass plate up her arm and tucked it into her brassiere.

"*What T.B.?*" Florence says pointedly. "All you're holding up is an empty trumpet case, Ruby Kozak."

And with those words, Flo turns and walks down the tracks where the streetcar glows smaller in the distance.

Florence's Little Fire

lorence bursts into the kitchen carrying the trumpet to find her mother sitting at the table, hemming an amputated trouser leg, her hair in pincurls. 'She looks like a plucked chicken,' Florence thinks. Henni's needle dips up and down rapidly and assuredly in the halo of the coal-oil lamp; it *flies.*

"Guess what, Mother? I *won!*" Florence chimes, setting the trumpet on the table in front of her.

"*Shhh*" – Henni warns in a lowered voice – "you'll wake up Mack."

"Who the heck is Mack?" Florence asks.

"These are his pants, and he's taking a nap. He's all worn out." Henni points the needle to the beaded doorway of her bedroom.

Florence sighs. Mack, nap. Some things never change. But Flo isn't going to let her mother spoil this night. "And guess what else, Mother?"

"Well, what else, Florrie?"

"We're going to have a little fire," Florence says, beaming, and grabs the matches from the kitchen counter.

"It's not even September yet," Henni complains. They don't need a fire. But Florence ignores her mother, and

237

waltzes into her bedroom, returns with the red scarf. "I'm *done* with this!" she cries, unfurling it.

"Quiet. Mack," Henni whispers.

"I don't *care* about Mack," Florence says. "I'm getting rid of this *now.*"

Her mother's face crumples. "You don't *care?* You don't care that *Mack* lost his leg in the last war, and the powers-that-be are just letting him rot out there in his cabin? What's wrong with you, Florrie?"

Like Ruby, her mother is trying to storm on her parade. "I can't get Mack's leg back." But she *had* been able to save the stranger's skin.

Henni sews.

Florence lights a fire in the kitchen stove. She won't let her mother spoil her joy, not tonight. She tosses the red scarf into the fire and watches the flames gobble up the hateful fibres. "I've won. No more probation!" she sings.

"So you've won the right to be like everyone else," Henni says wearily.

As the last red threads sizzle to ash, Florence realizes once again that her mother is the saddest seamstress in the world.

The Red Ink in Muriel's Diary
August 31, 1942 (Continued September 2)

O yes we saw everyone's talents the other night, didn't we? Above all, I bore witness to the considerable gifts of deception of one Lieutenant Colonel Roper McLaughlin, the intelligence man who charmed me over the months until I, yes, I – fickle-mindedly, foolishly fell o fell in love but then looked down from the platform – my stomach tail-spun hard when I saw her, young, pretty, not crippled, the woman seated beside him, too close for a colleague; human bodies betray so much, don't they? Is this woman what he so badly wanted to speak to me about? His eyes met mine, then, just for an instant but long enough to know my thoughts, for he has learned to read my thoughts, and at that moment my thoughts were, "Roper, you betrayer."

I should have stuck with science, for science, like all rational pursuit, never hurts those true to its models – (how could he sit there like that, watching the singers and dancers and the rest, flaunting that young, pretty, uncrippled woman, in front of me?) Lieutenant Colonel Roper McLaughlin should have won that talent contest! MASTER *of* DECEPTION.

I will not cry. Engineers do not cry! Will go to bed instead.

Continued/...

Last night Thaddeus Brink appeared at my back door. So many months since I last saw him, I'd assumed he'd left these parts. Was frying sausage, sipping sherry. I let him in, asked, "What are you doing here?" His answer: "There's still work here." He'd shaven, looked so much better than that first frozen night. His face was filled with little lights again, just like when he was a boy. Of course he didn't know that a few days ago, my heart had been battered by that LIEUTENANT COLONEL OF DECEPTION. *I didn't let Brink know how good it was to see him. I lowered the flaps of my heart. But sherry and sausages opened them. Thaddeus took my hand and we ranged through the Vancouver days of our youth again. How the light hit English Bay in May. Blossoms. His hand on my forehead so many years ago, his voice saying he could feel my brains jumping around in there. We kept politics out of it for once. More sherry. We let politics in. Remembered our joy, delivering Red Flags, the sheer adventure of it, given those papers had been banned. Joy, adventure – until my mother caught us. I told Thaddeus how I'd never made it up with her after she'd had him locked up, and hearing this, he surprised me. "Maybe it's time you did, Muriel." And then, foolish woman that I am, I began to cry. Thaddeus Brink removed the pins from my hair and held me until I was a girl without polio again, loose-limbed and long-haired. He comforted me and if some spying intelligence betrayer was going to discover me there, in my own home, with Brink, so be it – I almost wished he would.*

Flying Makes Her Dental Fillings Hum—
Florence (at 20,000 Feet)

*F*lorence has a terrible case of butterflies, but Mr. Loftus is dandy. When he sees her clutching her seat as they ascend, he says to think of the bumps as potholes in a road. "Exact same thing," he yells, grinning across the cockpit at her. Potholes are something she knows *lots* about, she hollers back, shakily, and as the Mosquito climbs, her dental fillings hum. She wonders how all that weight of metal – her weight, his, all the sockets and seams and joints – can be held up by mere *air*.

'Please God, let my rivets hold,' she prays silently.

As the plane reaches its cruising altitude, Florence begins to relax. She's chosen October for her prize-flight. She's so taken by the golden haze, flecked with dark evergreens, below. The light and dark of things. Loftus banks the plane out towards Lake Superior. She'd no idea how vast it was, how blue. "Look!" he hollers, and points down at a moose slogging through muskeg. It reminds her of her own heavy slog through her life, now, with Jimmy gone. But the golden blaze of autumn leaves brings back the trumpet, the stranger, the new yellow scarf she was given at work the day after the talent contest. Audrey Foley, her friend.

Florence follows the moose's jagged course. The animal's running reminds her of the men who'd escaped from the Angler Detainee Camp – they'd be specks if she were to see them from up here. Her sad, sewing mother, a dot. The man Mack, half a dot.

Orville Loftus flies south. He gradually lowers the plane a couple of thousand feet – "you'll see more that way," he says. 'Mount McKay looks like a big squashed muffin,' thinks Florence – wait 'til Audrey Foley sees that! They pass over Flo's old high school, where she'd failed to graduate. The fancy houses near Vickers Park, built by lumber barons, their turrets and all-around verandas, their gardening sheds larger than her entire house. 'They don't look as fancy from up here, they just take up more space,' she thinks. There's the Neebing streetcar, bumbling along its course. Now they're above Fort William Aviation (three enormous boxes, and a smaller one, Head Office, the tiny courtyard between). There's Sub-Assembly, where she'd riveted and welded and cried in the bathroom so often because of her red scarf. There's the plant parking lot where she'd sat with Jimmy in his De Soto, and suddenly, to her dismay, Florence starts to blubber. Jimmy has been writing to her from overseas, but his letters are spotty and strange. As they pass over Bishop's Field, she thinks about those letters, folded in the drawer of her night table beside the blue-grey toque.

I won't die, Florence. I won't ride no wooden Buick. The homegrown Canadian lorries are useless, my auto mechanics have sure come in handy. Tell my mother to keep the fluids up in the De Soto. Sure hope you're weld, Flo (ha ha). Some new words I've learned; "staghounds," "scorpions," "wasps." They have a whole new gist, where I am. If you ever see that holier-than-thou Reggie Hatch, remind him that I didn't squeal on him over the wires, will you? Nobody gave me any credit for that, did they?

On and on Jimmy wrote in this vein, while Florence wished for a little more *romance*. But in Jimmy's most recent letter he'd at least said he hoped she was still waiting.

She is.

They fly directly above her house and, although Florence is still bawling, she picks out the pig hut, the sauna shanty. The little boxes of her life. The chicken shed, where she'd practiced the trumpet so hard. Ruby Kozak can keep the trumpet case forever. Who cares, it's just a case – nobody's case. Flo gazes down on the stranger's neat stack of firewood (tiny matchsticks from the air) where she'd hidden the brass plate. She half expects to see him duck among the trees, another speck, but he hasn't been around in so long. Perhaps he considers his debt to her mother paid, but why would he have left without saying goodbye?

Florence snorts back a big, tearful gulp of air. Orville Loftus glances across at her, concerned. He asks if the flying is making her sick – "It can if you're not used to it," he tells her. Florence says the flight is grand – she's awful sorry, this is no way for a winner to act, is it? And does Mr. Loftus maybe have a tissue?

There's the Gruff rock below. She sends it a tearful wave.

Loftus tells her that the Mosquitoes don't come with tissues, there's only an oil rag tucked under her seat, and he's sorry it's not better for *a lady.*

"I'm not a lady," she croaks, reaching for the rag. "I'm Florence."

She honks loudly into the oil rag as they junket back, lowering, towards Bishop's Field.

'So this is what winning feels like,' she thinks.

She thought it would feel better.

November, 1942 –
Muriel writes in her diary
in red, red Ink:

all that higher learning
and such a fool am I

*M*uriel McGregor furiously erases a wrong angle from her drawing as she sits at her drafting table, smoking and fuming. She's behind on her work. For part of the fall, she'd been in Toronto, carrying out some research on freeze-down problems. The engineering library at the university has some papers she'd needed to consult. Each girlish face she encountered on those streets brought to mind the attractive woman with Roper McLaughlin at the talent show. Could that woman be a *wife?* Why had he not told Muriel? Why had he allowed her to humiliate herself during their spirited conversations in her office? – the office she's now back in, struggling with freeze-down, fighting to forget him. Her. *Them.*

Thank goodness for Audrey Foley's chatter and muffins, flying or not. Muriel would have died of loneliness otherwise. She lifts her eyes to her outward-facing window, briefly. It's snowing. Good for testing skis at least.

Her telephone rings. Fraudena from the switchboard. Lieutenant Colonel Roper McLaughlin is there in the foyer. Might he have a few words with Miss McGregor? 'Oh, so *now* he wants to talk,' Muriel thinks coldly. She's busy, she tells Fraudena – tell him she only has a minute to spare for him.

Soon, his knuckles tinkle against her office door. She swivels on her stool, her heart racing.

Roper McLaughlin enters, a file folder in his hand. 'A folder no doubt filled with telephone numbers of his women,' she thinks. She remembers the pained remorse on his face when their eyes had locked for an instant at the talent contest. He wears the same look now. *Good.* He also sports a new tweed jacket. Muriel won't comment on that. She takes a puff on her cigarette instead. He seizes the spare drafting stool and perches on it, a few feet away. He asks if she'd had a pleasant trip to Toronto. *Passable.* Mostly she worked. Ate many suppers alone. How about him? He's been all the way to the west coast, he says.

She blows a wreathe of smoke. "How nice for you – *alone?*"

"No, Muriel."

"With your *wife?*" she says, her voice barbed with icicles.

"Yes. And I also have a *daughter.*"

Now Muriel is confused – which one was at the talent show, wife or daughter? "Well, you have a *whole family*, how lovely for you."

He rises from the drafting stool and scrapes it along the floor. He's less than a foot from her now. The closest he's ever been. *Too close, too little, too late, Mr.-Intelligence-Man-with-a-Family-in-his-Pocket.*

"Muriel – *you* are my daughter."

She sends him a cynical laugh, a rind of disbelief pickled in vinegar.

Roper McLaughlin looks frantic. He sets the file folder on the floor beside him. Muriel's laughter has soured to a stop. He grasps her hands, says if she could only *listen.*

"Oh, this will be a *sweet tale*, Mr. McLaughlin. I'm adopted. My mother was a juvenile court judge in Vancouver. She had many contacts with orphanages. She chose me."

Roper is still grasping her hands. A deep sorrow furrows his handsome face. "Your mother and I met in Vancouver in 1905, in spring. You know that famous tree in Stanley Park? It's ancient and hollow. I met her there, inside the tree."

'Oh *please*,' she thinks.

"No, truly I did," he says. "Your mother was a bit of a naturalist, as you're also aware. She took my breath away. She was brilliant. I was nineteen, Muriel. We had wonderful moments, the deepest of my life." He gazes at her. "You have her eyes. And you have my chin."

Muriel studies his chin carefully. It *is* hers. She hadn't noticed before. The world is full of chins. "If you're my father, why did you leave?"

"I didn't. I stayed for several months. I loved your mother. She isn't easy to leave – *or* love. She's always had her own ideas. She wanted to go to law school. Even when you were well along the road to life, she steered true to her course. She didn't need a man, she told me."

"So she didn't love you?" Muriel asks.

"I think she did, in her way. But your mother is a free spirit."

"Oh yes, a *free spirit*," Muriel says bitterly. "Let me tell you about my mother. She was *so* free, she kept me in a bubble. How is that for a contradiction? She thought friends would sully me. That's why I spent so much time alone. I wired my van Amstel replica dollhouse when I was five years old, taught myself how by reading books. At last, when I was thirteen, I made a friend – a boy I met at the library. His name was Thaddeus Brink, a sort of wild, socialist spirit. He got that from his father. It was during the last war and they wouldn't give him a library card because he was on some blacklist having to do with banned socialist newspapers. Their refusal didn't seem fair to me, and that's how I came to notice him. After that it was only natural that we stuck together. He had no friends. Neither did I. We were both misfits, made for each other. He meant everything to me, Roper – adventure, friendship, love. One day, my mother caught us together. 'You must never see Thaddeus Brink again,' she said. Shortly after that, she had Thaddeus convicted and locked up for two years along with a ring of juvenile subversives. She hoped that taught me what happens to people who go against the Dominion of Canada, she said. So how is *that* for a '*free spirit*,'" Muriel laments "– *that's* my mother, and you're right – she isn't easy to love. She stole love from her own daughter, snatched it right *out of the world –*"

Roper gazes at her intently. "But she also *brought* love into the world. Besides, if you don't mind my saying so, you were so very young then, and you've likely had many admirers since this Thaddeus Brink."

"A few. But engineering school was difficult, and then I got polio. There was no one I loved like Brink until –" Her eyes rest pitifully on Roper.

"And I turn out to be your father."

Suddenly Muriel snaps her back straight as a Morse taper. "Wait a minute. You just came from Vancouver. You *saw* her, didn't you?"

"Yes. I told her I was going to make myself known to you. I wanted her blessing, I suppose. She'd just returned from a resort at Ladysmith."

"She was ill last year. Is she well now?"

"Mostly. She enjoys retirement, though she's hardly idle. She gives public lectures on juvenile crime throughout the lower mainland. She is fierce and mobile. She drives a 1937 Cabriolet Streetrod, can you imagine?"

Muriel sniffs derisively.

"She misses you, Muriel."

"*Really.* So she spends her days as a spinster and a pedagogue."

"I think you're being unkind."

Muriel doesn't grace his statement with a response. "That's why you came here, isn't it? All this *intelligence business* was just an elaborate ruse."

"Muriel, I had to see you. I'm not getting any younger."

Roper confesses that once the idea of meeting her entered his mind, not even the Luftwaffe itself could dislodge his dream. As for his work in Fort William, he'd been "inventive" in the security areas, but the workers and the men in the detainee camps who were desperate to break free had helped him out. He hadn't relished the *whimsy* aspect of his work, but he felt strongly he couldn't simply write Muriel a letter announcing his relationship to her without being present to corroborate the news. He'd corresponded off and on with Annabelle McGregor over the years. She hadn't wanted him to interfere with raising Muriel, or even disclose his identity to his daughter. But she'd had a change of heart. Roper didn't mind saying that Muriel's mother was not *quite* as hard-boiled as she might think. She, too, was moving towards the final phase of her life's journey. Muriel sends Roper a smile laden with grudge, but a smile, nevertheless. She swivels her drafting stool back and forth in a twitchy way.

"Tell me something," she says. "Does your wife know that you – that I –?"

"She doesn't. That is another difficult task ahead of me. I had to see you before I got much older," he repeats dumbly. "One never knows."

"Well, here I *am*," Muriel sighs. "A complete fool."

"Those words are the farthest from the truth of any you've ever spoken, Muriel."

"They're closer than you think. Look at this," she says, indicating the pedestal drawing on the drafting table. "Years of trying and I can't even figure out winter landing gear."

He comes over, instantly interested. "What's the hitch?"

"Freeze-down. Other engineers have tried everything. Even vegetable oil – until that got scarce as hens' teeth."

In the manner of someone recalling some lost thing, Roper reaches down and retrieves the file he'd laid on the floor. He passes it to Muriel. She accepts it warily, as if it might contain some further unwanted genealogical news.

"It's a gift," Roper says. "For you. For your last birthday

and all the birthdays before that. I'm sorry to be so late. Oh, and by the way, it's top secret information – we had to pay handsomely to get it, but I think it might solve your freeze-down problem."

Muriel opens the file. The papers inside have RESTRICTED stamped across them in red. They have been translated from Japanese into English. Her heart thumps as she reads. *British Intelligence Subcommittee Report on Secret Interview with Disaffected Japanese Engineer: How the Japanese Solved the Freeze-Down Problem on Winter Landing Gear (Skis).* The papers contain calculations Muriel can follow, aspect ratios, lengths and widths of skis. Then her eyes fall on everything she's needed to know for the past year: *freeze-down of skis was eliminated by the addition of a celluloid strip to the bottom of the ski. On the aluminum alloy ski a thin layer of cotton was placed between the metal and the celluloid. Celluloid strips wore well after one hundred landings and takeoffs.*

Muriel closes the file. "So the Japanese know."

"Yes," Roper says.

"How long have you had this file?"

He looks sheepish. "I brought it with me when I came here."

Muriel lobs him a cross look. "Why did you wait so long? You and I spent hours talking about aviation. You could have told me in one of those conversations. The Allies' progress could have been hastened if I'd known this. The war –"

"Not everything's about the bloody war." Roper struggles with the impatience in his voice, and fails. "But to answer your question, it took many months for my people in London to verify the information. It's solid, though."

"So why now? Why do you give me this today?"

Again, he looks sheepish, but faces her gaze directly. "I was waiting for the right time. There are wrong moments to give a woman a gift, and there are right ones."

Muriel sends him an anguished look. "Even if that woman is your *daughter*?"

"*Especially* if she's your daughter," Roper replies, and for the first time it strikes Muriel how very tired he looks for a man who's just returned from a month of vacation – with his wife.

Almost as High as the Moon
Far Above the Wolves
Where Eagles Soar
And this –
This –
Is What Winning Feels Like! This is how Wonder Woman Feels!

*W*hoo *hoo!* Here I am on high – flying in a spanking new Mosquito. *Flying.* My dream. Mr. Loftus sure is old but it doesn't matter; I feel snug as a bug up here. He does these dipsy-doodle tilts and twists because he knows what a supreme kick I get from them. But when I ask him to "make 'er spin, whoan-cha *whoan-cha*, Mr. Loftus?" (you have to holler to be heard in this bird) he shouts back, "no way, kid." But stagger me, this is the best thing in the world anyway, even
    without
        spinning
           down
And down
There are birds. Hawks. Foraging winter gulls. And some wild-feathered thing I can't recognize, so I'm going to call it *the Audrey Bird* – no, *wait!* –

WEDNESDAY'S NEW WARBLER ☺

Ha! – that's about perfect because today's the first Wednesday of the year. And no ordinary year, either. I turn eighteen; I'll mark it with the bird. You guessed it – soon I'll be the age I *said* I was two years ago, almost like I've grown into my own story. "Take a gander at that dandy bird out there, keeping up with us, Mr. Loftus!" He nods. Flies.

Stagger me, look at all the animals galloping down there! That dark, lumbering dot is a bear, Mr. Loftus says. Then there are these shapes that flash like lightning. Deer, I guess. And the tiniest moving glimmers between bare thickets. "Foxes," he yells to me. It's like there's a whole zoo on the run down there! I didn't see any gophers, though, and when we flew over Churchill Ladies' Residence, I knew I wouldn't spot Marilla, even if we *were* flying low enough – she'd have rolled herself into a small ball on my quilt and, not having x-ray eyes, I can't peer through roofs.

But guess what? I swear on Ruby Kozak's lipstick – right now –

a red flash! Flying right past the plane – *Woo hoo* –

Wonder Woman! – I'm *serious.* I mean, why couldn't it be? I've seen so many things this past year, why not? Look, the toes of her red boots just over –

They're gone now. But she was there a minute ago.

Guess what else? I'm learning how to type. Ruby Kozak said I could practice on her typewriter during lunch hour. We set things to rights just before Christmas. Sure, before Ruby would be nice to me I had to tell her she'd made me everything I am. But *not* talking to her, since she fired me, made me feel *rotten.* After all, I got *un*fired. Why couldn't we be *friends?* I asked and she buckled. She was going to need someone to write the *Voice* after she left the factory and got married to Reggie Hatch and became a *real* reporter. I stood high on my hind legs, hearing that –

'Oh could I   COULD I   COULD I?'

Ruby admitted that I couldn't push a snack wagon all my life, and typing, while dreary, would prove a useful skill for me. So she showed me a few basics: home row, finger positions. How to strike with pads, not nails. Posture. How not to mush the keys, how to avoid lazy wrists. Exercises for nimble fingers (and guess what? I already have them!). Then she gave me her old *Handbook for Ontario Typists*. She said once I speed up she'll let me write small parts of the *Voice*. I'm still the snack-wagon girl, though – who can juggle as many muffins as me?

Typing is swell! I don't slam the carriage like Ruby used to do. Typing is just another kind of juggling, *finger* juggling. And I still have my Wednesday reports, only they're to Miss McGregor now. We have tea. She gives me cigarettes and I tell her what's happening in the realm of "the worker" (she always asks about "the worker" like all those hundreds of girls and fellows on the line are one big chunk of peanut brittle). And sure, Florence Voutilainen and I are still friends and is she HAPPY without the red scarf! Stagger me, I can still hearing them yelling "off with the rag!"

The only fly in my ointment is that no amount of muffins will persuade Florence to forgive Ruby for getting Jimmy fired. Flo's got a stubborn streak when it comes to Ruby – she won't back down and that makes me blue.

Oh look! Here comes the moon on the rise – see, right over there –

The Moon

Silver sliver

Cool coin of the future.

Mr. Loftus says he's "takin' 'er in, now" – he means the plane, and I'm so sad that the flight is almost over. But I'll write about it for the *Voice* – that'll perk me up some.

We land like cream on the airstrip at Bishop's Field. I don't want to get out yet so I just sit, strapped in the navigator's seat, keeping on my swell aviation helmet that's so big it wobbles on my head.

After he's shut down the engine, I say, "I have to ask you something, Mr. Loftus."

"Yes, Miss Foley?"

"I've been here over a year and I haven't seen – I mean, I want to know, and maybe you can tell me, with all your knowledge of planes – how do they *fasten the wings?*"

The test pilot peels his helmet off and he looks beat, tired. He breathes sort of long and slow before answering. Finally, he says, "they get fastened like anything else in life, kid – *one piece at a time,* and you just pray that at the end of it, the whole thing hangs together and keeps you up there."

So Long, Good Stranger

*S*ummer, 1943. Lake Superior's headlands shimmy with heat. Wild carrots teem in the ditches around Fort William, releasing their peppery aroma. Florence Voutilainen hasn't heard from Jimmy Petrik for months. His mother had insisted that Flo and her mother take his De Soto, for, Louella Petrik said, they live much farther from town than she does, they need it more, and Jimmy would be pleased to know they were keeping it running. Florence can tell Jimmy's mother has given up expecting his return any time soon. *Flo,* on the other hand, has not. Although she polishes Jimmy's car regularly, she doesn't drive it to the plant. She's used to walking and her legs have grown strong.

She hasn't seen the stranger in months. Then one hot day as she's hoofing it home from the factory, he springs out of the alder saplings at the side of the road near the Gruff rock. He scares her almost half to death, just as he had the first time she'd encountered him with his axe.

She gasps. She tells him she'd thought he'd left.

"Soon," he says, though he admits that for him, the word "soon" has some give to it. But he wants to say goodbye to the daughter.

"No," Florence protests.

He emerges from the ditch and matches his stride to hers. "My work here is done," he remarks. They walk along for a while. She asks if he isn't worried someone will spot him. He is, but he needs to see her. He asks her how she's been.

"Good and bad," she shrugs, kicking at a small stone. "Good, since I've gotten rid of the red scarf. Bad because the world's a pretty lousy place when a girl's best friend will ruin her happiness."

The man asks the daughter to explain. She does. As they walk along the road, he lights a cigarette, and she tells him the whole story.

He sends her a sad look. "There's good in the world, too, Florence."

"Where? I'd like to know."

"Here. *You.*"

She lowers her eyes. "What's so good about me?"

The man smiles. "You were kind to me."

"I think it was my *mother* who was kind to you, mister," she says with a knowing look. Then she's sorry for the nettle in her words.

"You were kind, Florence. *You* were."

"It's strange," Flo says at last. "You're sort of the – *criminal* element, I guess."

He smokes, doesn't disagree.

"And," the girl continues, "knowing you has been in no way cricket – yet you're the best person I've known."

He pats her arm. "That means a lot, Florence."

Suddenly her eyes light more fully on him than they have in a long time. "I've got it," she beams.

"Got what?"

"A way for you to leave."

He smokes. Waits for the girl's revelation.

"You'll drive away in Jimmy's De Soto. Take it. It only makes me sad."

The stranger gives her an affectionate look. "That is a grand, unselfish thought, but it won't work, Florence."

"Why not?"

"License plate. They'd track the car to you. It'd get you into serious boiling water. I'd have to stop for gasoline. I'd face prying eyes, loose lips. An automobile's a cinch to apprehend. But thanks anyway."

Florence wraps her arms around him for the briefest moment, and then she backs away. She takes in the smell of his smoke. She swats at a tear. He smiles, and his face fills with tiny lights the way it did when she first met him. He wants her to remember something he told her long ago.

"What?" she asks.

"That you're loved."

Before she can find a way to speak around the lump in her throat, he touches her hair and then, in a fleeting second, he sprints into the ditch. Flo watches the alder leaves settle back into place after he's slipped through their green. She knows he's skilled at making his way through the thick bush, yet she doesn't envy him being there with a million blackflies, and nowhere proper to sleep.

"So long, good stranger," she says, and though he's already beyond earshot, she senses he can hear.

```
tYpinG

hair goZe

are U reddy PINKie  ?????
Redd      dre!!
          Aefaef  aff   aef   jil   jol   joll   jol
[Shift

          AEF   AUD   AUU              DRE   OAUD   REY

                                 Iiiii        meeeee

          AuD       ADDR EY

            AuDReYYYYYYYYYYYYYYYYYYYY!!!!!!!

                         PiNg is FUNnnn %
                         Lik fLyng ^ !
```

*R*uby has been writing *A Soldier's Story* for months, crafting her installments from Reggie's letters, and printing them in *The Factory Voice*. In August, an editor from Boreal-Dominion Publishing in Sault Ste. Marie wrote to ask if she'd any interest in pulling her *Voice* pieces together into a book. People would eat Ruby's story alive, he'd written. *Interest?* After that, Ruby's platform heels didn't touch the ground. She'd floated over to her hope chest, lifted the lid, kissed the editor's letter and dropped it inside. And Reggie's most recent news was the best installment of all. In fact, Ruby won't even need to buff it up; she plans to run it as is, for that extra bit of authenticity.

September 25, 1944

Dear Ruby,
So much to say, but dislocated shoulder of arm of writing hand, penmanship may be patchy, point form. Please forgive. Nurse will help. She'll mail this letter, too. I can only imagine how worried you must have

been all these weeks, not knowing what became of me. I've had quite a time of it. I got hurt bad in early August. On mend, now. Shoulder mighty sore, memory came back slowly, in pieces. Brain felt Bren-gunned for days. I couldn't even tell them my name.

But your face, I never forgot. Could only grasp part of your name, but I knew it was you from a photo the nurse retrieved from my uniform and showed me. It was you. "Who's Rue?" the nurse kept asking.

What I remember: I lost my gunner. Fire ripped through rear of plane, heard Matt Paltry scream, "Jesus, Hatch." That was it. Plane handling badly, in spin. I'm almost glad you never met Matthew. You'd have gone for him. Eyes bright as those tall blue flowers with spikes (kind?) in your mother's garden. Never will I forgive those swine.

We were somewhere near X (better not take any chances), trying to keep air clear of dogfights for our boys on the ground. I don't know what hit us. Came at speed of light. Paltry was a first-rate gunner, not one to miss anything spottable with the naked eye. Maybe it was the Germans' new V-2 rockets, they fly over three thousand miles per hour. Next thing I knew, trees, ground, coming up hard, fast. I radio mayday. Rear of plane's a cauldron of flame. Then smoke. I'm coughing, don't know where I am. Voice below: "Get the hell out – now!" Pardon my French, Ruby, but if I could have moved a fucking muscle, do you think I would have sat in that burning cockpit for the fun of it? Black lines in crazy directions in front of me, branches. Tree, must be.

Next thing I remember, some chap's smashing through the windshield, pulling me out. I'm bawlin' "Paltry, get Paltry!" Don't ask me how whoever was rescuing me got back down the tree with me in tow. I must have blacked out. Maybe he threw me down. I'm on the ground. He must have yanked off my flight *helmet, he's slapping me. "Hatch, stand alert!" How does he know my name? I was terrified of being taken prisoner by the Germans, but this voice held no accent. "Reggie, wake up!"*

He's dragging me from the plane. I can half stagger along, my arm across his shoulders. He tows me into a cluster of charred trees, only then do I recognize Jimmy. I ask him what in Christ he's doing here. Always the smart Jimmy. He says, "aren't you a little under your assigned altitude, Ace?" I don't know why he's joking, we both know plenty of German snipers roaming around. My shoulder takes notion to saw itself, without ether, from my body. But out of my mouth come words anyway, "what're you doing here, away from your division?" Petrik gives me the evil eye. Barks, "never you fucking mind." He sort of bucks me up. "See that path through the trees?" he points some distance away. "We follow that for a half mile, there's a whistle stop. I got friends there, amis, they'll fix you up. Only thing is, we cross some open grassland before we link up with the path. Won't be easy. No choice." I'm still wailing over Matt. "Matt's gone," Jimmy tells me. I hurt so bad I tell Jimmy run, leave me. He says, "fuck that, Hatch, do you know how good it is to see somebody from home?"

I can't answer. I'm fading. Feel Jimmy dragging me along somehow, hear him grunt. He's galloping at a decent clip considering me in tow and he's dodging bullets and trying to fire his gun as we move through the open grassland. Then I hear the crack. Something warm on my face, they've got me, no, no, they've got him. He's still dragging me, cursing like I never heard before. My head's drooping like a dishrag but I look up long enough to see he's wasted a sniper not twenty feet away. "Go," Petrik cries, "Crawl now, or I'll shoot you, Reggie." He means it. I start crawling, pulling him with my good arm. He only groans for a minute.

I feel his chest, nothing. I make sure. Nothing. I must have nabbed his weapon. I don't remember after that.

Who knows why Petrik was out there? He saved my life, that's all I know. Jimmy the wheeler-dealer of Fort William Aviation, of all people. Tell his girl, you know, your friend. Her name is the same as some town in Italy, huge feet. Tell her I'm alive thanks to him.

Nurses here sweet on me since day one. Especially Hampstead redhead. I told her I've got a girl named after a stone. I can't get your name, at first, too muddled. I say Rue, Rue. "A rue stone?" the nurse asked, scrubbing me down (maybe I made eyes with her just a bit, sorry). Then I remembered. "Ruby," I told her. "The Factory Voice. Fort William Aviation. The prettiest, most precious gem in the Dominion of Canada. She's my life."

You still are.

Love, Reggie

September
The Perils of Intimate Apparel

*F*lorence Voutilainen's dire undergarment situation can't wait another day. She hasn't bought new underpants for over two years, since the spring of 1942, for the bowling date that went sour. Not to mention a single slip, brassiere or corset. This fall, the factory needs her more than ever, so she rarely takes Saturday off, but the truth is, the news of Jimmy Petrik's death has brought her very low. She's tired. She doesn't tell Frank Parks she'll be missing work to buy undergarments, she says dental emergency. The intimate apparel is an emergency in its own right as Florence has gained a good deal of weight since Jimmy died. She's comforted herself with bread, molasses and licorice allsorts. The elastic waistbands in her underpants have ravelled and snapped. With the rubber shortage, underwear is expensive, even if she'd had time to buy some. Then, that morning, Flo awoke and realized she didn't have a single pair of knickers to wear to work, so she telephoned the factory with a chipped-tooth story. She'd already received an award for least days of work missed, so Frank Parks told her to take the day off with his blessing.

It snows lightly as Florence strikes out from home to where Rosslyn Road joins Neebing Avenue. She takes the Neebing streetcar to Simpson Street, and from there walks the short distance to Chapples Department Store. The intimate apparel section is on the top floor; there's not much there, these days, but Flo hopes some bigger sizes will be left. The store's top floor is airless, funereal. She tugs at her wool dress, which rides up over her billowing midsection. She's twenty-five now. She needs a girdle, a heavy-support one. She'll look for underpants next. "Front Line Family" plays on a radio, through the store's intercom, as Florence glances at a brassiere display over which hovers a large sign printed in loopy letters – *Revolutionary Smart Separation.*

Flo can't say for sure why she talks to herself, out loud, the tedium of shopping alone, perhaps, but she does – "There's no such thing as smart separation," she laments.

"You've got *that* right" – a voice behind a nearby rack of nightgowns.

The voice startles Florence. Ruby Kozak stands there, glowing in a maroon coat. She looks like a movie star. She's wearing platform shoes even though the fall "snap" has happened, and it's cold, and it has already snowed. Flo stares at her own heavy boots. She hasn't been this close to her enemy since Ruby had chased her down at the streetcar stop. Friend of her youth.

"Hello, Flo."

"I go by Florence now." She decides that this very instant.

Ruby finds this droll, these stuffy words coming from the rumpled, big-footed girl she's known since Jehovah (Flo can still halfway read her old friend's thoughts). Ruby laughs, but slices her volume down the middle. Girdles herself in. To Florence, Ruby looks like she expects harsh words and – Flo dares to think – perhaps even believes she *deserves* them.

Florence suddenly finds her own name-claim ("I go by Florence now") amusing. She breaks into laughter like seal barks, the tears not far behind. Ruby pulls a handkerchief from her coat pocket and gives it to her.

"You never did have a hanky," Ruby says.

Florence blows her nose. "I never will."

Ruby tells Florence she's shopping for her trousseau. She and Reggie are getting married, not for a while but never too early to plan. Maybe Flo read about the engagement in *The Factory Voice?* Florence says she hadn't heard, and breezes her congratulations. For months Flo has felt far too blue to read the *Voice.* She says she must be off. The chickens need feeding. Flo hasn't selected any intimate apparel, other than the girdle. The underpants will have to wait after all – running into slender, trousseau-seeking Ruby has thrown Flo off too much to shop. Florence swallows the deep hurt of knowing her friend is getting married and she hasn't been invited, never mind asked to be maid of honour like they'd vowed when they were girls. But as Flo heads downstairs to the cash register, girdle in hand, she wonders if she'd even *go* to the wedding if she *was* invited. Her thoughts flood with confusion.

Ruby Kozak has followed her to the store's main floor.

Florence takes her girdle to the cash register and pays, and waits while her change comes bouncing and chattering from Head Office, all the way across the store, along the long trough suspended from the tiled ceiling, like a little road in the sky. Ruby stands there and fiddles with her raffia handbag and blows at the strands of hair sliding down over her pretty forehead. She says she wants to walk Florence to the streetcar stop.

"What about your trousseau?" Flo asks.

"It can wait."

Florence shrugs. "Whatever floats your canoe."

Outside, late afternoon is leaving slivers of mauve light everywhere. They reach Simpson Street, not speaking, simply moving along beside each other like they used to after school when they were girls. Silence chills the air as they walk to the trolley stop. They can see their breaths. Along the sidewalk trots a dog. It snuffles in a small ridge of snow, continues its trot. Suddenly a giggle catches in Florence's throat and she swipes at a tear. Ruby asks what's wrong, why is she laughing and crying at the same time? Florence answers that she's just been thinking how funny it is, running into Ruby in the girdle department.

"I mean girdles hold things in," Florence says, quaking, "and I've held in my fury at you for condemning Jimmy for so long and then there you *are,* just *standing* there. For you it was just a story, Ruby. For me, it was my *life.*"

Silently, they pass the Red Cross building's *Have you Joined the Gallon Club?* sign.

Ruby straightens her back as she steps along. "Try to understand, Florence. Through this whole awful war, they've told us to nip corruption in the bud, be a model citizen. I was just trying to do my part for my country. I was striving to be a good citizen."

They reach the streetcar stop. The trolley tussles towards them. Florence laughs, not her earlier seal-bark laugh, but a woman's short, wistful one. "I've known you since you wore ringlets, Ruby. I can see right through you. There's one thing you'll never be, and that's a good citizen."

The streetcar looms, brakes. Florence says so long. Ruby returns the words with an odd little wave. Florence trudges up the trolley steps in her big boots. A couple of commuters scurry to board after her. She chooses a window seat on the side of the car closest to the sidewalk, then looks out the window at Ruby, still rooted there in bald, cold light. Ruby looking up at her, still glowing like a movie star. Florence is surprised Ruby hasn't already run off to write some story or other.

The streetcar rolls forward. Florence closes her eyes for a quick moment. 'It's cold in this trolley,' she thinks. A honking automobile horn, and Florence opens her eyes. She looks out the window; Ruby Kozak is sprinting alongside the streetcar, her raffia handbag flapping against her unbuttoned coat, her hair coming unpinned. "Florence! Florence!" she shouts as she runs, and Flo has no idea how Ruby can run so fast in platform shoes.

The trolley gathers speed. Ruby is right below Flo's window now. Florence can't *not* look at her. Other passengers gawk at Ruby, too. She sprints frantically, like she's trying to catch the last trolley in the world. More horns goose the air. Florence Voutilainen has never, in her twenty-five years, seen her friend so dishevelled.

"*Florence!*" Ruby screams. "Be my maid of honour!"

Ruby is running out of breath, Flo can tell. She's dropping back. Florence's stomach churns. What should she do? This is, after all, another performance starring Ruby Frances Kozak. Flo could simply turn away from the window. There'd be no better way to say what she longs to say – she's sick of *The Ruby Show*. Florence hears her name screamed again, and something in the anguish of those two syllables stirs a strange ecstasy in Flo, and makes her believe her days of being so much less than the beautiful, brilliant Ruby could spin into a new era.

Ruby must have found her second wind, as she sprints closer to Flo's window now. She's right under it, panting "*maid – of – honour*" through the glass. She pounds her palm against the window; her sapphire ring catches light like a hard little white fire. Every passenger stares at the crazy runner out there.

Suddenly, Florence opens the window, thrusts out her arm, fumbles for Ruby's hand, and shouts, "*Yes.*"

In a final surge of energy, Ruby Kozak leaps into the air and grabs Flo's fingers and, for a split second, while airborne, grasps them, not like a Hollywood star, but like a working girl from Fort William, Ontario.

Love typing – sweet swit tYping–
so mooch baeter now – Watch this–
)Exsir   cises from Ruby's BooK: : : : :

My dog dislikes porcupines. My dogdislikes pro-
copines. MY dog dislicks percipins.
(frst one always best 4 sum rasion

THE RAIN IS BEESTLY UNPLEASNAT. THE RAN IS
BEASTLEY UNPLEASNT. TE RAINS BEAST LYUN
PLEESANT.

My canoe is the cruiser typ. My cano is the
cruiser type *(ha!)* My canoe is the cruiser type –
uh huh reddy to move on! –
THE HARDEST ONE from Rooby book here I go – postoor –
back strite

"Oh, very imprudant indeed, Master Coperfield,"
returned Uriah, siGhying modestly. "Oh, very
much so! I'ts a topic that I woldnt touch upon,

to any one but yo. Even to you, I can only toUch
upon it, and noo more. If any one else had ben
in my place during the last four years, by this
time he wod have had Mr. Wickfield under his
thumb," said Uriah, very sloely, as he stretched
ot his cruel-looking hand above me table, and
pressed his own thumb upon it, until it shook,
and shook the room.

I showed Ruby and she said, "practice makes perfect, Audrey,
practice makes prefect." Stagger me, I'll make it PREFECT!
Just Lik the muffins I mad theM purrrrrrrrrrrrrrrrrrrrrrrrrrrrrr

> You SAw me sawed ME
> With yer vury own IZ!

Five Daffodils

*a*pril 1945. Someone leaves five daffodils on the steps of Muriel McGregor's back porch. She arranges them in a crock on her kitchen table and admires them as she sips sherry and eats her grilled cheese sandwich. The light taps she hears now at her back door don't startle her. She's grown used to living with ghosts. She goes to the door and there's Thaddeus Brink. She's not seen him since right after the talent show. That seems so long ago, now, the night he'd held her. He's older in some way that doesn't mesh with mathematics. But handsome still. She waves him towards the empty chair across the table.

"I grilled more sandwiches than I can eat," she says, pointing to the frying pan. "Plates above the sink. Help yourself. And maybe you remember where the sherry glasses are."

Brink nods. He pours himself some sherry and takes a sandwich. He eats like a starving man, and doesn't speak until every last crumb is finished. "Still building war machines?"

Her cheeks prickle and burn. "We're almost done with the work here."

"I've missed you," he says, sliding his worn hand across the table.

"Thaddeus. Don't."

"I've always loved you. Even the work you do can't change that."

"Brink, *please.*"

"They're still looking for me, Muriel. War's end isn't going to let me off the hook. As far as they're concerned, I'll *always* be wearing that yellow jacket with the big black circle on the back."

"No gloom tonight, Thad. Please." She brushes the tops of the daffodils with her hand. "Speaking of yellow, is it *you* I have to thank for these?"

He rakes his hair with his fingers. "It is. They're a goodbye present. I have to leave for good, Muriel."

"Where?"

"North."

She laughs. "This *is* north, Thad."

"I mean Alaska."

"You'll ride the rails? Hitchhike?"

"I can't risk either."

They drink their sherry. She's lost in thought until he calls her back by touching her forehead. "What are those jumping brains thinking?"

She lights a cigarette. "I'm tying to figure out a way to help you, Thad."

He shakes his head. "You didn't report me, Muriel. You've done enough."

She tents her hand over his, briefly. "You don't understand, Thaddeus – you're my last remaining problem to solve, and I *will* solve you. When you see three clay flowerpots on my back step, return here. It means I'll have it figured out."

They sip their sherry. Finally, Brink says, "My Muriel, is there anything you can't figure out?"

"Yes, plenty. But when it comes to moving people through space, from one place to another, maybe I *can* find a way."

They drain their sherry glasses in quiet, conspiratorial sips. When she asks him what he'll do until she devises a plan, he answers: hide in the trees until he sees the clay pots. He rises to leave, and Muriel asks him to promise her something.

"Anything," he says.

"Don't forget me."

Thaddeus Brink laughs. "Muriel, that would be impossible, you're the bee's very knees" – and then he vanishes into the cold spring.

The Last Albatross

*T*he rumours of layoffs that have swirled through the sweltering production sheds are now true. Muriel McGregor knew this even before Audrey Foley blew into her office one Wednesday to tell her, but she'd let the girl surprise her with the news. The last Mosquitoes have moved down the line. The last rivets have been riveted, the final test flight flown. When Muriel McGregor and Orville Loftus land the plane without a hitch, he peels off his aviation helmet, and turns to her.

"There's something I got to know," Orville says.

"What?"

"You once told me that two albatrosses hang around your neck – your mother, and a man. Do you recall?"

She does.

"What I need to know is, is the man-one still there, or, just maybe, is he gone?"

"Gone," Muriel answers.

"Gone sounds good," Loftus says. "And on that note, I'm wondering if you fancy a ride in a Sopwith – an *extended* ride, as a matter of fact."

"Perhaps. But there's something *I* need to know, Orville."

He's smiling, now. "Ask away."

"This letter you've been waiting for – from this fellow, Harry –"

Loftus' face shadows over. "Hawkes."

"Yes. Him. Harry Hawkes. Did that letter ever come, Orville?"

"Nope."

Muriel pulls her helmet off now. Her hair tumbles down. "Then considering what you've told me – that you can't fly the Sopwith until you get the, you know, *absolution* – how can you make a trip?"

Orville Loftus studies her wavy chestnut hair with its few grey strands. He pauses for a long moment. "Because I realized the person who has to forgive me is – me."

"Now what?" Muriel says.

"What do you think?" he asks, his weathered cheeks growing flushed, his eyes riveted to hers.

The colour in Muriel's cheeks rises to match his. When he wraps his warm hand around hers, she doesn't pull it away.

"What about that trip?" Orville asks.

"Where?"

"Whole dang country," he says. "At least the western half – Fort William to British Columbia."

Muriel hesitates for a moment. "Yes. I'd like that, but I've a favour to ask."

"Ask away."

"Can we bring a hitchhiker?"

Orville doesn't take his hand away, and doesn't hesitate. "Long as the seat right beside mine is filled with *you*."

She blushes again and thanks him. She'd appreciate it if he didn't say anything about their passenger – *ever*.

"Got the law on his back?"

"*Some*thing like that," she smiles. "We all have our albatrosses to bear."

"Mum's the word," Loftus says, and then asks Muriel if he might have a favour in return for ferrying this fugitive.

"Anything."

"I don't want to fill out any dang flight report *forms* on this trip."

She laughs, and doesn't bother to remind him that *she's* been the one filling them out for the past three years anyway – as if he didn't remember.

"When do we leave?" she asks.

"Soon. All right?"

"*Yes.*"

MORE YELLOW JACKETS ESCAPE! And Pretty Well Everybody Else Out Too!

*W*ell blow me up, workers – while operations are winding down in our production sheds, they've been buzz-buzz-busy not far from here, out at the detainee camps at Red Rock and Magpie! TWENTY *prisoners from those camps bust out and are at* LARGE!

Lock up your gophers!

These menontherun are wearing bright yellow coats. They broke out the same way as those fellows at Angler back in '41, by sawing through the window bars with heavy-gauge wires. Cudgel me, I say GOOD FOR THEM! *Your new* VICE *– stagger me, I mean* VOIce *– knows what it's like to run hard. Long may they*

RUUNNNNNNN!

I might get fried for printing that and let the moon smite me if Im wrong but I don'tthink I'll fet fired – Why not? *1. Because Ruby's not here to fire me. 2. Because I can type 60 words a minot now not prefect but they'll need a Voicefor the new streetcar contract the factory's going to retool for, and since I can keep the workers well fed (uh-huh, snack wagon, they'll always need food)* AND *well-red (Voice)*

I PREDICT THEY WILL

KEEP ME!–
Stagger me if I'm wrong!
What else is new? Ruby Kozak is getting married in a couple of weeks. Good for Huuurrrrr!

May her lipstick
        Shine through
                To eternity

(Ha!)

Three Tin Cups

*T*he trio of clay flowerpots Muriel leaves on her back step haven't been there long enough to soak in the morning sun when Thaddeus Brink knocks at her door. He carries a small rucksack. He's to meet her at the front of the house, where she goes, in her freshly ironed blouse and slacks, and tinted shades to protect her eyes from the late-summer sun. She takes a compact suitcase, leaving the boxes of files, four years' worth, stacked in her front hallway where they'll stay for a few weeks. When she returns to Fort William, she'll have a last supper with her father and his wife, Glynis, before they move back to London. The city is in a terrible state, Roper told her, but back they'll go, in time for their baby's birth.

Hearing the familiar hum of Orville Loftus' truck, Muriel locks her flat. Thaddeus Brink follows her to the vehicle, and the three of them squeeze into the cab. Muriel tells Orville that, foolishly enough, she feels a sudden nostalgia for Fort William. She asks him to take a longer route out, to use his imagination. He drives through the back streets of town, past the Royal Edward Hotel, McKellar Diner, the peeling sign hanging crooked and forlorn over the door of Petrik's Autobody.

They say nothing until the jade green De Soto passes them on Arthur Street. Muriel McGregor would have recognized it anywhere. She's taken so many rides in it. Jimmy Petrik's old car, driven, now, by an attractive, auburn-haired woman around her own age, probably just a few years older. The car has acquired a new feature – a large sign painted in bright purple on its side: *The Revolutionary Mending-Mobile.* Muriel doesn't understand at first; then she remembers. The driver must be none other than the Red Finn herself, Henni Voutilainen. Muriel's face lights with a wistful smile. Unlike Jimmy, his beloved De Soto has returned from the dead, used now by the Lakehead's eccentric seamstress. 'It has met its match, that car,' Muriel thinks, as a kind of strange delight overtakes her.

"Look at that cracked buggy, would ya, and the dame driving it – she's speeding," Orville says, pointing to the De Soto, now well ahead of them. A sky-wide grin crosses Thaddeus Brink's face.

They continue out of Fort William. On the highway just beyond town, a girl stands hitchhiking, worn carpet bag at her feet. There's just no way they can squeeze the hitchhiker in – besides, they're not going far before they'll change their *mode of transport.*

Orville Loftus declares it a shame, a kid like that out on the open road. Girls roam the roads like gypsies now, after getting laid off at the factory. He's seen them on drives to and from his farm.

"Reminds me of that sprout I took on the plane ride," Loftus muses.

"Audrey Foley," Muriel pipes in. She can see why he thinks this – the hitchhiker *does* resemble Audrey, but isn't.

"Wonder what happened to her, anyway?" Loftus asks.

"She told me she's staying on at the plant," Muriel says. "One of the few girls who *are* – she's fallen in love with *typing,* of all things."

"That *does* seem odd," Orville remarks as he downshifts for the turnoff onto the country road. "She struck me as a real *live wire,* and typing is such a sitting-still sort of thing."

Muriel laughs. "Well, I know the girl and I'll wager that her fingers will punch those keys into some pretty wild places, though her small rump be grounded on the chair. Besides, her snack wagon will keep her moving."

Orville Loftus shifts the topic to planes as the three of them bump along, farther into the country.

"You sound like some kind of flying ace," Thaddeus Brinks says to Loftus.

"Oh, you'll see, Thad," Muriel smiles.

After a while, they arrive at Orville's farm. Sancho runs, tail wagging, to meet the truck. The dog barks at Brink until Loftus orders it to be quiet. "The neighbour will feed you every day," he adds, his hand still razzling the dog's head. Sancho follows them into the barn and, once inside, Loftus lifts the tarp off the Sopwith.

"This thing flies?" Brink asks.

"Thaddeus, *please*," Muriel says.

"You want a ride or not?" Orville asks, testily.

"Orville, *please*," Muriel implores.

"Good thing you travel light, and you're thin to boot," Loftus tells Brink. "It's going to be a squeeze." Thaddeus wedges himself into a small space behind the plane's two seats, and winds himself into a paper-clip shape.

Loftus slides the huge barn door all the way open now, on its rollers. He backs his truck up to the barn, hooks a tow rope to the small plane, and tows it out into the yard. He's cut a swathe leading from the yard to the front field. "Airstrip," he tells Muriel, pointing, smiling. He closes the barn door, gives the dog one last pat and parks his truck beside the house. Loftus helps Muriel into the Sopwith and scrambles in too, bringing only a change of clothes, a loaf of bread, jar of jelly, a dipper, large thermos of water and three tin cups.

They rise into the sky, fly west. Tilt north into clear sky. Orville falls into a comfortable silence. Muriel's thoughts settle on the two men who share this antique flying machine with her. Both exasperate her. Both love her.

Suddenly, about fifty miles northwest of Fort William, Orville exclaims, "Son of a pagan dog, look at *that* down there!" He points to a large yellow mass, swarming over the rocks. Muriel is jolted from her reverie as she surveys the open rocky stretch of land below. From up here, the men look like bumblebees, each with a black circle on its back.

"*Good*ness, the bees grow large up here!" she calls to Orville.

"You didn't know? Northern bees. They're on the move this time of year."

Muriel turns to see Thaddeus Brink's dancing eyes, the dozens of little lights in them. Soon enough, the yellow swarm is left behind.

Winnipeg. While Orville refuels, Muriel diverts a couple of Nosey Parkers who ask for a gander inside the Grasshopper. She starts telling these Parkers about planes, and, dizzied by her knowledge, they forget about snooping. Saskatoon. Night. Thaddeus disappears into a stand of trees – he's used to sleeping in the bush, he says. Muriel and Orville pitch a tent beside the plane. They make a small fire as curtains of aurora borealis shimmer. The next morning, they rekindle the fire, and brew coffee. Thaddeus Brink emerges from the trees, and Muriel pours coffee into his tin cup. They fly over the prairie's sloughs and wooded tufts and grain elevators. Vs of ducks fly southbound. Orville and Muriel converse in comfortable spurts, in the easy way of those who have travelled together. They talk about work they've done, work they'll do, places they'll see. Muriel occasionally turns around to check on Thaddeus Brink. He's so quiet, back there. The engine drones him into sleep much of the time, that, and late summer's heat. Still he smiles drowsily at her every once in a while.

They land on the outskirts of Edmonton. Thaddeus goes for a walk to stretch his stiff joints. When he returns, the three of them eat jelly rolled in slices of bread. Orville and Muriel camp once again beneath scintillating northern lights. Brink vanishes into the trees. In the morning, when he reappears for coffee, they consider routes. Loftus was thinking they'd head towards Fort St. John. Where does Thaddeus want to be dropped off exactly? Prophet River?

"Or Watson Lake," Muriel says, poring over a map. "That's right on the Yukon border and you could nip over to Alaska."

Orville leans over the map, frowning. "Watson Lake? That whole neck of woods has crawled with military ever since the highway was built, but they should be thinning out now."

Brink says some of his brothers live up there; they'll help him along.

"Thaddeus comes from a *very* large family," Muriel teases, winking at Brink. He winks back. Orville says enough kidding around, they'd better make tracks.

They fly through lowering daylight and land, bumpily, at last, in scruffy country sliced open by a sweeping river, and fringed with a low line of trees that skims the horizon. Beside the Sopwith, an estuary, where a large bird lands with perfect grace. Orville helps Muriel out of the plane, then Brink. The breeze riffles with autumn chill. Loftus thumps Thaddeus on the back and says, "guess you made it, eh?" The men shake hands. Muriel tucks a map into Thaddeus's rucksack, and a few slices of bread. "You'll be all right?" she asks, grinding her cane into the cooling earth.

"Yes," he says, his eyes wandering over to Orville Loftus, "and so will *you*."

She smiles, but her eyes pool. Her bones tell her she'll never see Thaddeus again.

"Bee's knees, Muriel," Brink mutters, in an odd, choking way. He squeezes her gloved hand and makes for the horizon, not once looking back.

Orville Loftus grips the same hand Brink so recently released. "You got any albatrosses left?" he asks as they walk back to the Sopwith.

"I'm afraid so," Muriel says, dabbing a tear with her glove. "The worst one of all. My mother."

"Does she still live in Vancouver?"

"Yes," Muriel says. "That's the motherland, all right – she'll die there, too."

They don't speak until they've settled into their seats. "Is it maybe time to make things right with her?" Orville suggests.

"*May*be," she hedges.

"What the devil will she make of an old coot like me?" he asks nervously.

She hovers her hand on his worn-leather-jacketed arm. "She'll only want to be convinced you're not some kind of communist, socialist, anarchist or theosophist."

"How do you know I'm *not?*"

"I *don't*," she says, laughing. "We'll just have to fly over that bridge when we reach it, won't we?"

"Or go under it. Where to, Miss McGregor?"

"To the motherland, Mr. Loftus."

He dons his battered aviator's cap. "Affirmative south-bound destination," he calls out to her.

Employee exit procedures (Day 3) implemented in orderly fashion. 1,200 girls from shop, another 500 from Final Assembly, Stores, Salvaging, sundry other areas of plant (lavatory matrons, cafeteria and so forth). Total layoffs now without incident: 2,700. To ensure continued success of program, extra temporary constables stationed at congested points: personnel badge drop-off, also A-N and O-Z paperwork wickets. These constables also directing laid-off to Archibald Street Armories to inquire about assistance and bene-fits. Last of Mosquito line decommissioning, routine. Have briefed men on security issues around retooling for incoming streetcar contract.

C. Kozak

on Kozak drops his report in the internal mail chute and trudges up the wooden steps to his security cage. He heaves a sigh and lets himself into his office. He passes Jimmy Petrik's old desk. He sinks into his own worn swivel chair, lights a cigarette and reads that morning's *Fort William Daily Times Journal*. He brews tea and writes layoff notices for four of his own men. Good chaps. He's sorry to see them go, but building warplanes is one thing, homeland trolleys another. The plant will retool for a contract with the Toronto Transit Company. Almost all the girls have gone, though that chippy snack-wagon kid is staying on, a couple of cooks, and, Con's heard, one welder – Florence Voutilainen. He's pretty sure Florence chummed, donkey's years ago, with his own girl, Ruby. *Ah, that Ruby* – she's been charmed from birth, that one. Now she's off to work for the newspaper in Port Arthur. She's getting married soon, too. Her fellow, Reggie, is back, and Ruby is happy as a hummingbird in a honeysuckle patch. Her book, *A Soldier's Story,* is selling like hotcakes. Once again, Dame Fortune's blessed star has shone on his daughter. The war has been won. Still, they'll always need a watchman. And as for production – if they don't make this, they'll make that. The Dominion will always clamour for something – it's written in the book of fate. And their factory under the lopped-off mountain beside Lake Superior will retool faster than the lifts and drops of ladies' hemlines.

Acknowledgements

*T*his is a work of fiction; however, numerous books, articles and historical documents provided valuable source material. These include: *"They're Still Women After All": The Second World War and Canadian Womanhood* by Ruth Roach Pierson; *Saints, Sinners, and Soldiers: Canada's Second World War* by Jeffrey A. Keshen; *Careers for Women in Canada: A Practical Guide* by Gabrielle Carriere (1946); *Fighting for Dignity: The Ginger Goodwin Story* by Roger Stonebanks; Gordon Burkowski's history of Canadian Car and Foundry; Pamela Wakewich's article, "'The Queen of the Hurricane: Elsie MacGill, Aeronautical Engineer and Women's Advocate" in *Framing Our Past: Canadian Women's History in the Twentieth Century,* edited by Sharon Ann Cook, Lorna McLean and Kate O'Rourke; "Women's Wartime Work and Identities: Women Workers at Canadian Car and Foundry Co. Limited, Fort William, Ontario, 1938–1945" by Pamela Wakewich, Helen Smith and Jeanette Lynes, also in *Framing Our Past;* Peter Raffo's article, "'Murder' in the Bush: The Making of a Modern Myth" in *Journal of Finnish Studies;* Kelly Saxberg's *"Rosies of the North" (NFB, 1999).* The papers of Elizabeth ("Elsie") MacGill, Canada's first female aeronautical engineer, housed at Library and Archives Canada, also provided important source material. The epigraph to this novel is from Elizabeth Bishop's poem, "Questions of Travel," found in *Elizabeth Bishop: The Complete Poems* (New York: Farrar, Straus and Giroux, 1969). The passage from *David Copperfield* that Audrey types was taken from *Ontario High School English Composition* (Toronto: The Copp Clark

Company, Ltd., 1921).

I would first like to thank my editor, Sandra Birdsell, who brought enormous wisdom, energy, humour and imagination to this project. Sandra was an anchor of inestimable value. She inspired me to take creative risks. Working with her was a privilege and an extreme literary hike in the absolute best sense.

During the six years in which this novel was written, I have accumulated a huge debt of gratitude to the mentors, colleagues, friends and family members who read drafts, provided information, and offered encouragement at critical points. Thanks to Elizabeth Hay, David Carpenter and Trevor Ferguson for their superb mentorship during the 2002 Banff Writing Studio. Michael C. White was an astute mentor at the University of Southern Maine's low-residency M.F.A. program in 2004. John Fell, Kent Bruyneel and Noelle Allen made helpful suggestions on earlier drafts. My mother, the late Mabel Seim, read two embryonic versions. David Carpenter restored my faith in the project at a crucial point, and rekindled my belief in Santa Claus. Thanks, too, to: Merilyn Simonds, Wayne Grady, Leona Theis, Nancy Forestell, Peter McInnis, Richard Cumyn, Ron Kassner, Robert Currie, Nancy Mattson, Jeff Keshen, Anna Mather, Bonnie McIsaac, Anne Simpson, Jennifer Glossop, Clare McKeon, Sheldon and Dawn Currie, Holly Luhning, Jennifer Still, Darren Bernhardt, George Sanderson, Ian and Laura Cull, Peter Campbell, John Blackwell, the Pushor family, Laurie Stanley-Blackwell, Robert Zecker. Also to my Facebook friends for posting responses to a title short list. David Lynes offered canny suggestions, open ears and a generous heart. One draft of this novel was written during my time as Writer in Residence at Saskatoon Public Library; thanks to everyone at SPL for their generosity and collegiality. Finally, I am grateful to: the Canada Council for the Arts; the Department of Women's Studies at Queen's University; Library and Archives Canada; the Thunder Bay Museum; the Canadian Warplane Heritage Museum; Stegner House; the Banff Centre; and St. Francis Xavier University.

About the Author

*J*eanette Lynes is the author of five collec-
tions of poetry, most recently, *It's Hard Being
Queen: The Dusty Springfield Poems* (Freehand
Books, 2008), and *The New Blue Distance*
(Wolsak and Wynn, 2009). She has been a Writer
in Residence at Saskatoon Public Library and
Northern Lights College, Dawson Creek, and a
Visiting Artist in Residence with the Women's
Studies Department at Queen's University.
Jeanette has also been a faculty member at the
Sage Hill Writing Experience. She co-edits the
Antigonish Review and teaches at St. Francis
Xavier University. This is her first novel.